The Count of Cape Hatteras

WASHED ASHORE

D0882314

BRUCE WILKINS

The Count of Cape Hatteras: Washed Ashore
By Bruce Wilkins

Published by Studio East Press LLC
www.countofcapehatteras.com

© 2009 Studio East Press LLC
ISBN: 978-0-615-29046-1
First Printing

Cover photography by Bruce Wilkins
Book design and printing by Farmville Printing,
Farmville, Virginia

*All characters in this story are wholly fictional. Any resemblance
to actual people is coincidental and unintentional.*

Contents

DEDICATED TO

EDWARD B. "BUCK" WILKINS

PROLOGUE

September 2007

OUR STORY BEGINS not on Hatteras Island, but instead, on the opposite end of North Carolina's Outer Banks. Just as the sun rose above the horizon on Carova Beach, a lone Jeep bounced along northwards, heading for a family of wild Mustang ponies. They were gathered at the water line ignoring the approach of the vehicle.

Inside were two people of very different backgrounds. Frank was a former Marine who served two tours of Special Operations duty in Iraq and Afghanistan. He later spent time as a security specialist with Bluewater for yet another tour in Iraq. Disillusioned with the lack of understanding and support of his missions, he put his life savings on a down payment for a fishing boat which he had hoped to charter from Oregon Inlet. That didn't work out. As the bank began to repossess his vessel, Frank took a summer job as a wild horse tour guide in Corolla while deciding his next move.

Anna was a young, extremely intelligent college student from Russia who worked three jobs all summer long in Corolla to save money for her final year of school back home. She was a housekeeper at a hotel, a clerk in a grocery store and filled out her ambitious schedule as a clerk in a small gift shop. The summer had flown by for her and though she missed her family, she dreamed of spending more time in the United States. Like many young Russians, she had found the abundant opportunities of employment intoxicating. Though she had taken jobs that most of her young American counterparts would have refused, she was thrilled at the arrival of each new paycheck. Anna was proud of being financially independent from her family and she wished she had more time to take advantage of all the opportunities that surrounded her on the Outer Banks.

With the summer season all but over, Anna had talked Frank into taking her up to the four-wheel drive area so she could finally see the wild ponies. It was a Monday morning, a day after the passing of a violent tropical storm, and Frank had waited for an hour at the horse tour office for any possible customers. The phone didn't ring, since so many people had left the beach ahead of the storm. Those who stayed obviously assumed no tours would take place. So, Frank called Anna and she rushed over, happy to be able to fulfill one of her Outer Banks' dreams.

Frank continued driving northwards in the soft sand near the dunes in order to keep the horses they were approaching on the storm-packed sand at the water line. When they were within a few hundred yards, he casually steered the vehicle onto the hard sand, keeping a slow pace that hopefully wouldn't make the horses leave. Anna's face was almost at the windshield, staring excitedly at the gathering of horses. Then, simultaneously, they both saw something else...what appeared to be a human body, surrounded by the horses.

"You stay here," Frank said, as he stopped the vehicle about fifty yards away. "I'm going to check this out."

"No, no. I go, too," Anna quickly responded, climbing outside even before Frank's sandals could touch the sand.

Sure enough, the prone figure was human. It appeared to be a man, quite thin and light-skinned, with a mat of soaked, white hair covering his face. A small wave from the outgoing tide washed over him as Frank and Anna came closer.

Meanwhile the lead stallion of the group peered at the new arrivals with a strange sense of duty to protect who they had found. It took several attempts by Frank, waving his arms skywards, to move the horses away. Last to leave was the black stallion, stopping to look back with a stern glare of warning. After all, like the man on the beach, so too did their ancestors wash up on the shores of North Carolina.

Another wave passed over the man and a muted cough startled both Frank and Anna. Frank rushed to his side and checked for broken bones or open wounds with one hand, while feeling for a pulse with the other. Anna stood above them, her hands to her mouth as she watched in concern.

The man coughed again as Frank gently rolled him over onto his back. Slowly, his eyelids opened, displaying bloodshot blue eyes which weakly flickered in the growing light. His eyes fought to stay open as he slowly gazed upon the two strangers.

"Are you all right?" Frank asked with a quickly growing note of suspicion. His new inclination was that the man was some reveler who had partied a little too hard the night before and passed out on the beach. "How'd you get here?"

The man tried to speak, but failed in his first attempt. He could only gaze slowly from Frank to Anna, as his parched and battered lips tried to open.

"Okay, dude, what's the problem here? If you need medical attention, we can get it for you. Did you ride the storm out at one of these beach houses?" Frank asked, pointing over his shoulder to the homes rising beyond the sand dunes.

"I...." was all that came out in response. Then, with what appeared as a superhuman effort, the man said, "Thirs...thirsty."

Anna ran back to the Jeep to retrieve a soft drink she had brought along, while Frank again checked the man's pulse. He could see that strength was finally coming back to the man's body and that his eyes were becoming more focused.

Anna returned and she held his head up as she put the drink to his lips. The man's grateful eyes rose skyward, then shot directly at her's. "Than...thank you."

"Okay, you don't have any broken bones or wounds and it appears you're getting your strength back," Frank said matter-of-factly. "But I'm still going to call the Sheriff's Department to have them handle this. Let's just get you on your feet and up the beach a ways so you won't get run over before they get here."

The man struggled quickly in an attempt to rise, but then fell back to the sand. His eyes were now full of frustration at not being able to communicate. He finally caught one deep breath and then slowly began to speak. "Please...don't call anybody. First, did you find anybody else? A friend of mine...he should be here somewhere, too."

"No, buddy, just you and the horses. We've driven all the way up from Corolla. 'Course, there's still a few miles to the Virginia line, but I think you're going to be the only one out here today like this."

A wave of sadness shot across the man's face, as he took another big breath to speak again. "Please do not involve the police. Or anybody else. I can't explain anything now, but if you help me get off the beach...somewhere I can rest a bit...then...I'll..."

"No way, dude," Frank countered. "We don't know who you are, where you came from, or what you've been involved in. Neither this young lady or me need to get involved with anything like this. We're going to turn you over to the authorities and let them take care of you."

"No...please...no."

"Well, who are you?" Anna asked suddenly. "If you promise you have done nothing wrong, then we may help you."

"Anna, I don't think..."

"Has anybody helped you out with losing your boat? No. Has anybody helped me out to extend my visa so I can work here longer? No. So, we can at least help this man...we can take him back to a phone where he can call his friends for help."

"I...don't...you are my friends," said the man meekly, while Frank reflected upon the situation.

The horses had only walked a couple of hundred feet away before stopping and looking back. Like Anna, they appeared to be concerned with the man's survival. Frank still agonized over the issue, while Anna gave the man another drink of her soda.

Then the unknown man on the beach looked at each of them with a sudden sense of honesty and power. "This I will say to you both right now," he said. "If you help me today, I promise that not only will all your problems be solved, but you will live a life that will surpass your wildest dreams."

Frank and Anna gazed silently at one another, as alternate looks of doubt and hope flickered between them. Finally, they smiled and turned their attention to the man. "Okay, we'll get you back where you can rest and we'll keep things quiet. But…"

"Thank you, thank you," the man interrupted. He weakly lifted his head and looked as far north and then as far south as he could. With a faint smile that stretched his weather-beaten lips over long-neglected teeth, the man lowered his head back to the sand, muttering above as if deep in prayer.

"So, what about you?" Anna asked, as Frank began to lift the man to his feet. "What is your name?"

Gaining his balance and now supported on each side by his two rescuers, the man looked directly into Anna's eyes. "We shall see."

PART I

CHAPTER 1

August 1991

"I JUST DON'T UNDERSTAND why you have to go. I don't like it one bit." It was a statement Leeann had told her boyfriend, Brent Williams, time and time again. Her blue eyes were staring far out at sea, as a look of extreme worry discolored her naturally beautiful face.

"We've been over this so many times and you just have to trust me on this. I'll only be gone for ten days and when I return I'll have my Divemaster rating. Then, I'll be able to work on that dive boat in Hatteras."

"But I still think you should work on your father's boat, crabbing. Let's stay in Colington. We've graduated. We both had steady jobs. You keep telling me you want to get married and yet, you take off down to the Caribbean for ten days to learn a trade that, for all we know, won't support us. It just doesn't make sense to me."

That had been the ongoing argument for the past several months. Brent had a dream of operating a dive charter business on Hatteras Island, which he firmly believed would be an extremely successful venture. One that would give them the independence and freedom to leave Colington Island and truly be on their own. Not that working on his father's boat wasn't satisfying. But eventually owning his own vessel and taking people from all over the world to the shipwrecks of the *Graveyard of the Atlantic* would be, to him, both fascinating and financially rewarding. Then Leeann would no longer have to wait on tables and the two could have the family they both dreamed about.

"I know it's going to be tough for a few years, but we'd be getting in on the ground floor of the dive industry down here. Even my Dad is almost convinced. It's one of those risks we must take if we're going to get ahead in life. I don't want you waiting on tables all your life. I want us to be able to have whatever we want. With the crabbing up here, we'll just be scratching along year to year."

She sighed, having heard his side of the issue for months. While the rest of their friends were enjoying the water, they remained on their beach towel, both agonizing over their future.

One of their friends, Lawrence, noticed their dark mood. He walked from the waterline and sat down close to Leeann's outstretched legs. "Are you still upset?" he asked, with a thin smile across his face.

"Yes, I am!"

"Leeann, we should both be thankful," Brent pointed out. "If it wasn't for Lawrence here, I wouldn't be able to afford to take this trip."

"Hey, cheer up, Leeann. We'll be back in just ten days. If he took the Divemaster course up here, it'd take months and months to complete. At the resort hotel I go to on Rogotha, it'll take just little more than a week. I'll look after him. Everything's going to be fine."

She looked at him with a polite, yet wary smile and thanked him. Indeed, being the son of a wealthy banker on the Outer Banks, Lawrence could easily afford to front the expense of the trip and the training course for his friend. But Leeann had never really liked, nor trusted Lawrence. He had made passes at her before, but then again, he had made countless passes at so many girls for as long as she had known him. Short, overweight and loaded with a massive ego based on his father's money, Lawrence was just a tad short of being unbearable.

"Yeah, Leeann, Lawrence is going to let me pay him back without interest," Brent continued. "We leave tomorrow and we'll be back before you know it. This should be a happy occasion for us today. So let's go in the surf. Let's enjoy ourselves!"

Leeann's face finally brightened up a little and she relented. They stood up to join their friends in the water, but Lawrence remained seated. "No, you two go on. I'm going to relax here a bit." Leeann and Brent walked hand in hand to the water. Behind expensive sunglasses, Lawrence's eyes never strayed from her captivating figure.

CHAPTER 2

THE RESORT HOTEL COMPLEX on the north side of the small Caribbean island nation of Rogotha resembled nothing of its inherent nature. Among its swimming pools and crisp, white beaches that blended into turquoise water, there existed a sinister nature of wheelings and dealings of various nefarious factions. Not the least of which was the nation's very own government. In short, it was Lawrence's very favorite destination in the world.

He had vacationed there with his family every year since he was a toddler. Consequently, as he had gotten older, he became more and more connected with those local legions of graft and corruption. He started as a thirteen year old, buying marijuana with his cousins. Later, he made the graduation to cocaine which had taken over the demand structure of the region as the illegal drug industry itself skyrocketed to higher levels of marketing. By now, Lawrence was a valued and veteran customer of a middleman smuggling operation based in Rogotha City.

On this particular day, while Brent was gleefully taking dive classes on a coral reef miles away, Lawrence was making a rather dramatic move. He was graduating from cocaine distribution to solicitation of murder.

"So, my friend, let me get this straight. You want me to have your friend thrown in jail and then murdered? Is this not so?" The young Rogothan named Manuel Pantez stared across the pool side table at Lawrence not with amazement, but with a mild sense of amusement.

"That's right. I want him gone. I want him gone in a manner that, first, he will never come back, and secondly, that no finger will be pointed back at me. This is important. For that I will give you ten thousand US dollars. That in addition to the eight grand I'm giving you for my next load of coke."

"But...murder...that is indeed a much higher level. Of course, we can have it arranged so what you want will occur, but are you sure you want murder on your hands? Let me tell you from personal experience, once you commit murder or even being behind a murder, you are a changed person forever."

"Oh, I'll be a changed person all right. If you have the abilities to have him falsely arrested then murdered shortly afterwards in jail, then not only will I never be a suspect, I'll make it look like I was the only one who tried to gain his release. And that will secure my goal."

"Which is?"

"Well…it's like this…."

"Never mind. I already know. This is over a woman, right? One that he has and you cannot. At least as long as he's alive.

Lawrence took a huge gulp from his mojito and smiled at him. He put his hand out and they shook, sharing wicked smiles that knew no boundaries of conventional morals. "Manuel, it's always a pleasure doing business with someone as smart as you."

CHAPTER 3

HANDCUFFED TO A HEAVY METAL CHAIR, Brent was still in a state of shock. His arrest just hours before as he stepped into his hotel room was swift, sudden, and without any explanation whatsoever. Even Lawrence was nowhere to be seen.

Brent was thrown into the back of a dark police van and the vehicle sped away a split second after the heavy metal latch was secured. He bounced around inside the windowless compartment, falling once with his head striking the steel bench that was welded onto the floor. All the while, his thoughts were beyond questions on why he was arrested. He could only think about Leeann…the love of his life who now seemed a billion miles away.

It was at least an hour of such travel before the truck stopped. He heard muffled voices in Spanish, then the truck continued forward for another minute. Once again it stopped, the transmission thrown into reverse and again, Brent fell to the floor. Suddenly the doors opened and huge hands reached in, pulling him outside and onto his feet. In the scant seconds that it took him to be transported into a holding cell, Brent shot rapidly between thoughts of terror and of Leeann.

Two guards stood on each side of the chair, as he waited for what came next. It didn't take long. A side door opened and in walked an older man, dressed in what appeared to be the uniform of a captain. He was accompanied by a younger man not in uniform — almost his own age, a little older — who carried on an intense discussion with the captain, nothing of which Brent could understand. The younger man finally stared right at Brent with a somewhat detached look, then nodded his head to the captain. If Brent had known Spanish, he would have heard him say, "That's him. Have it done."

The two guards unlocked his wrists from the steel back supports of the chair and led him down a long, narrow hallway that eventually opened into a courtyard that was surrounded by tarnished stone buildings with bars on the windows and razor wire along the roof lines.

"What have I done? What have I done?" Brent shouted, which only resulted in a physical rebuke from one of the guards and muted laughter from behind the barred windows. "Why are you...."

This time the guard struck him on the forehead with the butt of his rifle and it was the next morning before Brent awoke...with dried blood all along his face and on the moldy stone floor of a tiny, dark cell. Indeed, he was a billion miles from Leeann.

CHAPTER 4

"No, no, no, I don't believe it for a second!" Leeann exclaimed to those gathered in the tiny living room of Mr. Williams' Colington Island home. "He...he's about the only one I know our age who doesn't do drugs!"

That may have been the case, but the word from Lawrence was that Brent had tried to buy cocaine from an undercover agent. This, of course, had not happened in his presence, he told Leeann over the phone. Also, of course, he was staying down there to search for Brent's whereabouts and to see what kind of bail is needed. "I am so sorry this has happened, Leeann. I feel I'm responsible. But I'm not going to rest until this misunderstanding is cleared up."

How could this have happened, reflected Leeann, as she sat in a rigid chair next to the window that overlooked Colington Road. Less than a week ago, they had been hand in hand, arm in arm, nestled together as if they were indeed one. Then, for him to be arrested! And in some foreign country she had barely even heard of!

She continued to well up in tears with each passing moment, jumping in anticipation each time the telephone rang. But it was always family or a friend asking for updates and if there was anything they could do. Without her best friend, Crystal, seated next to her and constantly consoling her, she perhaps would have drifted off into some kind of incoherent state of despair.

"I just don't understand this," Mr. Williams kept repeating. "This isn't like him. He couldn't have..."

Calls had already been made to their congressman and efforts to immediately find out about Brent's exact whereabouts were well underway. Hours went by that first evening and when Brent's aunt perked up after answering yet another phone call, the room instantly became silent. "Yes? Yes?" she practically yelled into the receiver. Then a few seconds later, she said, "Leeann, it's for you. Finally, it's Lawrence again."

"Hello? hello? What have you heard?"

"Well, it's good and bad, Leeann. So far, anyways. Brent is okay, but he's been transferred to another jail that's forty miles from here. I just called and they said they were not receiving visitors because of some emergency at the place."

"What…well…he's all right, isn't he? You said he's all right."

"Yes. Well, as far as I know. I'm sure they would have told me otherwise. They were quite insistent that no one was allowed there until the emergency had been taken care of. They told me to call back tomorrow. I think everything's going to be okay. But I plan to be outside the gates there tomorrow morning at sunrise. I'm not going to rest until Brent is back safe."

"Oh, thank you, Lawrence. We're still making arrangements to fly down. Brent's dad and me and his aunt are going to be there as soon as possible. Maybe the day after tomorrow. I don't care if he's released tomorrow afternoon. I have to see him. I need to see him!"

"There's no real need in that. I mean, since it looks like he may be released soon. I'll be here and bring him home as soon as he's out. Just you all stay there. You can trust me on that."

"It's just that I'm going crazy up here and so's everybody else."

"I know, I know. Me, too. In fact, I just feel responsible for all of this. I was the one who got him interested in coming down here. I should have told him to forget that dive business he wanted to start. Find something else that was safer, easier. So you two could be happy forever."

"You are so sweet, Lawrence. I will never forget what you are doing. But I still must come down. I love him so much…I can't stand this any longer!"

"Okay, I understand. I'll call you tomorrow to let you know the latest. But you just hang in there. Wait 'til you hear from me again until you come down. Everything's going to work out for the best. Just you watch."

When Lawrence hung up, his very next call was going to be swift and cold. The false anxiety over Brent was replaced with true anger towards Manuel. *It's been almost two days*, he thought. Brent should have been dead by now.

CHAPTER 5

IN AN INSTANT, THE JAIL CAFETERIA erupted into a violent brawl of mayhem. Chairs were flung, tables overturned and guards were attacked. Brent, sitting alone at a side table, was not part of the revolt and unable to understand Spanish, he knew nothing of its origin. He dropped to the floor behind a table that was on its side and peeked around its edge to see what was happening.

Three guards broke free from the inmates, rushing into a storage room that was adjacent to the main dining floor. They managed to slam the door behind them, a split second before several inmates literally bounced off the steel of the door. Another guard was not so lucky. Several inmates pounced on him and from Brent's vantage point, all he could see were flailing fists pounding onto the hapless guard, trapped on the wooden floor.

It was at that point that Brent first smelled smoke.

The flames crisscrossed the room as if matching the speed and ferocity of the rioting inmates. The old building, despite its stone exterior, was essentially a kindle box and the added-on steel doors and door frames, as well as the bars at the windows were quickly going to be among burnt rubble.

How it started would later be studied by government authorities. But on that day, as soon as the flames leaped to the exposed ceiling joists, all manner of confusion ruled, allowing for the riot and turmoil to expand outside and throughout the jail complex. The first inmate to attempt an escape from the fire was met with gunfire that pushed his body back over the main doorway's threshold. The sheer number of inmates who pushed through next were also met with gun shots. They managed to quickly overpower the guards who rushed to the scene.

Brent stayed low and worked his way around the baseboard, ducking from flames that licked from all directions. He reached a window, peered outside quickly and saw that inmates from other buildings were now being released by the initial rioters. As the noise of the riot had moved outside, only Brent was left to hear an eerie sound, just behind the steel door of the storage room.

The trapped guards were screaming for their lives and pounding hard on the steel door. One of the first flaming beams to drop landed against the door. Flames raked over the wood surrounding it and Brent could actually see the vibrations from where they were unsuccessfully trying to pound their way through.

He glanced out the window once again to see if help was coming. It wasn't. Instead, a group of inmates had already commandeered a truck and were heading out the gate, some firing weapons they had taken from the other guards who had been beaten. It was at that second that Brent knew he, too, could escape. He bolted for the door, stepping over several bodies that had already been touched by fire. Just as he reached the front doorway, he again heard the muffled cries of terror from the trapped guards.

With one quick sigh, Brent made his decision. He turned around and bounded towards the storage room. The joist was old and heavy and mostly covered in flames. It didn't even budge at his first attempt and he saw that it was wedged. Before he could attempt to move it again, he felt a searing pain on his arm and saw that his sleeve was on fire. Rolling his arm along the floor and through a puddle of orange juice, he put the flame out. Then he turned his attention back to the wedged door and the screaming guards.

With strength he had never known, combined with the rest of the ceiling falling apart and falling, he pushed the joist away. The door only opened little more than a foot or so. He reached inside and grabbed one of the guards by the shirt, pulling him through. The other two guards quickly followed, as yet another flaming joist dropped inside the storage room, igniting spilled bottles of cleaning fluids and cooking oils.

The front doorway was now nothing but flames. With the building disintegrating, Brent and the guards pushed their way through a severed window seal, its steel bars flaying in different directions, allowing for an opening just large enough for one person to exit at a time. Of course, Brent was the last one out, having helped each wounded guard to safety.

After crawling from the remains of the building, Brent was immediately surrounded by the three guards who peppered him with obvious thanks and genuine smiles of appreciation. Other guards came over, as the rest of the jail complex was quickly being retaken from the few inmates who didn't escape by vehicle or into the surrounding jungle.

Still unable to understand a word that was said, Brent meekly returned their smiles. As he caught his breath and got beyond the spontaneity of his actions, he begin to see a faint ray of hope. Maybe his efforts would cause authorities to let him go free.

But just as he could not comprehend words that he had heard, he also could not understand the complexities of life that had swirled around him since his arrest. Once again, he was taken under armed guard to another distant location.

CHAPTER 6

THE DISCUSSION TOOK NO MORE than half an hour with a substantial part of that time spent on everyday life on opposite sides of the island nation of Rogotha. Two government officials, in the privacy of a quiet courtyard that overlooked the Caribbean on the remote southern side of the island, decided Brent's fate. Then they reflected upon the changing dynamics of Rogotha's volatile politics.

"Well, the Pantez clan has demanded his death, but how can we do that after what he did for my men?" asked the warden of the jail where Brent had been kept. "Surely there is a way that maybe you could find some place that we could keep him here, over the mountain range from Rogotha City, since none of the Pantez people ever come over here."

"Yes, yes, there is a risk. They were paid for his murder, no? But, yes, the man can be hidden here," the local police captain and highest ranking government official of the tiny hamlet pointed out. "No one comes here, after all. It would be just as if he were dead. Disappeared."

"That's what I was thinking. Besides, from what I hear, the Pantez people are losing their clout anyways. The days of the smaller smuggling families are all but over. No one's going to risk pitting themselves against the Colombians or the Mexicans. They'll just be doing small time deals with tourists. We should not have to worry about them. As long as the prisoner remains hidden, of course."

"Yes, I agree. We can hold him here, then two or three years from now, the Pantez family will be out with the current government, and we can set him free. No one — that I can promise you — will ever find here him," assured the captain. "Depending on when and how long the current government stays in place, no one shall know. You and I have seen…how many different governments…three? If those in power go, we'll release this man to the gringos and buy some good will there. It shall all be good."

"Yes, I like that," the warden said. "If he had not shown such bravery, I would not have taken this chance. He saved his life that day, as well as the lives of three of my men."

"Then, it's agreed. I know the perfect place for him. Not even a jail. It is an old holding cell in a cellar…a dungeon really, of the old courthouse building. We do not hold court there anymore. It's just a tax office, but it's also where we hold political prisoners from time to time. Haven't held any in years. He will be adequately fed, but there is no chance of escape. Only you and I will know why he is there and only on my orders will he be set free."

"That sounds perfect. Now, on my end, I will turn some charred remains over to American Embassy. They have already been asking many, many questions. This will buy us time with them and the man's family. This will also save us from the wrath of the Pantez. Everything is working out, I feel good about doing this, even at the risk we are taking."

"Yes, but it is the least we can do," the captain pointed out. "A couple of years from now, he can go home and his family will be so happy. We will have a new government and we will go on. Now, tell me about your family. How are they doing?"

Indeed, Brent would have been saved and eventually released, but unfortunately, two years later in the midst of the violent days of the government's overthrow, both the warden and the captain were killed.

Leaving no one who knew who Brent was and why he was being held. The only thing left was an order that the prisoner was never to be set free.

CHAPTER 7

LEEANN WAS EMOTIONALLY wiped out. Her despair was as deep as Brent's, who she was now sure had been killed. Not able to look at the casket in front of her, she was held tightly on one side by Crystal and on the other by Brent's equally devastated father.

It was a packed funeral with vehicles parked alongside the curve in Colington Road where the cemetery looked out over the sound. Leeann's painful moans were in contrast to the sound of gulls nearby and the the occasional breeze that played along the nearby loblolly pines.

She could barely hear the preacher giving the last rites, just a word or two here and there that did not connect in her mind. Brent's funeral was an event that she never would have expected. She found herself wishing she was also in a casket, leaving a world of complete agony and misery.

Mr. Williams clutched her hands from time to time and she could hear him stifle sobs as the ceremony continued. Crystal, strong as always and knowing that she was indeed needed that day, propped her up. Tears were also a frequent occurrence throughout the remainder of the crowd, as Brent had been one of those extremely-likable neighbors who treated everyone in the exact same, down-home fashion. Along with sadness, the most transcending nature of those in attendance were shock and surprise.

All except for one person who — on the surface — appeared as sad and shocked as anyone else: Lawrence Parker.

He was initially miffed at not having a seat next to Leeann, but he did mange to squeeze in immediately behind her on the second row, practically pushing aside one of Brent's elderly aunts. Several times he leaned forward to pat Leeann's shoulder or to offer his hand, but she was in such a state of shock she did not even know he was there. That was in spite of the kindness she had managed to show him earlier in the week upon his return. "I will never forget everything you did to try to help Brent," she had said to him on several occasions.

Lawrence sat back impatiently in the folding chair, waiting for the preacher to finish the service and for the burial to take place. *A few more weeks of mourning on her part and then she will be mine,* he thought to himself. Then he looked at his Rolex and frowned, thinking, *How long is this funeral going to take?*

CHAPTER 8

IT WAS A QUIET DAY on the beach, hardly anyone around, with just a sea gull here and there lounging at the waterline. Leeann and Brent had a rare mutual day off. They took advantage of the weather for a quick excursion to Pea Island, with their four-year-old daughter. After all, young Amanda already loved the beach as much as they did.

"I'm still so sorry for the way I acted back then," Brent apologized as they sat on their beach towel, watching Amanda playing nearby in the sand with her favorite pony figurine. "It was a crazy period. I don't know what I was thinking, trying to go off on my own doing something I knew so little about."

"Oh, forget about it. It just made us stronger," Leeann said. "You had to get it out of your system and I knew that. I knew things would eventually work out for the best."

"Thank God you did."

"Yes, it's been nice, hasn't it? We didn't need all that trappings so many other people seem to crave. Look at Crystal. She's on the verge of going through her second marriage already. That rich lifestyle must not be all the glamour people think."

"Going down to the Caribbean island to that horrible place with Lawrence? What was I thinking? All that trouble and legal expense...glad that's behind us."

"You and me both. That was such a crazy time. Thank God for our congressman."

"Yeah, just imagine what we could have done with the money that it cost us for all the legal bills and those flights down there?" Brent added, his eyes looking not just at little Amanda, but also at her future. "We wouldn't be renting now and we'd have more money socked away."

"Oh, we'll do all right. We'll make it through. Anyhow, we can't change things. We can only enjoy what we have now. Would you take anything for her?"

"Of course not and even if we hadn't had her, I'd take nothing for you. I'm just sorry that I was so bull-headed back then. That I let all my money worries get to me and caused me to behave like I did."

"You don't have to apologize anymore. You've been doing that for years. We're back on our feet now, like I knew we would. It's just that we're a little behind from where we would have been. I knew the pressures you were under. I knew you didn't mean the things you said. You don't express your feelings very well, but they are real and strong and deep inside. That's what matters to me."

"Thank you. And you're right. Things have turned out great. I'm glad we made it."

They snuggled up together on the towel and stared at Amanda, who was now carefully burying one of her feet into the sand, then pulling it out to make a little house. She tried to put her toy pony into the hole, but the top of the roof caved in and she looked up at her parents with an exasperated frown. Brent and Leeann laughed, then stood to walk over to their now smiling child.

"Oh, that's okay, dear," Leeann pointed out. "That's the way life sometimes is. Here, let us help you make a bigger stable for your pony."

Brent reached down to help and he looked into his daughter's precious little eyes which reflected the sand and water and sky.

"Wake up! Wake up!" The loud command was followed by a sudden kick of the metal door, echoing throughout the dungeon and waking Brent from his recurring dream. "Food! Food!" the guard added in his sparse, heavily-accented English. "Eat!" Then he was gone, leaving the tray of thin soup and stale bread in the door slat.

It was over five years since Brent had seen or heard hardly anyone else.

CHAPTER 9

HE SAT IN THE SAME CORNER of the large, deep dungeon, waiting for the one highlight of the day. The point in time when, for several minutes, a narrow ray of sunshine ventured into his cell. It came from a two-foot wide, steel-barred window that was near the very top of the fourteen-foot high ceilings. Not that the room was spacious — it was less than two hundred square feet — but the high ceilings made his long stay there almost bearable.

Actually the window was just about at ground level outside and if he had arrived in the daytime all those years ago, Brent would have known that he was not being held in a jail, but a largely unused government building. Left alone in complete emptiness — no books, no radio, and of course, no letters — he plowed painfully through each minute, heartbroken at what could have — should have — been.

The low depths of the dungeon often had its pitfalls, especially during hurricane season. At the bottom of the room, there existed a drainage hole about a foot wide that apparently worked its way down to the opposite side of the building. In the countless hours of reflection that he had, Brent realized the building must have been built on a hillside and that he was on the high side. When a heavy rain occurred, water rushed in from several drain holes, doubtless serving as a catch basin and drainage area for courtyards or roofs from above. In turn, that water went out through the storm drain to no doubt, a nearby stream or river, perhaps even the sea.

There was just one other major physical element to his world and that was a huge steel door that opened only twice a year...at least that was the best he could figure. Then, a doctor would come in accompanied by several guards and he would give him a brief examination for reasons unknown even to them. He was given a haircut and even a new toothbrush and tooth paste. Food was still served on a tray through the slat in the bottom of the steel door. And, of course, the drainage hole at the bottom of the cell floor served as his toilet.

His days and nights were spent meandering from the deepest inward reflections to the most silly of useless thoughts. He battled for years over the question of God. He missed his dad, his aunt, and everyone else who shared his life back home. He labored incessantly over the most trivial of details. Why did common terns and elegant terns intermingle so well? How did the small speck of dirt on his floor come together? But mainly, he thought of Leeann.

He had long since given up on talking to his captors. During one of his first few months, there was a guard who would often speak to him, basic phrases in English such as "How are you today?" and "See you tomorrow." But after a year or so, he was gone. That guard apparently gained his freedom from wherever this place was, reflected Brent. Mostly they just ignored him, and he, them. Which as he later appreciated, gave him that much more time to focus on his memories of Leeann.

He could close his eyes and envision her warm, beautiful smile and the long blonde hair. And of course, those luscious, unforgettable blue eyes. He could see that confident walk, her friendly, talkative nature and the way she could make virtually anyone seem as if close kin. If not for that memory, Brent knew what he would have done long ago.

He would have given up.

The ray of light vanished from its daily path along the floor. The barely visible cloud of dust that always stretched from the light's source was also gone. Another day and perhaps another year had died and he was yet even further from a prior life that only prison had made him realize was so precious. Now, his only friend was despair.

But soon, that would change.

CHAPTER 10

IN THE SMALL but global community of multi-dimensional espionage, Ray Dampier happened to be what he hated most about modern society: a celebrity.

Intricately known and both revered and admired, Ray's astonishing skills were legendary. His services had once been sought by everyone from the heads of every national intelligence service to the billionaire barons of major drug cartels. But now, he was being thrown into a dungeon on the south side of one of the poorest and most remote islands of the Caribbean.

Ray was not only the leading expert on computer espionage, but one of the field's early founders. Earlier in his career, he had brought down countless individuals and criminal enterprises, as well as Cold War spies and modern terror cells. He was a master at identity creation and used those talents to foster the success of countless operations. But after seeing a largely ungrateful nation belittle the agencies he proudly served — from his early days in Intelligence as a young U.S. Army Captain in Vietnam to his equally unknown but spectacular successes in Iran and Afghanistan, Ray Dampier became disillusioned, jaded…and even angry. Too many idiots safely sitting on their sofas back home, degrading and not even understanding the dangerous nature of things that needed to be done.

That state of mind caused him to veer from his service to country. It led him into raiding a massive cocaine fortune — through the invisible computerized streams of global equity — to keep not for his country, but for himself.

Ray's superiors at the Central Intelligence Agency could have sent him to prison in the United States. But even they were wary — both from a sentimental concern over his past great services and a pragmatic desire of not wanting him as an enemy — to directly do him physical harm. The drug cartel that he stole from would no doubt take over that task, they rationalized.

Well, they thought wrong. Despite the fact that Ray had used his computer and financial skills to pirate away hundreds of millions of dollars from one of the drug cartels, his life was not in physical danger. Quite the contrary. With such unique and invaluable skills, they instead wanted his cooperation which would be worth far more in the long run than a relatively benign theft of just a few hundred million.

The top cartel members tried every conceivable "civilized" manner to bring about his cooperation. There were the promises of huge rewards and living a lavish lifestyle, not to mention the forgiveness of the sum already taken. They brought in the most beautiful women and offered him the most beautiful of villas, but to no avail.

Inevitably, they switched tactics to subtle threats, which he quickly met with a counter threat. He explained to them that if he could not type in a certain code once every two weeks, that much of their vast holdings would automatically be brought out into the open for the CIA, DEA, and Interpol, not only to see, but to confiscate. Obviously, Ray's unmatched reputation came not just from his computer and financial skills, but his solid grasp of Machiavellian talents as well. He was, quite simply, the perfect modern day pirate.

Even indirect steps at physical threats were unsuccessful. He virtually lacked any family, having never been married, except of course to his work. When they managed to track down his only family member — a moocher brother he detested — Ray even begged them to do him bodily harm. He had them checkmated at that angle as well.

Just before giving up, one of the leaders of the cartel came up with a novel idea. As a chief who worked his way through the ranks on distribution operations throughout the Caribbean, he vaguely remembered connections with some officials on the island nation of Rogotha and how they had places hidden even to the CIA. Perhaps a little time in one of their tiny, forgotten prisons would persuade Ray to lend his immense talents to their greater good.

CHAPTER 11

"WELL, WELL, OLD FRIEND, imagine meeting you here, of all places, in Rogotha. And on the south side, at that." It was a statement made in an almost pleasant, but certainly friendly tone, from a high-ranking member of a Colombian drug cartel to the one person on the planet who they truly needed. "In fact, Ray, I'm going to stay a couple of nights here myself because we're sure you're not going to like your accommodations here one bit."

"Excellent, Pasco," Ray responded in an equally pleasant one. "So, you'll be staying with me. That'll give us a chance to catch up on things. You can tell me all about your family."

The local governor of the south-central province of Rogotha — who understood very little English — stood attentively nearby, knowing the importance of the meeting that was taking place. Virtually out of the blue sea, this well connected and mannered visitor, along with several serious-looking bodyguards, arrived in his office with the scruffy, older North American in leg shackles. Only hours before they had walked up the steps to the tired old building. The local governor's phone rang and it was his regional chief who had the honor of living on the more-populated northern side of the island. "Do whatever this man asks," was the gist of his orders.

"Oh, no, no, no, my friend," Pasco said with a smile. "You'll be staying in what I have been told is a dungeon. I'll be staying in the little hotel down the street. Granted, the facility certainly is nothing that I am accustomed to, but then again, just wait to see where we are going to put you. Hopefully, Ray, you'll do the right thing and return our money and come work for us again. Then we can both get the hell out of here."

"Now, Pasco, you know throwing me in a 'dungeon' isn't gonna change my mind. The relatively little I took from you folks still doesn't make up for the great benefits I've given your financial operations. I deserve it and you know it. We're all just making money from the saps and suckers up north who continue to buy your products. Their problems are not ours, we know that. What I bring to the table is not just the best wealth creation, but also the best wealth protection. How many identities have I given you? What? Three? Four?"

"And my heirs for generations to come will thank you for it. But, as you know, I have my orders. We want most of our money back and we want you to work for us again. You were paid greatly for what you did. My friend, admit it. You never had to take any physical risks. And that's what this business has come to. That and being spirited off to the US and federal arrest. You just sit in an office and type letters and numbers into a computer. For that you were made a very rich man, don't you think that is fair?"

"We've been over this time and time again. Do I not deserve the kind of compensation that people on Wall Street who also type numbers and letters into computers deserve? Look at the payoffs those megastars have. I'm one of them, too. I just work down here instead of up there."

"Pfftt…Ray. You compare yourself to that faulty system? To those swine? Even the majority of shareholders of those firms believe such people are grossly overpaid. I, myself, have how many hundreds of thousands of shares in those companies? I will also say they're overpaid."

"Funny, I never see you complain about the outrageous salaries of those ball players who escape from Cuba," Ray pointed out with a laugh. "Are they not overpaid, for what? Hitting a ball with a stick, they make tens of millions?"

"Ahhhh, but that's real work. That's working with their hands. They are very skilled."

"Well, there you go. I work with my hands and I am also very skilled. I will keep my money and when you folks finally accept that, then I'll work for you again. I will continue to build your legitimate world that allows you to come out from the shadows."

The man smiled at Ray, turned his attention to the local governor and rolled his eyes, then looked back at Ray. "I do believe it is impossible to dislike you, my friend. Perhaps, that's another reason why there has never been a call for your life. You are really one of us, no matter where you were born or raised or lived. We are the true realists of the world, making money from those who are weak and lost. And, yes, yes, you are indeed very uniquely skilled. But...again, I have my orders.

"I have talked to your new overseer here and we have a little surprise for you. Yes, you are going to be thrown in a dark, deep, dungeon. I have no doubt a person of your experience and inner strength will be able to survive. But, we are going to throw in a little wrinkle for you. One that we all feel will finally make you see that our continued business association needs to go on. And all this bickering over payments will end."

"Oh, so, you're probably going to have me chained up on the wall like in those old gothic novels. Well, do your worse, that won't bother me. Matter of fact, my back needs a little stretching, come to think of it."

"On, no, no, no, Ray. None of that. We have another surprise for you. You won't be alone in this cell. There will be a *norteamericano* in there with you. One who's been in there for almost fifteen years. From what we've been able to learn, he was thrown in there...possibly by a so-called friend. Anyway, his life was completely wasted for selfish reasons. And for that, which even he does not know why. Or doesn't remember. You see, he went *loco*. He hasn't spoken a word in over ten years, they tell me. Oh, we'll have a guard posted outside your first night, just in case he tries to kill you. But other than that... unless you decide to come back and happily work for us under our terms, you are going to be locked up with a lunatic...so, good luck, my friend. I'll be waiting for your call in the morning."

Chapter 12

"Yep, it's just like they said. You're too far gone. Well, I guess I'd probably be pretty much the same if I had been in here for as long as you. You sit there in the corner staring at me, sleeping like a cat, then staring…yeah, I'd be just as crazy as you.

"But you should at least be thankful for one thing. You've been in here, what fourteen, fifteen years? Well, at this point in history, it would at least be the best fifteen years to throw away, if you ask me. The whole world's gone to hell. Yeah, I've heard that cliche all my life, but now things have really changed. When things got like this in the past, it wasn't so bad. The world was sparsely populated and social storms would just float on by with time. But now, the world is teeming with people. Can't walk for 'em. And they're all connected. All by what you couldn't dream of. The Internet. Lot of knowledge out there running around, but very little morals. Very little discipline, very little class…terrible. Everybody is 'me, me, me' and America especially has become a wasteland, absent of brains and grace.

"The schools are so dumbed down and when they took the paddle out the school, only violence took its place. No child left behind, I'm okay, you're okay, if it feels good, do it. On and on and on with all sorts of bullshit like that. Good thing you'll probably never come back to your senses or get to go back home. You would be dumbfounded at how the weenies took over. There's no freedom of speech unless it's to tear apart the government or the church. College professors tell their dumbed down fodder how evil their parents are and the kids wholeheartedly agree, riding around in the Beemers and having their credit cards paid for all the while… by those 'evil' parents.

"Parents aren't parents anymore, anyway. They're their kids' buddies. They want to be thought of not as parents, but as cool. Don't spend direct time with the kids. Take 'em to a planned activity.

Dance to soccer to karate to baseball. Everything's gotta be planned and organized...and conducted by somebody else. 'What? Me be a real parent? I don't have time. I have to work extra hours to pay for all these planned activities! So, I don't have to be a real parent.'

"And everywhere you go, people are on their cell phones, not for anything important, but just to make everybody else think they're important. Just because they're talking to someone. 'Hey, where you at?!' It's the new cigarette. Only the dumbest of humans still smoke, so the rest apparently have to have something to do with their hands, so they make these endless stupid cell phone calls. 'Where you at?!' This lack of discipline, this religion of immediate gratification has torn a once-great society into a mob of ignorant and egotistical ingrates! No, sir, you haven't missed a thing!

"There's no longer any music. Just loud, arrogant, demeaning shouts of depravity. Hasn't been a good band since Lynard Skynard. Yet the powers that unfortunately be call this new crap poetry. Tattoos are everywhere. Tattoos were once worn only by sailors, Marines, even prison inmates, those who struggled in the hardest of conditions. Now, anyone, regardless of how easy their lifestyle is, they have to have that tattoo. To show that they're 'tough.' You know, immediate gratification. It takes too long to see thirty countries as a merchant seaman. 'I'll just go to the mall and get a tattoo this afternoon instead. Then I'll, too, be tough.' No true substance to anyone, anymore.

"People can't read maps nowadays. They have to have printouts from computers to tell then how to get somewhere. Maps are too much trouble for these idiots! Even their kids can't tie a shoe. The more done for you, the better life is. They wouldn't last ten minutes in the bush. Our society is disgusting and if you dare say so, then you're an outcast because you're not supposed to tell the king he has no clothes on. But the king now is 'everybody.' Well, everybody who subscribes to the dumb-downed laziness of modern day America.

"And don't bother to get married anymore. At least not without a pre-nup. Marriage is a business all about the con, instead of about the love. The more they say that's not true, the truer it is. If you ever get out of here, take my advice, don't get married. Look at what they said happened to you. Your best friend set you up down here. I'll betcha anything it was over a girl. It's terrible out there, I don't have to tell you.

"And don't have any American kids, you'll regret it. You can't even raise one right if you wanted to. All the pseudo parents and their kids would brand you as uncool. And if you tried to instill discipline in your kid, they'd call social services on you. Nosiree, you didn't lose out on not being able to have any children.

"Nobody's at fault anymore either. If shit happens, who do I sue? You get injured in America, you win the jackpot. 'Ohhhh, I have mental anguish, somebody needs to pay. Oh, I'm not suing you, I'm suing the insurance company.' Only a dumbed down society can produce people like that.

"American work ethic? Ha! They expect to be highly paid and to work as little as possible. Glued to their cell phone all day is more like it. And of course, manual labor is too good for them! Auto workers surf in the rubber room and the car buyers look overseas. If it wasn't for immigrants, the country would shut down. Who'd do the real work?

"Sure, other countries are already far down the drain. You can't get fired in France. You can't turn in a potential suicidal bomber in the Mid-East. But, still we must refrain from criticizing American Pop Culture, or we will be branded as Neanderthals.

"So, just be glad you're locked in here. You're away from the ugliest sight in American history, uglier even than the Civil War, uglier than even race riots down South, uglier than even soup kitchens in the Depression. You're away from the final downward spiral of social implosion. You're away from an unspoken calamity of impending social upheaval. The self-destruction of a once-great country. I've shorted every bit of stock I have. I've hundreds of millions now, but if things in America disintegrate as they're going and if the dollars sinks like I think, I'm gonna be sitting on a mountaintop. Blue chips and Swiss Francs. Gold bullion and silver American Eagles. Well, sorry about America. Nothing lasts forever..."

Then, before Dampier could utter another word, his cellmate slowly and awkwardly stood, looked straight into his eyes and said in a low and halting, but determined voice, "I'm going to escape. I'm going back home. And I'm going to marry my girlfriend and we're going to have kids. American kids."

Dampier looked at him with a warm, proud smile and nodded his head. "Welcome back, son. Now, let's figure out how to get the hell out of here and accomplish all of our dreams."

CHAPTER 13

IT WAS LESS THAN A WEEK before Pasco flew back to Colombia, leaving orders with the local officials to alert him as soon as Dampier changed his mind. He thought it would only take a night or two, but he should have known that — if anybody could — Dampier would be able to retrieve the inmate from his madness. No problem, Pasco reflected. The old man loved the finer things in life. Maybe it would take a month or so of that barren existence for him to finally give in.

Dampier had other ideas. If he could just open a tiny crevice into the world outside, he knew he could organize an escape. It would certainly be risky and he would have to call in some big favors from many of his equally shady and talented friends, but it was indeed possible.

His first link was a nightshift guard, a young man who spoke a little basic English, one who spent a lot of his shift talking on his cell phone. Looking through the food slat at that tiny telecommunications key was a nightly "high" for Dampier. In perfect Spanish, he soon managed to convince the young man to carefully overlook the strict orders for them to be held without any communications to the outside world. He did so by promising him access to a far better way to communicate. With just a few calls and in less than two weeks, the young man was now the proud owner of an iPhone that was shipped to his home. Giving a man like Dampier access to the Internet — if only for minutes in the deepest period of the night — was almost like giving him a drill, pick, and shovel.

Dampier did far more than just make attempts to have help getting out or having help on the outside waiting if they did escape on their own. He set up an entire new identity for Brent, but also a large sum of money in various accounts waiting for his arrival. It would be a Georgian passport and identity and Dampier had to smile when he explained to Brent that Georgia was a country of the former Soviet Bloc and not the state down South.

Although the weeks grew to months, the two wasted not a bit of their time. From a stage of barely knowing any international geography, Brent soon was tutored so expertly on the world that he could draw out his own globe if he wanted. Dampier went much further than mere geographical boundaries. Their days were spent in complicated discussion on politics, economics, history, and even computer science, something as alien to Brent as the country of Georgia had been.

Dampier had tried his best to convince the guard to smuggle in some books, but he balked. Too tangible a way to be caught dealing with him, the guard pointed out. Allowing the use of his iPhone was dangerous enough. But with each passing day, enlivened by hours and hours of true intellectual pursuit, the naive young waterman from Colington Island was becoming quite enlightened to a world he barely had time to learn about on his own.

Twice, Pasco flew in to try to talk some "sense" into Dampier. Pasco assured him that there was no means of escape and that only a "God-given miracle" would grant him access to the real world and to his hidden riches. With polite small talk and a "no thanks," Dampier would send him on his way. He was left each time with his strong faith in God, a hope for such a miracle, and the joy of having a bright young student. The son he never had.

CHAPTER 14

A MIRACLE DID OCCUR but in the disguise of disaster. Her name was Clarissa, a massive hurricane that wreaked havoc throughout the Caribbean, but especially on the island of Rogotha.

The first real hint of the seriousness of the situation was not the high winds and rain that swept into their tiny window, but instead, a harried visit by several guards who left them with more than a day's supply of food and water. In fact, they brought enough for several days and left with a dire bit of advice. "Let this last as long as it can. Good luck. God be with you."

Brent experienced hurricanes before while in the dungeon, but never the deep concern expressed like this by the guards. Years before, a hurricane passed through that raised the water level in the cell to above his knees. Essentially being the storm drain center for the roof system of the building, the torrential rain that came with the hurricane had created a waterfall on one side of the cell and a suction drain on the other side. But even then, no extra precautions had been taken by the prison staff. Now it looked as if the guards were going to leave the building and perhaps even the entire town itself.

"Must be a big blow coming," Ray said as the steel door was locked behind the disappearing guards. He was right.

By midnight the entire building seemed to be shifting on its foundation. Rain overflowed the drainage pipe that was built inside the wall and seeped through a crack at the ceiling in the corner of the wall. The wind began to whistle through the small window with a howl that sounded like a wounded animal. Each time the water flow and wind increased, they felt as if it could get no stronger. But it did. Time and time again.

Then they heard a loud bang as if dynamite went off, creating a crack several inches wide that streaked up the height of the front wall, as if a huge snake was trying to escape the rising water. Ray shouted, "Look! Look at the window! The window is going to give!"

"Lot of good that's going to do us down here," Brent shouted over the wind's roar. "Probably a good thing though. Otherwise, we'd be drowning now!"

"Drowning?" Ray said with a big grin. "I thought you told me you were a diver!"

That was just like Ray, not allowing the bleakest of circumstances to defray his composure. Looking at his friend, Brent started to smile in respect, but he suddenly noticed a look of amazement on Ray's face. Another huge pop went off and the crack widened another couple of inches and even caused the steel rods in the window to gap inwards. Ray peered up at Brent with a smile as wide as the growing gap in the wall. "Brent, get the foam mattresses. Quick! Let's block that drain hole!"

In a sudden, complete understanding, Brent grabbed the mattresses, furiously balled then up and pushed the thin foam pieces into the storm drain. No sooner had they done so, the water level quickly began to rise. So powerful was the flow of water coming into the cell that the level was rising about a foot a minute. In the entire Caribbean and the East Coast of the United States as well, the only two people hoping for the massive hurricane to continue were Ray and Brent. At least until they could reach that window.

Ten minutes later they were within reach of the window seal, which by now had cracked open, with huge chunks of plaster and concrete falling into the still-rising water. They were treading water, Brent almost effortlessly, while Ray was beginning to fight to keep his head above water. There was an unfamiliar look of fear on his wrinkled face and Brent realized that the older man wouldn't be able to stay above water much longer.

As the rate of the water's rise began to slacken, with so much pouring through the large crack in the wall, Brent had to reach high and fast with his hands to grasp the loosened steel rods of the window. Quickly looking down over his shoulder to check on Ray, he braced both feet on the wall and pushed as hard as he could. Two of the bars jutted out and even came loose, as a broken concrete slab peeled back from the window.

The water was up another foot or so and Brent managed a quick glance outside. It was dark and rainy and a group of palm trees across the street were bent over almost double. He grabbed hold of two more bars and braced his legs again, repeating the successful move he earlier made. Two more bars peeled away — plenty of room for them to escape through — and with a big smile he turned around for Ray. But his friend was nowhere to be seen.

With his natural comfort of water, even in such circumstances, Brent dove beneath the still-rising surface and methodically felt around in the darkness. After a few seconds, he came to the surface for another breath of air, knowing the water depth was more than fifteen feet. He pushed off from one of the bent bars and descended as fast as he could, thankfully bumping into Ray's body halfway to the cell's floor. He expertly shifted behind his back, grabbed him by both shoulders and resurfaced. Brent let out a loud gasp, while Ray began a spasm of coughing. The man's eyes were rolled up in his head and his face was even whiter than the "prison tan" they both wore.

"Ray! Ray! Are you all right?" There was only a silent, weak response as Brent guided Ray's hand to the window seal. "Hey man, hang with me! We're going to get out of here!"

Brent extracted himself first, never letting go of one of Ray's hands. He was about six feet off the ground level outside, but there was a foot of so of flowing water over the walkway that would cushion their fall. Branches of trees, roof shingles, and even metal garbage cans were shooting through the air as if mere toys. But the storm of turmoil was nothing compared to the prospect of remaining inside that prison.

Brent braced his feet on the outside wall, then grabbed both of Ray's arms and began to pull. He was almost deadweight in his barely-conscious state, but that no longer mattered to Brent. If Ray's feet were in concrete, he was still going to come out of that cell!

The swirling winds and loud noise seemed to awaken Ray as his head and chest appeared from the window. He started breathing louder, gasping for air but at the same time still able to gaze around at his surroundings. A weak smile tried to appear, as does the one small patch of blue sky at the end of a fierce thunderstorm.

"Okay, man, now feet first...hold on, turn around," Brent ordered. "Now, we're going to drop together. You ready?"

Ray managed a weak nod of the head.

"Okay, Ray, let go!"

They safely fell into the water and mud, bracing themselves automatically for the sustained wind whipping through the street. Ray was still silent, and fighting hard to be as self-sufficient as he could. Brent helped him to his feet and they began to move as quickly as they could away from the damaged wall. Like downed pilots behind enemy lines, their first mutual reaction was to get as much distance as they could from where they "landed."

Thirty minutes later they had made their way a half mile down a deserted street, protecting themselves as best they could by using the tattered buildings as cover. They reached an alley that led to the beginning of the wooded area that surrounded the small coastal town. After a dozen yards into the thick tropical brush, they both literally fell to the wet ground in near-total exhaustion.

"We...we made it!" Ray managed to say. "See, I told you!"

"Well, so far. But we have a long way to go. What do we do now?"

"No problem," Ray pointed out, between heavy gasps. "We make our way to the next town, about ten miles from here. It has a real port and I know just about every ship captain and first mate in the entire Caribbean. We'll hitch a ride to the States. Yep, we're home free now. Home...free..."

Brent looked around at the lush jungle foliage and dark clouds above. The heavy rain suddenly felt great, and the ache in his limbs began to subside. They had made it!

"See, now admit it, Brent. Even in the midst of utter turmoil,

God can grant at least some justice. This certainly may not be a miracle to anyone else, but it is to us. Funny how this universe sometimes works, huh?"

Before Brent could respond, Ray dropped off to a sudden, much-needed deep sleep. He smiled at his aging friend, then peered around at the swirling trees and swift dark clouds and realized that this time on earth wasn't meant to be any "Heaven."

Looking through the dark clouds above, Brent felt a presence that he hadn't felt in a long, long time…one of comfort and reassurance in the midst of chaos. For the first time in almost sixteen years, he felt like some immense force was watching over him.

Then he thought of Leeann. Though still a thousand miles away, he felt suddenly unburdened and happy, knowing at least there was no longer a wall between them. He would let Ray sleep a little while longer and then it would be time to leave.

It was time to return to the Outer Banks…and to Leeann.

CHAPTER 15

AT NOON ON THE THIRD DAY of freedom, they were still traveling through the dense and jagged mountain range that bisects central Rogotha. Such a detour was necessary because of the number of soldiers and police officers who swarmed over the tiny town from where they escaped. Quite possibly the two were considered missing and drowned, swept away by the hurricane's storm surge. If so, that was exactly what both men wanted them to believe.

With the authorities blanketing the roadways that meandered along the coast around the island, the only alternative was to make a bee-line jaunt through the jungle to the north shore. The closer port on the south side of the island would no longer be safe for them. Widely considered as impenetrable by even most locals, the jungle initially proved little match for the determination of the two men.

Ray handled himself relatively well for the first day, even proudly comparing their trek to the Australian forces taking on the Owen Stanley mountains in New Guinea during World War II. Which, of course, had been one of the countless history lessons he had given Brent during their captivity. Now, history for them had become real.

However, Ray's age and his long-time living of the "good life" before he was jailed finally caught up with him. On the third mountain they encountered — one around the 2,500 foot level — Brent had to carry him virtually the entire way. At one point, it appeared Ray was having a heart attack, but instead, it was a spasm caused by being far past the point of exhaustion. Ray, who had survived U.S. Army Ranger School four decades before, managed to regain his composure and continued the journey more or less on his own power.

During that third day, Brent was the first to reach the peak of what was the last mountain they needed to climb. Meanwhile, Ray rested a hundred yards or so down the summit. Brent rushed back to his friend with a huge grin after having seen the northern port city of Dagmire which was their tactical destination. Through hooded and bloodshot eyes, Ray's face cracked into a smile when told about the view.

"Yep, that'll work. Help me up, son," he said with a sudden refurbished spirit. "We're getting there. We're getting there."

It took fifteen minutes for them to reach the peak, as Ray had to stop twice to catch his breath. He was probably coming down with the flu or a fever from the jungle trek. Meanwhile, the level of Brent's strength and agility was increasing with each passing minute of freedom. He had been relatively well-fed during his captivity and as his mind had often drifted off into the imaginary scenarios with Leeann and their "daughter," his physical routine had actually been quite demanding. Old fashioned calisthenics and isometrics had been a vital part of his way to handle his incarceration. The exercise and his dreaming about Leeann kept him from breaking. The last year with Ray and all of the real-world education he received added to his mental well-being.

The older man slumped into exhaustion upon reaching a point where he could see through the dense foliage at the port city. A huge smile suddenly appeared on his face, followed by the echoing sound of a large happy burst of laughter. "That's it, son! Now, we're home free!"

"Oh, no. We still have a long way to go. What are we going to do when we reach the town?"

"Brent, I said we are home free! Look at that old freighter moored to the right. Isn't that old rust bucket the most beautiful ship you've ever seen?"

"Well...errr..."

Ray beamed at him with yet another big grin. "Son, that's the *Rakeman Maru*. I know the Captain. I even know the owner. I've done business with them many times. We go way back. I'll bet you anything that ship is headed for Norfolk or Philadelphia. Just the direction we're headed. But it looks like they may be heading out pretty soon, so let's get a move on."

"You think… you mean we can hitch a ride?"

"Well, hell, yeah! They owe me all sorts of favors and they're the most discreet and trustworthy people you'll find down here. They'll hide us, drop us off wherever we want and then we really will be home free. They'll probably be going right by the Outer Banks."

Brent's smile matched Ray's as the two stared at the old ship. But suddenly, as Ray was beginning to stand, his smile disappeared. "Brent, Brent. Don't move," he ordered. "Be still. There's a snake. A poisonous one right next to you."

Brent froze, but without the slight bit of fear. His eyeballs slowly moved downwards, gauging the location of the almost perfectly-camouflaged snake. It was staring at Brent, poised to strike if it deemed the human intruder was a threat.

"Brent, man don't move," Ray quietly continued. "One bite from him and you're a goner. Just sit still and it'll move on."

But in the space of a split second that was too quick for either Ray or the snake to fathom, Brent took utter control of the situation. The snake's tongue was out and its mouth wide open in pain. Brent's fingers were expertly dug into its throat area as he almost delicately held the subdued creature near his face.

"Oh, not to worry, Ray. I've met many of his cousins before. They used to come into my cell through the storm drain, but they stopped doing so after a few years of realizing their friends never came back again. A very good staple of my diet there for a while."

Ray was full of respect for the younger man, who he realized had made the very best of his time trapped in a dungeon. Brent was strong, adept, smart, fearless, and most of all, his spirit had never been broken.

"Kill it, Brent! Man, I hate those things."

Brent stared into the dark eyes of the snake which he alone knew were anything but blank. The snake knew he was at the complete mercy of the powerful force that had entered his kingdom. It was in complete acceptance of the fate that he, himself, had dealt out to so many creatures who had come around before.

With a rapid, powerful twist of his wrist, Brent threw the snake into the foliage where it quickly regained its composure and scurried away into the underbrush as quickly as it could.

"Dude, those things are evil! You shoulda killed it!"

Brent stood slowly, his thin muscular frame glinting in a ray of sunlight that pierced the overhanging leaves. "No, Ray, that snake isn't evil," he pointed out in a quiet, assured manner, while turning his gaze towards the old freighter.

"I know where true evil does live," he continued, thinking of his impending return to the Outer Banks. "And he's not getting off so easily."

CHAPTER 16

EVER SINCE THE RUGGED COASTLINE of Rogotha disappeared over the horizon, Brent remained on the port side of the fantail, quietly gazing towards the north and west. Indeed, the ship's captain had been delighted to see Ray again and he quickly set about solving the two escapees' transportation needs. But looking from the deck of the ship was proving to be Brent's fondest joy.

They were given the worn clothes of boatswain mates and even hearty meals during their two-day passage northwards to the shipping lanes off north Florida. While Ray slept in a make-do stateroom of comfort, Brent chose to remain topside with its God-given salty air of freedom.

For hours on end, he scanned downwards where the rusted, barnacle-encrusted hull would slice through the water. The sea foam would curl into a whiteness that would quickly dissolve, waiting for the timeless passage of yet another vessel. With each drop of water, Brent reveled in the fact that he was getting closer and closer to Leeann.

"Son, you'd better get as much sleep as you can," Ray said, penetrating his friend's reverie. "It looks like we'll be there in a coupla days."

Brent smiled at him, then turned his attention back towards the north. Seconds later, he dragged his eyes away from the twinkling stars over the horizon and looked at Ray. "I still can't believe it. I'm going home. I'm going to see Leeann again."

Ray leaned against the railing and withdrew a Havana cigar, one of a dozen that the captain had given him. He expertly lit it with the captain's lighter, then took a grateful puff while staring into the darkness.

"I taught you a whole lot the past year or so, but I just want to be assured that you're prepared for what you may encounter," Ray offered, choosing his words carefully. "Your girlfriend's probably married now, so just keep that in mind. Just remember not to get your hopes up too high. But even I know that's asking too much."

"I know. We've discussed this enough already. Believe me, I realize how much time has gone by and what could have happened up there," Brent said. "I'll remember all the things you taught me about patience and taking my time and getting as much information as possible ahead of time. I'll do all of that, don't worry. I'll be fine."

Ray took another puff from the cigar and frowned, knowing that the younger man was no doubt going to be disappointed. "If she wants you back, fine, if not, that's okay, too," Ray said. "With the fortune that's waiting for you, if things don't work out with Leeann, your outlook is still really gonna change for the better. So, count on that."

"Look, Ray, I appreciate all the concern. But for all you know, the government may have tracked down all the new IDs and bank accounts you have and we'll be arrested as soon as we show our faces. So, believe me, I don't have my hopes up so much on any account."

"Good to hear that's your attitude. Actually that's quite a healthy way to look at life. But don't you worry about my end of things. Those documents and money are just waiting for our arrival. I've set aside a sizable fortune for you and you know how to go about getting it. I've also got mine…in fact a couple of them, so we'll both be fine."

Ray grew silent, knowing that all the money he managed to stash away would still not be able to match the gift that Brent had already experienced: true love. A concept he never had time or focus for during his intense intelligence career.

"Too bad the love you and Leeann have can't be bought," reflected Ray. "I was never so lucky. So, son, you'll always be richer than me."

"Thanks, Ray. Anyway, I don't deserve the money you're giving me."

"Oh yes, you do. I'd still be lost in that jungle right now if it wasn't for you. Hell, I never would have made it out of the cell. So, enjoy what's coming your way, no matter what happens with your woman."

"Well, thanks again. Man, if it happens."

"Oh, it will, I tell ya. Anyway, Brent, let me change the subject for a second. That's why I came up here. Here's what the captain is going to do for us. He can't stop the ship or even slow it down because that would trigger the tracking systems of the DEA and Homeland Security. They keep a close eye on vessels like this. But he is gonna veer to about eight or ten miles off Hatteras, lower a skiff with us aboard, tow us for a while, then signal us when it's time for them to let us go. We can motor right on in to Hatteras in just a few hours, if everything works out all right."

"That's sounds great!"

"Yeah, we'll even be able to guide our way in by the Hatteras Lighthouse."

"Yep, that'll work."

"Now, Brent, do you think you still have any good friends on Hatteras Island? Ones you know you can trust and who'll take us on to where we need to go without saying anything to anybody?"

Brent reflected for a few seconds, started to reply, then fell silent for a few seconds more.

"Brent?"

"You know, as much as I hate to admit it, I don't think I'll be able to totally trust anyone again. Well, aside from you and Leeann. But no one else. Besides, I never really knew anybody down there, just a mate or two from the dive boats. I'm from Colington. Anyway, the last time I totally trusted someone, I spent fifteen years in prison, as you well know."

"Hey, look at it this way," Ray said. "At least that's a good attitude to have with all the money you're going to get."

"Well, I trust...yeah, I still trust the Hatteras Lighthouse. Steadfast and immobile. There's my trust, right there."

Ray laughed out loud and took another puff from the cigar.

"Hate to tell you this, son, but they moved it a few years ago. But not very far."

"Wow! Are you kidding?"

"Yep, picked it right up, then put it back down a piece, but it'll still be there shining for us in a coupla nights," Ray pointed out, just before breaking into a huge grin and then into a laugh. "Hey, that's what you'll be from now on, Brent...yeah, that's just perfect!"

"What? What are you talking about?"

"You're gonna be...The Count..." Ray proudly said, as if he had just named a son. "The Count of Cape Hatteras."

CHAPTER 17

As soon as the signal came to cut the skiff loose from the freighter, the infamously unpredictable winds of the Outer Banks suddenly began to roar. The midnight seas had indeed been rough, but as luck would have it, a fast-moving squall appeared seemingly from nowhere. Such was the fate of so many other vessels that wandered through the *Graveyard of the Atlantic*.

It had been precarious enough when the skiff was close to the churning water of the ship's stern, but now — disconnected and tiny — the skiff was plowing over passing swells that were increasing in height and fury by the minute. The engine had cranked on the first try, but before the lights of the freighter disappeared to the north, they hit one swell completely wrong, causing water to swirl into the craft. The violent collision almost swept Ray overboard, but a compass in his hand did drop to the depths below.

"Hang on, Ray! Hang on!" Brent shouted over the wind, while attempting to re-start the outboard motor that had been stalled by the wash over.

"I lost the damned compass!" Ray shouted back. "Dude, can you believe it? I'm an idiot!"

"Not to worry, Ray. This squall will pass in a little bit and then we can sight our way in by the stars. Then we should be able to see the lighthouse. So just hold on, man. We're going to make it."

The timing of the drop-off, in retrospect, was certainly bad, but they really had no other choice. Had they stayed aboard, they surely would have been discovered when they reached the first port. It had been the proverbial "now or never" situation, so they took the gamble with the deteriorating weather. So far, they were losing.

A flash of lightning illuminated the turbulent water as if it was mid-day and then another massive swell rushed by. Their boat was thrown down the trough so fast that its bow sunk into the water. Both Ray and Brent were pitched forward violently, their bodies crashing into the sea. Brent surfaced first and experienced a second or two of complete horror, until he finally saw Ray's head emerge nearby. He swam quickly to the older man, who was in a coughing spasm with an unaccustomed look of terror on his face.

"Let's stay together, man!" Brent said. "The boat's gone, so we're just gonna have to ride this one out!"

"We…I'm…I'm not gonna make it, son…not gonna make it."

"Hell, yeah, you're gonna make it! We didn't come this far for nothing. Just you hang on!"

Another violent stroke of lightning hit the water a short distance away, with the thunderclap following a split-second away. The wind was increasing and even Brent, who had grown up on the sea and the sound, was amazed at the intensity of the storm and the size of the swells.

"I can't…I'm…I …," was all Ray could say. "I…you had…"

"Hang on, Ray! Hang on!"

Then what appeared as the mother of all swells came upon them, violently forcing Brent's grip from his friend's arm and shoulder. They were a foot part, then three, and by the time the swell passed, he was ten impossible yards away. Brent yelled into the wind, "Ray! Ray! Ray!"

His mentor could only return a weak smile of acceptance, mixed with a final look of fondness for his friend. A flash of lightning gave Brent one last glance at Ray, just as the old man yelled, "May God be with you." Then Ray was swallowed by the rage of the sea.

"Ray! Ray! Ray!" But there was no answer.

Brent had to work hard to keep his head above water and he could feel the heavy current carrying him along as if he was lost in the rapids of a mountain stream, rather than out at sea. Minutes and then hours passed and he felt the beginnings of final and total exhaustion. Then he felt the arrival of something even more devastating: the sense that it was finally time to give up…that life had handed him the last bad hand.

"God, just go ahead and take me, okay?" Brent calmly asked in the midst of utter turmoil. "You took me away from the love of my life and now you took away the best friend I could ever ask for. I still believe in you, but...I just can't take it anymore. It seems to be the fate you have for me anyway. So, let's get this over with."

Brent felt an utter calm; a sense of final peace. The weariness of every muscle in his body suddenly felt like it had been overcome by a huge, warm blanket that wrapped him in safety.

Brent smiled upwards towards the Heavens one last time just as another flash of lightning shot directly overhead. *It just wasn't meant to be*, he reflected. Then, as his head began to slowly slide under the trough of water through yet another huge swell, his last conscious thought was of Leeann.

It was now all to end. But at least he had known that true love, if but for such a brief while. He smiled again, realizing his grave would be in his beloved sea, next to his beloved Outer Banks...the home of where his true happiness would have been....

PART II

CHAPTER 18

"TELL HER I'M NOT HERE," Leeann told her secretary. "I don't feel like talking to her today."

That was such a recurring order that it had become pretty much of a joke to the staff at Darebridge Mortgage. Entering its tenth year — and originally funded by the estate of her second husband — Leeann's company had done splendidly well in the boom years. Many, many people who couldn't qualify for a mortgage loan from a conventional bank were seldom turned down by Darebridge.

Leeann was also the expert at using her sweet smile to conjure up images of second homes paying for themselves, allowing baby boomers to look forward to a paid for home at the beach when they retired. *Oh, don't worry about balloon payments, or variable rates, this is the Outer Banks! There will always be somebody waiting to buy your home at your price!* Well, at least until 2007. Then, like so many other such businesses, her's went on a massive nosedive and her only calls were from frightened homeowners on the verge of foreclosure.

Leeann didn't need any such calls today. She was going to make the final decision on something she had been putting off for much too long. Today was the day she would finally decide on what tattoo design to put on her lower back. With her desktop covered with photos of tattoos and even her laptop displaying several of her favorites, she pondered each design as she smoked her fourth cigarette of the morning.

Indeed there were many more pressing concerns, most of them financial. Her business was on a very shaky foundation, but so far, she had not had to make any past due mortgage or utility payments. Her Mercedes was paid for and her IRA and 401K were safely hidden away from any potential creditors. She did carry a lot of credit card debt. There was still about eighty thousand she owed on a bridge loan to a home she had unwisely taken on a year ago, just a small home between the beach road and by-pass that she had planned to use for meetings with any of her boyfriends. So, all in all considering the economy, things were not too bad. As long as the lull ended by the end of the year or the Spring of 2008, she'd pull through fine.

Tight times had happened before, but she was pulled through by her current husband. But now, even though Lawrence never confided in her with his business dealings, she was beginning to notice that he was also going through some financial strains as well. Not that either one of them still weren't supreme experts at living way beyond their means. Several times they had huge negative net worths, but anybody not in the know would think they were billionaires.

Somehow Lawrence always managed to come up with big cash at the tightest of times. Leeann never asked about that after her first couple of attempts early in their five years of marriage. It was just family money, he told her, so don't worry about it. After all, he did practice law and had a busy practice, often in the middle of a lot of serious real estate dealings. He had a pretty good record in such personal deals, though he had managed to buy his way out of several complete disasters by God knows how.

So, she wasn't worried about the temporary tough times. Instead, her focus was on her tattoo design selection. One of her young boyfriends had been pushing her to get one, even though at thirty-seven she initially thought she was just too old for one. But, she rationalized, who's to say? Who makes the rules?

Leeann reached the point where she had narrowed it down to about four designs, when her receptionist again walked in to ask if she would now take a call. "Who is it?" she angrily responded, not looking up from her design photos.

"Your daughter."

Leeann frowned and quickly scanned each of the four designs one more time. She put her cigarette out and said, "Oh, okay, put her on hold and tell her I'll be with her in just a minute."

CHAPTER 19

How could all of this happen so quickly? One year he was a wealthy attorney focusing on real estate. Plus — and unknown to virtually anyone else on the Outer Banks — he was the linchpin of the region's largest cocaine ring. A mountain of equity on one side and a mountain of cash on the other. He was the local king. Then, almost as suddenly as his rise occurred, his kingdom began to falter. Fast, dramatic, and painful. And yes, with the very distinct possibility of personal violence. Upon himself.

From the very first day he left Rogotha, Lawrence had utilized his newfound connections on the island to begin a distribution operation that had lasted for over twenty years. Arranging the elimination of the boyfriend of the woman he wanted was just the start. He kept in touch with Manuel and visited the island about once a year. Smuggling the cocaine into Florida and then transporting it up the coast to North Carolina was Manuel's part.

Lawrence was in charge of regional distribution, using his connections along the Outer Banks, but more importantly in the cities of Tidewater Virginia. It had become quite a mutually-beneficial and long-standing relationship, one that made Lawrence a multimillionaire and Manuel more than just a member of a relatively small crime family of a tiny Caribbean nation. While they both became rich and powerful, they also shared a future predicament: they were headed for a rendezvous with a ghost from their past.

Lawrence was not feeling so rich on this warm, cloudless day in late September. His accountant had sent over detailed reports of his income and expenses, for both his personal and business concerns. His bills were staggering while his income had dwindled. Years had passed since he all but gave up on the typical title search and recording that many lawyers utilized to steady their income streams between big deals.

Now, Lawrence was caught on both sides by financial disappointment. In the past, when times were slow for his firm, he made do — extremely well — with his sideline cocaine business. In fact, for many years, he declared just enough income to keep any red flags from rising with the IRS. That money he handed over to Leeann, who could burn through it so quickly that even he would stare in awe. However, as the real estate bubble burst began in earnest, his cocaine distribution side was also taking tremendous hits.

There was the influx of Mexican gangs who were quickly and violently taking over the Tidewater Virginia market, as well as a few key busts to his people that occurred during the previous year. As his remaining people either vanished or went over to the new forces in the region, he was left alone on the Outer Banks with the apparent death of his hidden prized cash cow.

Being the overall financing of the operation, Lawrence was safely buffered from the encroaching Mexican gangs. But spending the week going over all of his legal and illegal records, he suddenly realized that not only was he caught up in a wicked bear real estate market, he also owed his long-time Rogothan connection over two million dollars. Lawrence had always come through in the past, but this time, there was no wave of drug cash or real estate sale on the horizon that could bail him out.

It was now a time of panic and Lawrence knew just what had to be done first. He reached down to the bottom drawer, unlocked it with a key on his ring and withdrew his personal stash of coke. A couple of lines would settle him down and let him think things through.

However, even with his brilliant but tragically evil mind, Lawrence could not comprehend the true extent of what he would soon face.

CHAPTER 20

CRYSTAL SAT IN THE CORNER of the tiny den of her small home. For about one hour, sunlight would pass along the room's old carpet on any clear day. Buried amidst live oaks in the middle of a packed Kill Devil Hills neighborhood, her old flattop was not only all she could afford, but it was all she wanted. Or more accurately, more than she thought she deserved.

Her life had taken a quick turnaround from her days as a young woman, when she commanded the attention of virtually any man that had the luck of entering her presence. There was a line of men after her hand and she had the pick of any of them. She quickly went through one ill-advised marriage. Her second choice was ultimately based more on money than love, but she at least tried to merge the two motives in a way that would be best for her future. A friend of hers often told her, "Don't marry for money, but don't marry where there ain't none."

Crystal did indeed marry and she married well. Her husband was from a wealthy family and he was a good guy, though not exactly a workaholic. Actually, he was a surfer and since there was apparently an endless and growing stream of dividends from various stocks, funds, and even trusts pouring in, she didn't mind. They had a great life, something that unfortunately, she didn't fully appreciate until it was too late.

Several years before, her husband and daughter had taken one of those father-daughter bonding trips, but not to a museum or teen concert. Instead, it was to a week-long girls' surfing camp in Costa Rica. They wanted Crystal to go as well, but since she didn't surf and her ten-year-old daughter did, she had told her husband that she would stay home and look after the house. Staying on the Outer Banks that week was the most fateful decision of her life.

On the way back from the airport in Raleigh-Durham, a businessman friend of their's volunteered to give them a ride to the

Manteo Airport in his private plane. It crashed in heavy fog upon approach and all three aboard were killed.

In her early thirties, heir to a portion of a large family fortune, and still the most beautiful woman on the Outer Banks, Crystal made yet another fateful decision. Her deep hurt combined with an immense sense of regret brought Crystal to her emotional knees. She took just enough of her inheritance to buy a small cottage in a working class neighborhood and a small trust they gave her a thousand dollars a month on which to live. The rest she turned back over to her husband's family.

For four years now, she was alone and hurt. Hidden away in a quiet neighborhood, spending much of her time painting scenes from her occasional day-trips to the sound or to the north beaches where the wild horses still roamed. Even the beaches along the barren stretches of Highway 12 South, where she and her high school friends had often gone many years before. Her paintings sold well in local shops, but she only painted two or three a year.

Crystal only painted in that daily path of sunlight that ventured into her hidden, painful and guilt-filled world. Her hour on this day was almost up.

CHAPTER 21

FRANK MITCHELL WAS NOT your average beach bum who ended up barely making ends meet on the Outer Banks of North Carolina. He possessed, among other accolades, a Silver Star with combat V and a host of combat and security experiences that even he could never reveal. But the allure ended for him when he saw his country falling back just as it did with his father during Vietnam. Not appreciating the efforts that he made in order to fight a gray war that transcended geographic lines. The world had gotten too complicated for a majority of people who spent ten times as much time keeping up with the personal lives of Hollywood celebrities as they did historical global shifts of major proportions.

He came from a well-connected family in Savannah, a renegade in that he was fiercely devoted in school only to subjects that were not part of the curriculum. His high school grades were just barely passing and it took the help of a few of his father's business buddies to get him into a decent college. Frank spent two years there and to everyone's amazement, he had a 3.9 average and was considered one of the most promising students of history and political science that had come through in a long while.

What surprised everyone even more — though not his family — was his withdrawal from college at the beginning of his junior year to enlist in the United States Marine Corps. Another two years, he could have gone in as an officer, but Frank had something else in mind. A fast track to Special Operations.

He graduated from Marine Corp boot camp at Parris Island where he made squad-leader. His MOS was for radio school, but after a quick discussion with his Senior D.I. and a couple of personnel officers, Frank persuaded them to change his MOS to 0300… grunt. His skills and extreme motivation soon led to a quick PFC rank, then orders came around again for radio school. This time he did what he was told and graduated from field radio operator school number one in his class.

Sent back to his old infantry unit, he deployed on a six-month Mediterranean cruise where he spent much of his time taking non-required Marine Corps Institute specialty training courses. By the time he was back stateside, he was promoted to Lance Corporal and then he started to call in some political help from his family.

Frank got permission to attend jump school at Fort Benning and after another year with his unit, he garnered several more training assignments. He was as "at home" in the jungles of Panama as he was in Cold Weather training with the U.S. Army's 10th Mountain Division in upstate New York. Then — and this time without any family connections — he was approved to attend his dream assignment: Ranger School.

Months later with both his jump wings and Ranger badge, Corporal Frank Mitchell was on his way to Kuwait.

As he did everywhere else, Frank worked hard, focused, and was the proverbial team player. His baptism under fire went smoothly and seconds into hearing his first shots fired in anger, he felt as if he had been under fire since Iwo Jima. He couldn't say that he distinguished himself, only that he fit in perfectly, performed his mission and made it back with his fellow Marines.

By the end of the war, and Saddam's rout back to Baghad, Frank was one of a handful who was called in to work with a small group of military personnel that only later he found out was Delta. It was the beginning of his Special Ops assignments and he had finally reached his goal.

For over a decade Frank served in various hotspots around the world, Haiti, Panama, even Bosnia. He fought valiantly and expertly, learning something new every day he was in uniform…or in local costume, whatever the case may be. He was stunned and angered at 9/11, even angrier than he had been when the Rangers were put into Somalia with too little support years before. Assigned full-time to Delta, he was considered not just a creative, imaginative, and brave member, but one who all his buddies knew could be depended upon, no matter what. At that level, all the non-hackers had long-since been weeded out.

Years later in Iraq, Frank walked into a trap that even his immense tactical skills could not overcome. He and three members of his team were tracking the suspected launching sight of a mortar that had almost hit a convoy several miles from the Green Zone. There had already been a devastating suicide bombing earlier in the day and the situation citywide was indeed hot, even chaotic. As soon as they ventured around a corner, his group came under AK-47 fire and one of buddies was killed instantly.

Without even a blink, Frank sprinted off to what appeared to be in the exact opposite direction of his ambushers, while his surviving teammates had taken cover. With grim looks on their faces, they watched him disappear, knowing exactly what was going to take place. One immediately checked the condition of their teammate even though he instinctively knew he was gone. The other reached over the barrier they were using for cover and fired a few bursts to where the ambushers had originally fired, silently attuned to Frank's sudden "disappearance."

Two blocks west, four men and a teenaged boy rounded a corner laughing and congratulating each other for what they knew was a kill shot. They held their rifles high and continued with their jubilant celebration, thinking they had conducted another successful hit and run mission.

But no sooner had they turned their eyes forward, they saw their last worldly image. Gunnery Sergeant Frank Mitchell and his M4A1. They died on the spot, falling amid their own blood and weapons.

Several days later, at a base camp north of the city, Frank was alerted to a most amazing news story that was making the rounds. "Teenaged boy savagely gunned down by trigger happy soldier."

"Stupid press," Frank said to his captain as he read the story from the laptop. "Don't they know I'm not a soldier? I'm a Marine."

His captain laughed, even though he, himself, was Army Special

Forces attached to the Delta unit. They both shook their heads again, knowing full well that by the time the back home "experts" had their day, someone would have to take the fall.

Just as if he would have jumped on a grenade to save his fellow buddies, Frank volunteered to take the heat.

"Don't worry, Frank," his captain pointed out. "Lay low for a couple of months and those morons will be focused on Britney and Lindsey. Then, you can get back to work."

CHAPTER 22

ANNA LOVED HER HOMELAND and knew that Russia was striving towards greatness it had never known. There was good and bad in its continuing transition, as nothing so historically monumental could happen without livid growing pains. Which was exactly the current nature of her own personal life.

Traveling to the United States as a student was a dream she had since childhood. It was then she first saw *Pretty Woman* and barely before the opening credits she was hooked to a culture so unlike her upbringing in St. Petersburg. However, it wasn't the tawdry side of the movie that held her attention. Instead, she was fascinated with the operation of the Regent Beverly Wilshire. She dreamed of working in hotel management and how fascinating it would be to meet new and different people on a daily basis.

So, by her second year of college in which she was majoring in hotel management, she successfully applied for the extremely popular student visa program that so many young Russians utilized to work summers in the United States.

Anna stayed awake during the entire flight from Moscow to Paris to New York to Washington and then the bus ride to the small North Carolina town of Elizabeth City. There, she and three other young Russians were greeted by a local representative of the agency that managed the student worker program. In the middle of the night, they were whisked by a van along strange dark roads that even went through what seemed to Anna as the most dismal of swamps. Later on she would learn that, indeed, it was actually named the *Dismal Swamp*.

As the van turned onto a modern five lane highway and shot southwards, she felt a sigh of relief as she encountered dozens and dozens of roadside businesses that ran the immense range of life itself in America...from a modern, design-tested Sonic Drive-In to a boarded-up shack that sold fresh shrimp and crab meat to tourists.

The vast differences in appearances was oddly soothing and triggered her first realization that life all over the world was so much the same, despite naive notions of nationalistic pride on all sides.

Like the other girls in the van, her face was virtually plastered against the glass of the windows as the van made its way across the Wright Brothers Memorial Bridge. Mesmerized, they watched the endless line of soft lights that could be seen as far north and as far south along the soundside border of the Outer Banks. The drive from the bus station ended at a home in Corolla, a relatively small structure that was located halfway between the Atlantic Ocean and the Currituck Sound, a distance of less than a third of a mile. When taken to her room — which she would now share with three other girls in two sets of bunk beds — she was the only one who remained wide awake and who didn't plop down in deep sleep.

Instead, she walked softly to the living room of the sparsely-furnished rental house and stared out the large picture window. There were other homes in the cul-de-sac, similar to the one she was in and only a few of them were lit. Well, she thought, here she was... the beginning of a summer that would be full of work, but one that offered an unfathomable degree of adventure.

Anna stared into the darkened neighborhood when a slight movement from a shadow at a nearby home caught her attention. At first she thought it was a cat, then she thought it was a small dog. But as it peered from the shadow, she knew it was something different. She watched as its head slowly swiveled around to the left and right, then its neck turned slowly for a rear guard check.

It was a fox. A beautiful, sleek, smart, and tediously-careful fox. As its body emerged totally from the shadows and onto the asphalt pavement, it suddenly shot across the roadway until it found a safe haven of shadows on the opposite side of the road...in yet another yard of promise.

Anna smiled...then went to bed.

CHAPTER 23

SUZANNE WAS ELEVEN YEARS OLD and upset that her mom wouldn't buy her one of those new iPhones. Not that she was a spoiled child...in fact, quite the contrary. She wanted the new cell phone for its photography and Internet attributes, while her mother only wanted her to have one of those colorful cellphones that were all style instead of substance. "But none of your friends have one of those," Leeann had told her time and time again. "Don't you just love the lime green one I got you? It goes so well with all the clothes I buy for you."

The girl — very advanced in her years despite her young age — would just frown and shrug her shoulders. How different she was from her materialistic mom. Suzanne had gained her mother's good looks, but not one iota of her personal traits. She was very bright, a little bookworm, and one who had only asked for a set of the *Blue Planet* series of DVDs for Christmas. Instead, she had received a host of trendy and over-priced clothes that was the current rage of the shallow and superficial set.

Those who knew Suzanne's situation understood exactly where the young girl had gotten her love of the sea and her disdain for conspicuous consumption. It was from her real father, who died when she was only six years old. She was on the verge of hating her stepfather, Lawrence, who she had always held in silent contempt. It was just something about him that generated a sense of revulsion and she was still angry at her mom for marrying him a few months after her dad had drowned while surfing one day at one of his favorite spots on the Pea Island Wildlife Refuge.

The older she became and the more she talked with her dad's real friends, the more uncertain she was about his fate. Her dad was just like the dolphins that he would sometimes show her gliding through the unbroken part of a wave, looking back at them in equal curiosity. Suzanne knew that she was still young and not yet given the intellectual credit that she was due, but sooner or later she was going to find out the truth about what happened that day.

Another issue that bothered Suzanne was her inability to work anywhere. She wanted to have her own money to spend however she wanted. In a few years, she would be eligible to work if her parents would sign documents to allow her a waiver for the underage work laws. She doubted her mother would do so and that again made her feel like she was locked into a cage.

"But you don't need to work...you don't need any money, because I already buy you everything you could possibly want." That was the comeback she always received from her mom whenever the subject came up.

Suzanne was also constantly taken from one organized activity to another organized activity. Everything in her life was strictly organized, regimented, and orderly. There was dance, soccer, dance, softball, soccer, dance, soccer, softball...all the activities that her mom thought were important. But what was important to Suzanne was the spontaneous aspects of life. Catching a surprising glance of the full body of a dolphin, sleekly roaming through the surf or a line of pelicans expertly skimming inches over the water, rising and lowering with the wave movements, patiently looking for a meal. That was what she wanted.

The vast majority of girls her age were all wrapped up in clothes, MySpace pages, celebrity "entertainment" shows, and of course, text messaging each other with the most useless of messages. Young Suzanne was not among them. She was in love with nature and specifically, the sea. She didn't care that much about text messaging. She cared about how she could maximize her time learning about the sea and she could do that so much better on that new iPhone than the brightly colored little fashion piece that her mom insisted she carry.

While her mother would be ferrying her along the 158 by-pass from cliche planned activity to cliche planned activity, Suzanne knew all the points where she could catch a quick glance of the sea.

Its bright and moving surface visible between narrow alleys and cuts to the beach.

The sea was beautiful and majestic. It was already part of her soul...and where the soul of her long-lost father now resided... waiting for her.

PART III

CHAPTER 24

BRENT LAY THERE UNABLE to open his eyes. Not only did he have no idea where he happened to be, he also had no idea where he was metaphysically. In fact, his first thoughts as he slowly rose from his deep sleep was if he was even alive. He only knew that everything was so soft and warm, so still and quiet.

As if in a great distance, he imagined himself hearing very faint voices. It was as if his hearing was just as laggard as his eyelids. At one point he thought that he was still in the sea, floating aimlessly and helplessly as he did for so long. Then he began to reconcile the possibility that he was just going through another of his multiple day sleeping periods that had been a core part of his many years in prison. His mind encountered the possibility that he was dead, just hanging in limbo and waiting to see what else God had in store. Limbo…where he had already spent almost half of his life.

The voices slowly became more audible, but Brent still could not open his eyes. He could not even move. His body was not used to the extreme comfort that seem to envelope his entire being. The voices were still there and it wasn't the Spanish that he had often heard from prison guards when a shift change took place outside his cell door. It was laughter…excited laughter. It seemed to be children or what he remembered children sounded like.

Then a much louder noise occurred. It was a click, not as loud as the cell door click that occurred when guards came in to force him to shave or for when his meager food rations were slipped through the grate in the steel door. This was something else and the strange noise made him fight harder to open his eyes.

Brent felt the presence of someone in the room. He remained still, unable to move. He wanted to, but his body would just not respond. This was either a return to prison or an arrival at death. And there wasn't anything he could do about either one.

This time the voices he heard were nearby. They were faintly familiar voices. In English, but almost sounding like another language since he had communicated so little for so, so long. He finally managed to actually move a bit and his eyelids gave in from the deep sleep, starting to lift open to see from where the voices came.

"Hey, I think he's finally awake," Frank said.

"Yes, yes, he is," Anna agreed.

Brent shifted a little and opened his eyes enough where he had to squint in even the dim light from the open doorway.

"Dude, are you okay?" Frank asked. "You've been sleeping for the past two days."

The strength in his limbs began to slowly reappear and Brent gradually shifted upwards so he could sit in the bed. He stared at the sheets and the blankets that wrapped around him. He wasn't dead. He wasn't still drifting in water. He wasn't still lodged deep inside the dungeon of a forgotten prison on a barely-known island. And... he was indeed alive.

"Where...where am I?"

"You're in a home in Corolla. North Carolina. About five miles from where we found you the other day. Several people live here. Workers around here. This is my room, but I've been staying elsewhere. No worries about that, but we just need to see where you go from here."

Brent sat up, virtually draining the last of his strength from his toes into the first real bed he had been in for nearly sixteen years. His memory returned as well and he smiled warmly at both of the people in the room.

"We do not know if you are okay or not," Anna said softly in her beautiful Russian accent. "Are you okay?"

Brent smiled at her again and responded with a faint, "Yes."

"Yeah, that's good. We need to see about sending you on your way now," Frank pointed out. "The weekend's coming up and I'll be needing my room back. I gotta work or I'll be broke and out on the street like you."

Brent again smiled at the two people standing next to the bed and then paused a few seconds as an immense swell of physical and emotional strength began to overpower his long-tormented being.

"I just need you to take me to one place. A place I only know in my mind. And after that…money will no longer be a problem for any of us."

Chapter 25

Brent was left alone inside a small room next to the vault where people could open their safe deposit boxes. The ride up from Corolla to Norfolk had been generally quiet, with Frank and Anna saying very little while all Brent could do was marvel at the changes that had taken place since the last time he was home. Yet, those immense changes were nothing compared to the sight of the opened safe deposit box.

He was still a bit numb from how easy it was to get access to the box. It was just a matter of verbally passing on a coded message that Ray had given him to the bank manager. There was not even a hint of surprise or anything, just a "Come this way, sir." There was not even a request to sign in or out. Just the bank manager and an assistant retrieving the box, giving him one of the two keys, then leaving him alone with the beginning of his vastly different future.

The first thing that struck his attention was a folded length of gold Canadian Maple Leaf one-ounce coins, each preserved inside its own plastic sheaf. He lifted it up slightly and saw that there were at least thirty or forty in the roll, if not more. There were also stacks of US hundred dollar bills, with bands around each package saying "$10,000." There were also several large packs of Swiss Francs and a small leather bag with a pull cord that revealed a handful of loose diamonds.

What was even more mysterious was a thick envelope that Brent knew contained the real extent of his fortune. Inside was the list of names and contacts who would provide him with the vital elements of being able to spend the vast fortune that was now in his grasp. The passport expert, the historical documentation specialists, the passwords and codes for the mutual funds and offshore accounts, commodity and cash accounts that Ray had told him about.

Brent looked up from the box and smiled at the pleasant wall in front of his eyes, painted a soothing shade of yellow. He stared through its calm exterior, knowing that the steel reinforced concrete bunker was a wall — unlike in his past — that he had all the power in the world to escape.

He took only three of the ten thousand dollar packets. Just for security's sake, in case he could never return, he also grabbed the gold coins and the bag of diamonds. He walked out, told the banker that all the new information about his identity would be forthcoming and walked slowly out of the building towards the waiting truck.

Anna was standing next to the vehicle, where she had been angling for some sun. She had little hopes of what the stranger had told them would actually come true. Frank was still seated at the wheel and peered at him, expressionless.

Brent climbed into the back seat and Anna returned to her front seat. They looked back at their passenger and Brent smiled with obvious relief. "We're on."

Chapter 26

It was two minutes before the appointed arrival time of a most mysterious businessman. The real estate broker was standing with the beautiful young Russian woman in front of The Inlet Inn, a post-World War II structure that had seen its best days decades before. Twice already, the broker thought he had a buyer, but after the inspections and due diligence were made, the other potential buyers fled. No doubt, it would happen yet again.

Exactly at ten o'clock, a black Suburban with tinted windows appeared and pulled to a stop, blocking the battered asphalt entrance to the old hotel. Anna motioned for the broker to remain where he was, then walked over to the back window as it lowered. The driver appeared, walked silently halfway between the truck and the broker, where he stationed himself with eyes hidden by dark sunglasses.

Anna walked over to the broker, handed him a written offer she had retrieved and then said, "We want to buy this today."

"But...the...."

"Three million dollars. That's half a million more than the owner wants. My boss said the elderly man who owns this deserves the money. He just wants a quick and simple sale to take place. That will also make it easy for the minority partner involved."

"Well, I'll be happy to pass it on to the Mr. Breckinridge. I'm sure he'll be more than happy and that he'll agree. I have the name of the LLC you work for, but who is going to be the principal? Am I going to meet him? Is that him in the truck?"

"So," Anna said quickly, ignoring the questions. "We need to know today. We have a very tight schedule. The builders are already lined up to make the necessary improvements."

"Well, then in that case I can say that, yes, we have a deal. I am, as you know, authorized to accept any payment above the $2.5 million. So, yes, we accept."

"Thank you very much. Now, I need to know this as well. How

much is that new home right there, built next to the hotel? It is one of which my boss would also like to possess."

"I...I don't...I don't think it's for sale."

"Please find out the price and we want to close on that as soon as possible, too."

"But, it isn't even listed. I don't even...."

"Next Wednesday will be a suitable time frame for us. We want to settle on that at that date."

"I...again, it was just built. That is one of the most expensive homes on Hatteras Island. The owners, from what I've heard, have no reason to sell. I don't even know who they are."

"That's what we're paying you for. To maximize our investment in the hotel. My boss wants the house to go along with the overall purchase. They both rest on the soundside and they are both part of his plans."

"I think I really need to meet your boss. Is he in the truck?"

She turned around and looked towards Frank, who immediately pulled out his cell phone and made a call. The broker started to walk towards the vehicle, but Frank politely walked into his path, his stern expression making the broker stop in his tracks.

The back door of the vehicle opened and two men in business suits climbed out and gingerly walked over to the broker. He suddenly felt a tinge of amazement, something that he hadn't felt in years, having dealt with such a varied list of clients.

Before he could say anything, one of the two men spoke up, "I'm Mr. Smith. I'm a CPA and this is Mr. Jackson, an attorney. We are here to finalize all the necessary details of this transaction. And to speed up the process of the home purchase."

"But, as I told this young lady, I don't think it's for sale."

At that point the two men, Frank, and Anna all looked over the broker's shoulder at the approach of a thin, extremely fit man dressed in tattered shorts, a salt-pelted shirt and sandals. He walked from the marina that was just a block south and he had a dive regulator over one of his shoulders. He was in his mid-thirties, but already had a head of closely-cropped gray, almost white hair. The sun suddenly dipped behind a high cloud as he walked up to the gathering, nodding with a smile to each of the people present.

"Allow me to introduce you to my boss," said Anna. "He is purchasing these two properties."

They shook hands, but the man remained silent. His piercing blue eyes stared directly into the broker's eyes. Aloof, but faintly menacing. Seconds went by and the broker became off balance within the awkward silence, not even realizing until later that he never received a name.

"I...it is a pleasure to meet you, but I have told your assistant here that the home you now also want to buy is probably not for sale."

The man looked silently at Anna, a message passing rapidly between their eyes. He turned back towards the docks, started walking away and then said over his shoulder, "Not now, it's not."

CHAPTER 27

THE INLET INN had a minority shareholder — owning just five percent — but one with an ego the size of Wall Street. John Street was his name and scamming was his game. In fact, that's actually how he got his five percent. As a guest nearly a decade ago, he was drunk and tripped on a walkway, slightly injuring himself. Of course, being a modern day American, he and his lawyers pushed the settlement far beyond what the old hotel owner's insurance covered. So he settled for a share of the property.

When he was told that the dilapidated hotel had been sold for the amazing sum of three million dollars and his share of the sale would be $150,000, Street became furious. No, he wanted $500,000 for his share. These people obviously had the money.

For that, he was invited by the purchaser to go fishing.

Always loving to play the "big shot," Street left with pomp and ceremony, making sure everybody on the docks knew he was going deep sea fishing with the new mysterious people in town. But far offshore, the fishing trip didn't pan out as he had thought.

"Okay, put some slack in the rope," Brent ordered, standing in a dingy that was halfway between Frank's financially-rescued boat and the boat of Stuart McCloud, one of the top dive tour operators on the Outer Banks. "Yep, that's good, right there," he said, motioning with his hand exactly at the point for Frank to throttle back on his Sportsfisherman.

Handcuffed to the middle section of the rope — which was now in the water — was John Street, his huge white beer belly rolling in the sunlight and water. There was almost no wind and the surface 150 feet above the shipwreck *Tarpon* appeared as the proverbial millpond. Except for the panicky thrashing of the water around Street.

An hour before their arrival at the wreck site, dozens of miles off the coast of Ocracoke Island, Stuart had been chumming up the three or four dozen sand tiger sharks that were often seen around the historic wreck. She was a decommissioned U.S. Navy submarine that sunk in a sudden squall in 1956 while being taken to a scrap yard in Philadelphia. While being towed from New Orleans up the coast, the vessel — which was credited with sinking both a German and several Japanese ships during World War II — began taking on water during the storm and had to be cut loose. It was as if a loving sea was unwilling to let such a mighty vessel be recycled into cars or refrigerators. She was now a popular diving site and also became a breeding ground for the sand tigers. Today, her residents were going to help teach someone a lesson.

"So, you have the audacity to try to shake people down?" Brent yelled into the water, not just out of hate, but also to make sure Street could hear him over the turmoil that surrounded his helpless situation. "You've obviously gone through life living off the sweat and worry of others, but now you've definitely tried to shake down the wrong people."

A big sand tiger lurched suddenly forward towards Street and Brent motioned for slack to be taken out of the rope. It pulled the man's body up just enough for the shark to veer confusedly away at the last second, wondering where the inviting chunk of meat had vanished. Two more swept by in the same center point location, with a dorsal fin scrapping Street's back as it passed. Brent motioned with his finger to again put slack in the rope and drop Street back into the water.

"No! No! Help me! Help me!" the man shouted, his voiced cut on and off by the water that washed through his ultimate nightmare.

"Help you? Did you help out Mr. Breckinridge when you shook him down a decade ago? Do you not think that we would know every single detail about the history and operation of that property before we even made an offer? Did you not think that there is an entirely different world with its own set of morals and laws out here that transcends your puny world of legal backstabbing, pan handling, and deceit? Well do you?" Brent shouted now truly in anger, while motioning for Frank to go forwards a bit to pull the man out of the water.

"That rope you're clinging to is connected to two vessels of the sea that know all about that world. So you have your choice, you do exactly what I say and I'll take you back to the mainland. Otherwise, this will be what your last few minutes will look like." Again he motioned for slack in the line.

Instantly, several of the circling sand tigers shot in, one even grazing the man's body before the rope could be tightened again, lifting him from the water. The man's shouts were literally drowned out by the the water. His attempts to keep his head and body above the water line were unsuccessful. Street flailed even more, causing the sharks to veer in and out in excited passes. They tightened the yet line again, drawing the man inches above the waterline, his body still so low that a dorsal fin from one of the sharks again strummed across his sagging waistline.

"You parasite! This is where your type belongs. Another parasite like you took fifteen years of my life away. You probably did much the same for Mr. Breckinridge. He couldn't keep that hotel in shape enough with the money you drained away. I come back to this country and you're the first person to test my wrath? Not only are you a leech. You're an idiot!"

With that statement, Brent reached down in the dingy for his mask and fins and in a brief flash that even surprised the two nearby boat captains, he stood and hollered at the whimpering remains of John Street. "Let me show you who you've challenged!"

To the astonishment of his friends, Brent hopped into the water and dropped beneath the surface, in the midst of a half dozen sharks. They stayed away from him, two splitting angles of his muscular body, shooting past in what could very well have been respect. Popping above the surface next to the focus of his anger, Brent's hands went around the man's throat, his thumbs pushing into his windpipe. He pulled the head underwater, just as another shark made a close pass into the fray. Street came up spitting and coughing and in another flash, Brent was back inside his dingy.

"Okay, here's the deal. You get not one penny for your shares.

We take you back to the docks, you get into your vehicle and you leave the Outer Banks. For good. No one likes you or your kind here in Hatteras anyway. And if you ever want to challenge me again, if you ever have a desire to move back here and make another gloating fool of yourself, you're coming right back out here and this time I *will* allow the sharks to finish this episode instead of me. You go back and report us and you'll once again get a little education out here on how our world overrules your little world of lawyers and entitlements. Understand?"

The man weakly nodded his head and Brent signaled for the two boats to back inwards, simultaneously reeling in the rope until the shellshocked emotional remains of John Street were thrown down on the aft deck of Frank's vessel. Brent bent down over the sobbing man, grabbed him by the throat, and peered into his defeated eyes. "One thousand miles away. That's how far you have to stay away from the Outer Banks for the rest of your life. You get 999 miles from here and then I'll personally feed you to my friends." With that he dropped Street's head on the deck and walked towards the cabin.

Frank stared at Brent, as did Stuart who was alongside holding a mooring cushion between the two hulls. Frank softly spoke, "Chill, dude. You made your point."

"I am chilled."

"Well, I'm just a little concerned...hold back a little on the anger. Just a thought."

"Oh, this wasn't even close to anger."

"It wasn't?" Frank asked, smiling in awe. "Then what was it?"

Brent coldly looked back over the horizon towards the mainland, northwards towards Nags Head and Kill Devil Hills. "This was practice."

CHAPTER 28

IT WAS ONE OF THOSE BRIGHT, new commercial office buildings that began construction too late to halt for the sudden credit crisis of 2008. A one-story strip mall with glass fronted sections for five retail stores or offices, plus a secure, hidden, and windowless office section in the rear. The developer was on the verge of handing it over to the bank in foreclosure when help arrived.

That help was in the form of a mysterious LLC that swooped in and completed the purchase in less than three days. The even more mysterious owner of the LLC arrived a week later under cover of night. By dawn, he was ready for a day-long series of meetings with various people who had been feverishly working for him for all of three weeks.

Shortly after six a.m. the first scheduled appointment took place. In suit and tie, the man walked into the small confines of the office, where Anna was seated behind the desk. Frank was standing next to the side wall near the door and a newly-tanned Brent was seated in another chair to the right of the desk. A bit early for a business meeting, but for most of the first three weeks of Brent's return, by six a.m. he was already ten miles offshore and headed to a wreck site in the *Graveyard of the Atlantic*.

The initial presentation was rather long and involved since it dealt with the far-ranging financial assets that were now officially owned by Count Matthew Van Sant. That was the identity that had been pre-arranged by Ray Dampier and which had a designated segment of the drug cartel assets that had been spirited away years before. Van Sant was the lost grandson of a Count who was killed for spying on the Axis forces in Hungary during World War II.

Totally fictional, of course, but a brilliant and nearly untraceable identity that was virtually bullet proof from any prying authorities. Besides, the skills and techniques of handling a large fortune taught by Dampier during their captivity would now serve him well. He knew who to contact, who to support, and how to spend in ways that would further protect his identity and his massive fortune.

That fortune, by the way, was listed by the money manager as well over $152 million and growing. Shrewd and timely decisions, generally in terms of betting against the dollar and the U.S. stock markets way before anyone else did, accounted for the massive jump in assets. And, unknown by the money manager, this was just a tiny portion of Dampier's fortune. This and the Van Sant identity was just what he had allotted for his friend. Brent silently thanked his lost friend, hurt that the storm had kept Dampier just miles from reaching his ultimate destination of affluence and security. All the more reason for Brent to respect and, yes, enjoy, the fortune that had been left to him.

The money manager outlined all of the individual assets and how his firm intended to make that fortune grow even more vigorously, yet at the same time keeping the new Count's ability to provide for his every need and want. Brent, or rather Count Van Sant, thanked the man for his work, then sent him straight back to London.

The next meeting began promptly at eight a.m. It was with an experienced and top-rated real estate developer who was now on the Count's sole retainer. Lured away from retirement and his home in Charleston, the developer was chosen not only for his wide range of skills and foresight, but also as a dispassionate and locally-disconnected professional who would not be influenced one way or the other by the local real estate business landscape. After all, this would be more than just a wealthy man coming in to buy several properties. This was going to be an invasion. His job had already been defined quite colorfully. He would look for choice properties preparing for foreclosure and like pirates commandeering weak and unprotected vessels, he would swoop in for the kill.

Burnette was his name and he had already engineered the quick purchase of the strip mall as well as the purchase of the old Inlet Inn in Hatteras. Outlining his report on that issue, he told the Count, "I thought we were going to have a problem with the minority owner of the property, but luckily all of a sudden that issue just cleared up. In fact, all I was left with was a legal document signing his stock away to the majority owner. I still haven't quite figured that one out." Brent glanced at Frank and they each shared a quick, yet subtle grin.

Burnette continued with his presentation, outlining the united efforts that three general contractors as well as a host of sub contractors had for the conversion of the battered old Inlet Inn into a modern and immaculate travel destination. The incorporation of the home that was purchased next door as a haven for those high-end clients who sought complete privacy and ultimate security was also given. Brent already knew most of this, since Frank was the one behind the overall implementation of that particular aspect of the property, since security and privacy was the main feature of that section.

The meetings went on throughout the morning, ranging from nautical officials advising on boat docks at the Inlet Inn to the dry nuts and bolts of tax and insurance issues. Brent gradually lost interest in these meetings as most of that information would be ferried out among his other management liaisons. Only when the last of the scheduled operatives walked into the office did the Count perk up as if he was on a dive boat and had just arrived overtop a new wreck site.

Adam Johnson was one of the most talented private detectives on the East Coast. He was also a long-time friend of Dampier's, even though he did not acknowledge their mutual friend's name. He was at the top of the contact list that Brent had found in the safe deposit box. It was to Johnson that Brent had given a most important series of missions. To find out about the people in his previous life.

"First, we have found your father. He is safe, but not well. After he lost his home on Colington Island and became too sick to stay anywhere on his own, he was first taken to a nursing home. Later, for financial reasons, the government moved him to a small rest home in Plymouth. There are only five other residents. The facility is owned and operated by a really nice black couple, but unfortunately it looks like it's about to be closed down by another government agency. Not out of neglect, but because they can't afford the necessary improvements for their home. So, with a little paperwork, we can have your father out and to wherever you want to send him within the week. By the way, he has had a series of strokes and he can't walk and can barely talk, but in my judgement, his mind is still pretty much intact. Sharp, in fact. As for your aunt, she passed away."

Brent fought back tears but he remained as superficially emotionless as he could. The act did not fool anyone in the room. "I'll visit the rest home myself tomorrow and take care of that situation personally."

"Okay, now for the two women you asked about. I have an extremely detailed account of their lives for the past two decades as you requested. The dossiers are here and if you want, I can outline them briefly or we can move on to the Lawrence Parker individual."

"A brief outline on each would be appreciated."

"Certainly. The Leeann subject has been married twice and could best be described as a man-eater. Extremely materialistic, fashionable and though is self-employed, seems to be undergoing some financial constraints with the current economic situations. Not enough to slow down her high spending habits, apparently. She's known as cold-blooded and devious. Extremely superficial and shallow. In my humble opinion — of which you are paying me for — I would advise you or any man, for that matter, to stay away.

"The second woman, the Crystal subject, experienced a severe personal crisis and extreme loss in her life. She has withdrawn almost totally from society and while talented and also extremely beautiful, she no longer takes any efforts to capitalize on her assets, other than the sale of some paintings down on Gallery Row. There's not much to be known about her, as she has indeed led an apparently broken-hearted existence for quite some time. All the details on both are in the dossiers."

Brent looked at both Frank and Anna, then back at Johnson. "Thank you for that and before we move on to the other subjects, let me just say that your report sounds accurate except for one minor detail. You accidently mixed up the names of those two women. The first report is about Crystal, while the second one is about Leeann, instead of the other way around."

Johnson frowned, pulled his glasses down over his nose, quickly studied his notes and then said matter-of-factly, "No, sir. They are the correct names."

In an instant, Brent's tanned face went as white as the day he escaped from prison.

CHAPTER 29

LAWRENCE STROLLED FROM THE RESTAURANT to his parked red Corvette, glancing at his Rolex in an effort to make sure everyone nearby knew he had one. He looked quite out-of-place in his expensive business suit and tie, but he was always one to project the image of the extremely wealthy Outer Banks mover and shaker. Even though he alone knew the depths of his current financial problems. At least he thought he was the only one who knew.

Just as he was about to click his remote key, a white SUV with tinted windows pulled up abruptly and a rear door opened. Four people were in the vehicle. Two up front, one in the far back and one seated on the opposite side of the opened door. It was Manuel Pantez. He was holding a pistol.

"Get in, Lawrence. Now."

They headed south on the beach road, then took a turn westward towards the 158 by-pass. Turning south again, they headed towards South Nags Head, blending into the traffic patterns on the five-lane road. Lawrence felt the presence of a pistol held to the back of his neck from the man in the jump seat while his eyes were on the weapon pointed at him by his partner and business associate from Rogotha.

"Okay, sooo, how's everything going up here, Lawrence? Everything okay?"

"Manuel, put the guns away. Come on, man, look who you're dealing with. It's me. You've never done this before."

"Yeah, well, you've never been so far behind on your payments either. You know, despite all these years, I knew I should have put you back on COD." The weapons faded away, with the knowledge that they were still there.

"It's going to be all right, I tell you. I've got this big deal coming down. It's going to be real good. I'll have way more than enough to take care of things. You'll see."

The SUV reached the turnoff to Route 12 South and they headed towards Hatteras Island. Suddenly the marshes and needle grass seemed ominous to Lawrence and his tone began to break down a bit as the drive continued.

"I promise you. There's just been a lot of problems lately. I've told you about them. The Mexicans. Coupla of my people got busted. And there's no money in real estate this year, that's for sure."

"I thought you told me that you have a big deal coming."

"Oh, I do, I do. It's starting to fall into place and it's going to take a while. Maybe even to early next year."

"You don't have until next year."

"Manuel, hey man, it's me you're talking to! Have I always not failed to come through? When have you lost money with me? Look at all the money we've made over the years. I helped you build your empire."

"We've helped each *other* out. Many times. All the way back from that time with that *gringo* long ago. But that's then, and this is now. I'm starting to worry about the money. You're into us for over two million US dollars. We know you're having a tough time. Do you think I'm just going to lay low about that?"

"Of course not. But these are extraordinary times. Things have never been like this. The credit market has dried up business and the Mexican gangs have all but taken over Tidewater and now they're starting to come down here. You can't blame me for all that."

"I'm not blaming anybody for anything. I just want my two million dollars." Then to his driver, Manuel ordered, "Turn here. Pull into this lighthouse."

The vehicle made the rounding bend towards the Bodie Island Lighthouse and it pulled to a slow stop a couple hundred feet away in the empty parking lot. "Get out."

Lawrence was becoming more nervous with each escalation of his abduction. It was almost mid-October, but it was also mid-week, so no one, not even any local park officials were nearby at the moment. Manuel motioned for Lawrence to walk next to him and while one of his bodyguards stayed in the vehicle, the other two walked slightly out of earshot both in front and behind.

"Lawrence…didn't you tell me how you killed someone near here one time? Over on the beach. Remember when you were bragging about it? That other guy who married that girl you were always after. That makes two people you've murdered…or had murdered… over this one woman."

"Well…he was coked up and drowned…that's what the coroner said."

"Lawrence, Lawrence, come on. I know you were pretty coked up, too, when you told me the story, but how was it? He married your woman. He was a cokehead. You took him surfing and you gave him a few good lines and…well he couldn't make it back to the shore? Was that it?"

Lawrence remained silent.

"So, Lawrence, you don't surf, do you?"

"No."

"Well, then if…and yes, I'm going to give you some time to make that big real estate deal…so, if you don't come up with the money — which since we had to come up here and talk face to face, it is now up to two and a half million — then we're just going to find some other way to convince you. Now, I figure, yes, the real estate market will turn around. All markets do. So, killing you now will not do us much good. Since you're responsible for killing not just one, but two men who were in your way for this woman, then that will be our key…your wife."

"Manuel, no…"

"No, amigo. It should be, *Manuel, yes.* That's your new collateral. You should be happy you have some. Anyway, I'm going to be real generous about it. The season's about over up here and even I'm about to wind things down here as well, because the Mexicans have just about gotten to me as well. We all need to get out of this business. But you see, I'm going to get out with my money. Or, I'm going to make a good enough impression on them that they may let my family work for them. Either way, I'll be happy. Now, when is this deal supposed to take place?"

"Maybe in the spring. Early spring, maybe. It depends on a few things."

"Hmmm, that's a long time from now."

"Manuel, I'm good for it. You know that. You've just go to be patient. You've just got to understand what's happening around here. Everywhere. You and I both are going through some monumental changes. Things are out of our hands. But, we'll be back, just like always. We always do. We're both survivors."

Manuel led the group back to the SUV, then they climbed inside and headed back to where Lawrence's car was parked. Only after the vehicle made its way to the 158 by-pass did Manuel speak. "Okay, I'll give you until then, but only until then. I want to be kept up to date about this big real estate deal you're talking about. If I find out you're just leading me on, then I'm really going to be mad. And while we do have a lot of history between us, if you are conning me, I swear the first thing I'm going to do is come up here and kill that beloved wife of yours right in front of you. Do you understand me, Lawrence?"

"Yes. Yes, I do." Silence again took over the vehicle. As they made the turn to head for the beach road, Lawrence felt an immense wave of relief. Manuel said he needed him alive in order to get his money back. That he would kill Leeann.

As he was let off and he walked towards his car, he again was swept with relief and now hope. Kill his wife? Lawrence smiled as he climbed into the temporary safety of his car and said aloud, "Fine by me."

CHAPTER 30

IT WAS THE FIRST TIME Lawrence could truly relax in the past month, ever since his encounter with Manuel Pantez and his men. A deal had been conjured up, financing secured, and even signed, all in the rapid pace that was needed to literally save his own life and no doubt the lives of his family. He would make millions, enough to pay off the $2.5 million to Manuel and still have plenty left over to continue his life of extravagance.

The land deal centered around a 34-acre tract of land on the extreme northern end of the Outer Banks. It stretched along the soundside part of Carova Beach. Lawrence inherited the parcel and indirectly controlled a 97-acre tract that was part of his late-uncle's estate on Knott's Island, directly across the sound. Since Lawrence was the attorney in the family and his uncle had no children, he had been entrusted to look after it, to see that it remained undeveloped on the Carova Beach side.

Not having the immense amount of capital that it would take to fight anti-development efforts and to build suitable infrastructure and buildings, Lawrence had been in talks with a hedge fund from New York that financed such projects. With the rest of his finances — as well as his wife's — spiraling downward and out of control, it was time to put that deal on the fast track.

After several weeks of intense bargaining, due diligence, and delicate behind-the-scenes political maneuvering, a deal had been struck. A wholly-owned LLC of the hedge fund top advisors would finance the purchase of both properties where they would construct a huge hotel complex with a theme based on the wild horses. Homes and condos would be constructed on both sides of the sound, with the hotel, commercial shops and restaurants on the Knotts Island side.

The homes on the Carova Beach side would be accessible through private docks on each waterside that would continuously ferry vehicles and people across. Lawrence had been amazed at seeing photos of the flat bottom boats that were used in shallow river crossings in the Third World. He was also amazed that the group had already budgeted a million dollars just for gaining the political clout to approve such a deal, with more funds that could be brought in if necessary. It was definitely a high-dollar operation and one that would clear for him nearly four million dollars, after paying Manuel the $2.5 million.

The only potential deal breaker had been persuading his uncle's friends — and minority owners of the Knotts Island property — to go along with the sale. Lawrence knew they would never agree to such a project, so he basically had to lie. But in a way that would not resort to any judge changing his plans. The LLC that he set up for the deal gave him 51 percent voting rights and the elderly couple 49 percent. That was the only way to convince them to sign the deal. They would get their previously-agreed option price — which was relatively low compared to the overall deal — but have what they thought was sufficient enough voting power to make sure the deal would not destroy the allure of the area. No commercialization was what they wanted.

Of course, Lawrence had used all of his stealth and cunning to convince them that he was indeed a good family friend who had his uncle's wishes in mind. He also majestically kept them from appreciating that their 49 percent voting rights amounted to zero percent. To them it was all about trust. To Lawrence it was all about saving his own skin.

Which reminded him. Just in case Manuel became impatient over the winter and spring before the deal would technically close and the money changed hands, he needed to take a big life insurance policy out on his wife.

CHAPTER 31

WINTER SUNSETS ON THE OUTER BANKS quite often can be the most beautiful sunsets of the entire year. The crisp, haze-free skies bring out the blues, purples and yellows that highlight the daily event. On this particular day, Count Van Zant — or as we know him, Brent Williams — was enjoying the scene with his father. Something that had eluded him for the past sixteen winters.

The very day the occupancy permit was granted at the completion of the renovation, Brent moved his dad in from the small rest home in Plymouth. There was no sunset on those first two nights, but on the third, it was as beautiful as any sunset could be. Brent, however, could only marvel at being reunited with the last of his family. At the crucial point when the flash of green light shot towards them as the sun touched the horizon, Brent was smiling at his dad. Unable to speak due to his age and the several strokes he had suffered, the look in the old man's eyes as the sun disappeared said everything that Brent needed to hear. That his father's mind remained clear and so did his love for his son and their home, the Outer Banks.

When Brent first went to Plymouth the day after the private detective's report, he fully expected to find his dad neglected and in a squalid and unsafe rest home. Quite the opposite. While the small home could no longer meet the new state standards that were passed by the legislature, the home was as clean and neat and as safe as one could be.

The owners, Webster and Annie Austin, were in their fifties and they lived in a neighborhood that was often the scene of drug deals and violence. But even the most unruly of the young "ganstas" never brought trouble to the Austin home. No other couple was as well-respected in the neighborhood, not even the Baptist preacher. They were friends to one and all. In fact, the half dozen or so residents they supervized were always treated as family. Brent's dad was the last resident left to pick up before the rest home shut down operations. He also had been the only white person in the household, but color was no barrier around that home. The only thing that mattered was goodness of heart.

Upon Brent's arrival, he was ready to fund whatever it took to remodel the home and let them be able to re-open their business. He was thrilled that his dad immediately recognized him and though unable to speak, his expressions radiated happiness at seeing his son again, especially after believing for so long that he was dead and buried. It was the first bit of Brent's early life that he was able to recapture.

After a warm meeting with the couple and seeing how his dad adored them and they adored him, Brent did what any extremely rich and powerful person would have done. He hired them to work at his new hotel where they would also continue to look after his father. Their money troubles were now over.

As for the father and son, their new place and time was indeed precious. They still enjoyed the timeless qualities of life they so often shared when Brent was a young boy. Near the top of that list was sharing sunsets together. Watching the sea gulls and pelicans, the occasional osprey carrying a fish for their own young, and of course, the magnificent color show that led to the birth of tens of thousands of stars. His dad would be in his wheel chair and Brent would be seated nearby, with him talking and his dad listening, neither taking their eyes off the dropping sun.

It was moments like this when the mysterious and wealthy Count Van Zant was back to being Brent Williams, the humble son of a Colington Island waterman.

CHAPTER 32

LEEANN'S MOUNTING FINANCIAL WOES on several fronts influenced her to do one of her favorite things: go shopping. There she was in one of her favorite dress shops in Duck and just as happy as could be after finding just the perfect peach dress with a matching handbag. The afternoon excursion had taken her mind off her worries and while one clerk neatly folded the dress to put into a bag, the other clerk suddenly looked up with an expression of shock. The credit card was declined.

Leeann was embarrassed, of course. But even more, she felt the first powerful twinge of fright. She knew her finances were in bad shape, but not to that extent. She fumbled in her purse for another card, and passed over several until she found one that she hoped would cover the purchase. Especially since she had virtually no cash.

It thankfully went through and she hurried out the door and back to her office. The rest of the afternoon was even more unsettling, as she realized that her American Express account had been closed. She yelled at her secretary, demanding to know why she hadn't been kept informed of the bills. "We did tell you," her young secretary responded. "Several times." Leeann motioned for her to leave the office and to close the door behind her.

Okay, what to do? The first thing was to go on-line to study her balances in her checking and savings account. She figured her savings account was down to almost nothing, since she had made an on-line transfer from it to her checking account only two days before. Also, the initial thrill and relief from having her $80,000 bridge loan on one of her rental homes extended by three months had now evaporated. That extension came about by raiding most of what was left in her 401K. There was some money in her IRA, but that was the very last of the liquid assets she possessed.

Her shock and fear soon turned to anger. She was mad that no one was even looking at the spec home she had for sale. She was mad that so many people were trying to call her to complain about the sudden shift in the real estate market. She was mad that her world of being able to have whatever she wanted whenever she wanted was apparently coming to a close.

Oh, well, as much as I hate to, I'll have to ask Lawrence for money. Which of course, was the only reason she married him.

CHAPTER 33

BRENT LOVED DIVING on shipwrecks off the coast of North Carolina for more than the obvious thrill of adventure or to appreciate the vast complexity of underwater life. He also enjoyed his time underwater because only there was he able to escape the growing number of distractions in his life.

Having finished his first fall and winter back on the Outer Banks, Brent was enjoying his first dive of 2008. It was early spring and he and Frank were doing a two-dive day on the *Dixie Arrow*, one of his all-time favorite shipwrecks. The vessel was special to him as it was the first offshore wreck he dove on before his imprisonment in Rogotha.

It wasn't a deep dive — only about 90 feet — and it wasn't far off Hatteras — about ten miles — but the old tanker sunk by a German U-boat during World War II had a little bit of everything for the diver. There was still a lot of relief on the wreck, with bulkheads still upright, though not nearly as high or as wide as on his first dive there long before. There was plenty of wildlife, ranging form the smallest and brightest colored tropical fish up to the occasional group of sand tiger sharks. Last fall, Brent saw several huge manta rays on one of his last dives of the season with Stuart McCloud on the *Offshore Roamer*. They talked about that sight all winter long.

After gearing up on Frank's boat, Brent stepped backwards until he was seated on the aft starboard bulkhead, his back to the water. Yes, it was safer just stepping off the transom, but Brent loved the feel of going over backwards, plopping into the water upside down, then wrenching his body and gear back into an upright position. Old fashioned perhaps, but Brent also felt that such an entry into the sea pretty much symbolized his life. All of a sudden, taken from a comfortable world and being dropped head first into the mysteriousness and danger of the unknown, with no given boundaries of where he was or how long he would be there.

Brent put his right hand over his face mask, held his submersible pressure gauges and octopus rig with his left, then gently rolled backwards. His body penetrated the surface and in a second or two he was six feet deep before he turned upright. The rapid changes in so many ways from being topside to being underwater was a high point of Brent's new day. The water, though warm, seemed cool when compared to sitting in the sunshine loaded down with gear. The freedom of being able to levitate in the water compared with the constraints of gravity above was another rush. With his first deep breath from his regulator, Brent was now in what he considered his true environment of happiness.

He swam against the slight current towards the anchor line which stretched forward of the bow to where it dropped downwards until it was tied to the shipwreck below. The sun was bright in the cloudless sky, creating a ripple of reflections along the anchor rope and trail line leading back to the vessel. As he dropped a few feet along the anchor line, taking a second or two to clear the increasing pressure in his ears, Brent saw the entire *Dixie Arrow* gradually come into view. He already knew virtually every nook of her remains and descending further, he had a powerful sense that he was coming home. A feeling he still hadn't truly felt since his return.

Yes, this was how he wanted to spend as much time as possible. After all, he was free, healthy, wealthy, reunited with his father, and had a host of the finest friends sorting out the complexities of his life. Frank and Anna were just too perfect to believe, especially the way they all first encountered one another. His finances were incredible and despite spending a fortune on his hotel as well as so many other purchases, his $152 million estate had now grown to over $175 million. This was due to the top of the line expertise that came from the contacts left to him in the safe deposit box by Ray Dampier. Really, Brent could say that he truly had no real worry in the world.

Except for one.

Through the extensive network of intelligence experts that Brent had become part of, he had found out all about the hedge fund deal that Lawrence Parker had in the works, the one that would save him from bankruptcy and ruin. Even Brent's money and influence would not be able to stand in the way of that deal. Through sheer cold-blooded evilness and greed, Lawrence had talked his way into an avenue of escape that would do more than save his life. It would be one that would make him, once again, a rich man.

Brent was determined that would not be the case.

Sure, Frank and some of his Bluewater buddies could ruin Lawrence's life once and for all. But that would be an end that lacked the long-drawn out pain and anguish that Brent had suffered. No, that would be too easy for him. Lawrence was going to meet a downfall that would shake him to the very core. He would be emotionally gutted and nothing less. How that could happen was Brent's main concern.

There were other issues going on in his life. Most notably of these secondary concerns was how his close-knit group of advisers had been trying to get him to loosen up a bit and start enjoying the things he had all but forgotten about. Anna and Frank were spearheading these efforts which centered around finding Count Van Zant a girlfriend.

Several attempts were unsuccessful due to Brent's ongoing devotion to Leeann, despite the repeated and verified stories of how she had changed so drastically from her prior life. He was also way too busy learning about modern life and, of course, plotting his revenge was also very time-consuming. Besides, he had told both Frank and Anna, *Leeann will become the Leeann of old when the time for us to meet again is right.*

As he reached the deck of the shipwreck and began to spread hush puppy scraps for the eagerly awaiting fish, Brent had no clue at all that within minutes he would be swept away by a woman every bit as captivating as the sea herself.

CHAPTER 34

BRENT GLANCED AT HIS BOTTOM TIMER and saw that he had only about eighteen minutes left before he had to return topside. While watching the tiny, glittering tropical fish guarding their own little corner of the shipwreck, he heard the muffled underwater noise of an approaching vessel. A minute later it came into view and he immediately recognized the *Offshore Roamer.*

He watched as the anchor was thrown in and dropped in front of the *Dixie Arrow.* Brent saw the boat go into reverse, dragging the anchor until it latched into part of the shipwreck. He swam over to the anchor and tied it in with the attached stretch of nylon rope, securing the vessel for their dive.

Another beautiful day of diving in the *Graveyard of the Atlantic,* but it was soon about to end for him. He was completing his second dive of the day and he never pushed the limitations of the decompression tables. In a few minutes he would have to surface and again go back to the strange world that had evolved so surprisingly during his years of captivity.

Brent spent his eight months of freedom in a way that he hadn't imagined. Taking Ray's warning to the maximum, he waited before trying to mingle back into his previous surroundings. Certainly, finding out the drastic changes that Leeann had undergone was one reason for the delay. Secondly, being reunited with his father down on Hatteras was another reason he didn't have to venture back to the central Outer Banks. Thirdly, the destruction he wanted to rain down upon Lawrence was going to take a lot more time and effort than he thought. The hedge fund behind him may not have been a total white knight, but it was indeed powerful enough to forestall Lawrence's financial demise. It would just take Brent more time.

Yet another factor was instrumental in the slowness to rediscover his past life. The immense patience that he learned from being locked up for so long. He could bide his time. He had the resources.

He had the most secure and protected dwelling on the Outer Banks, if not the entire state. Brent could slowly move into the new world at his own pace. Just like Ray had advised so many times before. Kind of like not getting back on the boat until he spent as much time on decompression stops as possible.

However, the people around him were concerned that he wasn't taking his transition back to "normal" life fast enough. Anna, for a long time — and recently Frank — would drop hints that he needed to get out and meet a woman. Just to get back into things, whether he still loved Leeann or not. A couple of times they had tried to arrange dates for him, but Brent politely refused. *How can you date someone when you are in love with someone else?* Besides, she turned out the way she did from his choice to go down to Rogotha with Lawrence in the first place. He would rectify that problem, just as he would solve the Lawrence problem. But just not yet.

Frank and Anna had even suggested, along with some of his financial and real estate advisors, that he should go back to school. Or at least have tutors brought in that he could obviously well afford. Finally he had accepted that offer and was told that one of the top public school teachers in North Carolina would soon come down for about a week and help him adjust to modern times and conditions. When Brent was first told about her, he rolled his eyes. They said her name was Brandy. *Great*, he thought, *eighty years old with blue hair*. Well, at least it would temporarily appease his friends who were, after all, looking out for his best interests.

Brent heard a plop-plop and looked up just as two divers were coming into the water. That was probably his good friend Stuart and his wife, Monica. In fact, he quickly recognized Stuart with his dull and scratched twin-80s and the fact that he was only wearing the bottom part of his farmer john wet suit, with an ordinary sweatshirt for a top. Brent also saw blonde hair on the woman diver, so he knew Monica was coming down as well. The couple were the two closest friends he had in his new life, after Frank and Anna. They loved diving, had a great dive charter service, and also were well versed with the invisible world both above and below the surface that the majority of people never see.

They met on the anchor line at about the fifty-foot mark. Brent was headed up and they were headed down. He started to move off the anchor rope, so they wouldn't have to let go, but they beat him to it since there was virtually no current that day. Stuart gave him a thumbs up and Monica nodded as well, though he couldn't see her face because she had her hands underneath her faceplate squeezing her nosepiece so she could continue to clear her ears as she descended.

After a lengthy decompression stop, Brent made his way to the ladder that rose up to the transom. Frank was waiting on him and took hold of each fin as Brent passed them up, beginning the tedious process of gearing down. Ten minutes later, all his gear was put away and he had rinsed down with the exterior fresh water shower. As they always did, Brent and Frank de-briefed each other on what had happened during their dives.

A few minutes later, the glint of sun on the valves of Stuart's tanks shot cross the hundred foot stretch between the two vessels. Stuart climbed up and amazingly, Monica appeared from the air-conditioned cabin area dry and fully clothed. Before he could shout over, the second diver appeared and he watched as both Stuart and Monica grabbed her fins and mask and lifted her tanks from her back and pulled them over onto the aft deck.

The young woman stood on the transom and took off her weight belt. She stepped over into the boat, the sunlight glistening on the stainless steel of her dive knife strapped to her leg. She shook loose her hair and even from that distance, Brent could tell that she was both strikingly beautiful and extremely confident.

"I thought that was Monica," said Brent, as if to the wind and sky rather than Frank who was standing next to him and also looking at the woman. "Who the heck is that?"

"That's Brandy."

CHAPTER 35

SIXTEEN YEARS AND NINE MONTHS had passed since Brent had last surfed. After half a dozen rides on in, including three where he actually managed to stand longer than a few seconds, Brent was almost completely worn out. He had forgotten how physically exerting the sport happened to be. That was all but forgotten as he sat on his long board, a hundred yards off a decent sand bar near Avon, watching Brandy paddle back towards him.

Seconds later she pulled up, sat up on her short board and smiled at his weariness. "At least your intellectual and debating skills are not as rusty as your surfing."

He smiled back, taking the opportunity to lose himself in her pale green eyes. Back on the beach under the umbrella, she wore large sunglasses. Out here, she had those eyes totally in view. A magnificent view.

"Well, I really wasn't that much of a surfer back then either," he said, unable to take his eyes off hers. "I just came along. I was really a diver."

"You had your mind underneath the surface, I can see. Sorta like you do with your studies. With most students, it's difficult to get them to look beneath the superficial layers of a subject. With you, it's the opposite. You dwell too deeply in cause and effects. While that's good, with you, it's extreme. I think you often fail to see the beauty, power, and warmth that's mixed along the exteriors of life."

He was just about to respond to her polite — and very true — chiding, when her eyes turned suddenly from his, catching sight of an approaching and ridable wave. Instead of getting into position, he froze. He was lost in the vision of her sleek, but curvy body, the speed in which she whipped her board around, and the way she expertly paddled just enough in front of it to gain maximum momentum. Brent was mesmerized. Maybe he was finally starting to pay attention to *exteriors.*

In seconds she was standing up and her long blonde hair, wet and stuck to her back, shone in the morning sun. He watched her glide towards the beach, making one fierce and fun cutback along the top of the breaking wave. She stepped off the board, quickly studied the next series of waves, then paddled back out to him.

"You're not going to get your stamina back unless you ride more waves," she said to him as she sat up on her board, gazing at him with her captivating smile.

"You don't have to go back, you know. I will pay you far more than what you're being paid now."

"Oh, we've been through this before. Money couldn't compensate for the joy I have with my students. Yes, with you and wherever your money comes from, that would be great financially for me, but that still wouldn't match the satisfaction I have from my career with my students. I'm building lives…for the better."

"I'm sure that's why you were among those teachers chosen for the retreat down here at Hatteras. You're obviously one of the best."

"I don't know about that, but I do take my job seriously. And what you have paid me for this week, I will take to good use. I always wanted to take a trip to the Orient. That's what I will do with the money. Thanks again. You do know I would have done this for much less."

"Don't worry about it. Take a year off and be my personal tutor and I'll make it so you could travel for as long and as far as you want."

"Thanks, but, I've got my career back home. I grew up at Morehead City, so I've done the beach thing. I like where I live now. Anyway, I'll probably get popped the question by my long-time boyfriend any day now. Especially with this extra week on the Outer Banks being the tutor of the mysterious Count Van Sant."

They both laughed, even though Brent had told her practically nothing about his real background. However, little could be hidden from such an intelligent woman. Especially since Brent's sudden school-boy crush tended to make him play down his usual aloofness to people he hadn't known from his life before.

"Well, if you ever reconsider, you know how to contact me."

"Thanks again for the offer. I've had a great time, too. I'll be sorry to go. It's been quite the experience with you this week. You have an immense amount of knowledge on an array of subjects, but it still just doesn't piece things about you together. You're one of the most interesting cases I've come across."

"Which is why I needed your guidance. And why I need more of it."

"Oh, somehow I think you'll do fine. You'll find somebody else to fill in those lesson plans I suggested. Hopefully, it'll get you away from all those Bluewater courses you've been taking. Honestly, why do you need to take courses on close combat or escape and…what was it?"

"Evasion techniques?"

"Yes. And skydiving? You go to Louisburg once a week to make several jumps? I would think that you would have enough extreme sports down here with the shipwreck diving and surfing."

"Like you said, it's not what you know that hurts you, it's what you don't know."

"True, very true. But like I've told you all week, you just need a little more balance with more pleasurable educational pursuits."

He grew quiet and watched as she scanned and studied a series of waves that were making their approach. He became mesmerized again by her beauty. The little dimple in the middle of her chin that was magnified by the low rays of the sun. The white, almost porcelain quality of her skin, and of course those green eyes.

She turned around and caught his eyes raking over her. He was immediately embarrassed and looked downwards into the water. In that respect, he was not that much different from many of her middle school students back in western North Carolina, she thought with a smile.

"So, what are your plans?" she asked. "Are you going to stay on the Outer Banks or what?"

He managed to look back into her eyes and was more careful

of his obvious infatuation. He pretended that he was also looking for approaching waves while he responded. "Oh, I plan to stay. This is my home. It just doesn't feel that way yet. But, this is now my home."

"You should still spend a lot of time traveling. I know I would if I had your resources. There're plenty of things to do out there," she said, nudging her head far past the waves headed their way. "It's a big world out there."

"Oh, I still have plenty of things left to do right down here."

And for only the second or third time she witnessed a sudden coldness that swept across his face. As if the sudden image of the side of a turning barracuda or perhaps even a sand tiger, just beneath the the clear veneer of the water's surface. He was not this Count Van Sant. He was...someone totally different.

It almost made the warmth of the spring day disappear.

CHAPTER 36

LESS THAN A MINUTE after the sun dropped beneath the horizon, the dozen or so people who had been watching the brilliant sunset left the pier for the local restaurants. As usual, such people missed the beauty of the post-sunset light show with its hypnotizing shades of reds, purples and the blues. Not Brent and Brandy.

It was the night before her return to Charlotte where she would resume her public school teaching career and her long term courtship. The extra week on the Outer Banks after her retreat with fellow top North Carolina teachers had easily been the most unusual assignment in her career. The strange and hidden background of her pupil was as perplexing and intriguing as virtually all topics she had pondered over in her intellectual pursuits. So, now on the eve of her departure back to reality, Brandy was in the mood for some questions of her own.

When she was first hired during a break from her education seminar, Brandy was instructed — rather vehemently, in fact — never to ask anything about the Count's past or his background. She managed to build up a strong intellectual bond and like any excellent teacher, she was adept at being about to feel her way through her pupil's self-imposed boundaries.

"So, let me ask a few questions, since we'll probably never see each other again after tomorrow anyway."

"Why is that?"

"Oh, I just have some weird feeling about you. That you're going to disappear back into the world where you were before you came here. Even if I returned next year, you'll probably be gone. From what I've gathered and no, I haven't been delving into your background, but you seem to have come out of nowhere and you've managed to take the Outer Banks by storm…even more of a storm than it's used to."

"Quite the contrary. Very few people have even met me down

here and as you know, I'm either at sea or in my living quarters here. So, how could I be taking this place by storm?"

"Okay, your company has. The people who work for you. They all seem to be so professional and experienced. I know I've been a public school teacher all my career, but I know a few things about the corporate world. You have this relaxed beach kind of attitude around here, but beneath the surface everything seems...well..."

"Yes?"

"Well, it seems almost military. Like these beautiful surroundings and the lavish nature of this place is merely camouflage. Like there's some other goal that's on the horizon. I don't know. I just have that feeling."

"It's probably just a reflection of the people I have working for me. As you know, I'm not exactly impressed with the current American 'work ethnic' or entitlement culture for that matter. I was lucky to find a great, hard-working couple from Plymouth who manage the hotel. The people who are directly working for me are former Special Operations personnel, some directly from military service and some are former Bluewater, who were also former Special Ops. So, yes, there is a military bearing around me."

"But why? It would almost seem like you're preparing for war."

"You, yourself know that life is not a utopia. Wasn't meant to be. Look at the activities on the shipwrecks. The territorial nature of the fish and even plant-life. The constant battles that take place. The feeding that goes on. How ironic that battles at sea caused these vessels to sink and become havens for so much violent activity...or rather nature at work. It's rough out here and one must be prepared for the worst at all times. I'm just making sure that for me and the people close to me are in the best and most well-prepared environment for any such turf wars and battlegrounds that take place here in our so-called civilized modern society."

"You know, it's really not my place to say anything, none of my business of course, but that almost sounds paranoid to me. Why would you be paranoid? You seem like a nice guy. You are, granted, quite different than anyone I've met before. I don't know many people who spend one day a week making sky dive jumps all day... and even at night. I haven't given many lectures while on a boat heading to and from a far offshore ship wreck site. Like I say, I really don't know you, but there's such a serious side going on around you that I think may be a bit unnecessary."

He looked at her fondly and with a growing sense of respect. Brandy was indeed a beautiful woman, almost as beautiful as she was smart. He also knew exactly the motive behind Frank and Anna when they chose her to be his temporary tutor. They had often hinted that he needed to experience a little romance in his new life. He also knew they hoped such an attraction would pull him back from the anger and aggressive plans he was devising. Brent did indeed enjoy the warmth and friendship that came from his top two lieutenants and from this fantastic young teacher. He knew they were all looking out for his best interests, but nothing and no one would steer him away from his goals.

"Maybe — in this world we now live in — we need a wall of protection around us," he pointed out. "You know how I feel about things. Look at the culture. You throw some petit criminal up there with tattoos and gaudy chains and jewelry all over him and the so-called music and culture elitists fall all over themselves about what a genius poet or singer he is. When basically all he is doing is what we would have called in my youth 'talking trash.' This is a trashy society we live in. Admit it. You get some loser drug addict who may know three chords on a guitar and she's awarded the highest music honor of all. You have these idiot talk shows glamorizing the lowest common denominators in society and that just allows it to become 'respectable.' People marvel over graffiti 'artists' when they're really nothing more than vandals. You may have grown slowly accustomed to this society, but my sudden return after many, many years away has been quite unnerving. So, am I going to assure that I am safe and protected, that I have only morally good and serious people around me? You damn right I will. This country is in a social and intellectual free fall and I'm not about to be the one who gets splattered to the ground."

"Excuse me there, but you're not quite convincing me. You look more than strong and sufficient enough to ward off any threats, real or perceived. I think there's something else. Again, it's none of my business. I'd just like to leave you knowing that you'll start to see the brighter side of things in life. You can fume about those musicians, but I can counter any you mention with the talent of an Amy Lee, Mariah Carey, or Chris Isaak. You have to learn to overlook the bad and dwell on the good. Anyway, the sad thing is that I don't think you'll reach that point until you get past whatever it is that you feel you need to do."

He studied her again, looking past the perfect skin, the sweet smile, and the green eyes. He just smiled.

"When I leave tomorrow are you going to remember me?"

"But, of course."

"Did I help steer you in a more positive direction?"

"You certainly did."

"Will you promise to call me when you're on the verge of doing whatever it is that you think has to be done?"

Brent looked past her towards the western horizon at the deep purples that had now won out over the reds and yellows that had silently evaporated. He was silent for several long seconds, then sadly looked back at this bit of worldly perfection who could not be bought and could not be changed.

"No."

CHAPTER 37

THE FIVE OF THEM were staring out the window, two with binoculars, all with rapt attention as if they were seeing history unfolding on the grounds of the Inlet Inn. Annie, Webster, Brent's dad, Anna, and Frank were watching every single movement taking place in the parking lot as Brent was saying his final good-bye to Brandy.

"He's gonna kiss her! He's gonna kiss her!" Annie said excitedly.

They continued their vigil, completely invisible from the outside world, since they were nestled behind the heavily-tinted, bullet-proof third floor window of the ultra-private section of the hotel compound. In fact, they were at the end of the wide hallway that included two sections, one of which happened to be the heavily-guarded living quarters of The Count himself.

They were equally happy and amazed at Brent's mannerisms. For months, he had been the polite, yet stand-offish gentleman who treated everybody he encountered in a friendly, yet distant manner. He had shown no physical desires for any of the women who frequented not only the hotel, but for those he encountered wherever he traveled on the Outer Banks and beyond as well. Yet, arranging him to be tutored for a week by the extremely intelligent and oh-so-charming North Carolina public school teacher seemed to have been the impetus that launched his sudden comeback to his own natural physical nature.

"Naw...yes, he is! He's gonna!" Webster yelped with excitement that was shared by the people who were Brent's closest friends and family in the world. "Awww...no he's not."

Frank held his pair of binoculars for Mr. Williams, adjusting the vision until the elderly man signaled that the image of his son and the beautiful teacher was perfectly clear. Though his previous strokes had rendered him speechless, the worn lines in his face were in unison with the huge smile on his face.

They watched as the two continued talking and even giggled when it was so obvious that Brent was holding onto the opened door of her car, giving away the fact that he really didn't want her to go. How much he had changed in just a week, they each reflected.

Then the young woman reached towards him, put her arms around his shoulders and drew him towards her. It was meant to be a warm and friendly Southern style of affectation. Each lingered for a few seconds, then simultaneously broke apart suddenly as if they realized it had become more than just a hug.

Brent and Brandy were silent, staring at one another as if both acknowledged that it was a pity about the bad timing and the many invisible walls between them. There was a final handshake and then Brandy stepped into her car and closed the door while the driver's side window whirred downwards.

From the group's vantage point of over a hundred feet away and three stories up, they could see the "what if" look upon both of their faces. Then, with almost no warning, Brent lightly took her hand, bent over, and kissed it. They could see her blushing and Brent standing up stoically. They knew that finally a sense of true feeling had swept over Brent, which they — aside from his father — had rarely seen from him before.

The car pulled onto Highway 12, leaving the Count of Cape Hatteras sadly standing still, watching it disappear to the north.

The silence was finally broken from the group's hidden vantage point. It was Annie, who verbally made the decision that everyone else immediately agreed upon.

"I think he's changed. I think he finally felt something," she pointed out. "And I think it's time the Count had a party."

PART IV

CHAPTER 38

PAINTING IN HER TINY LIVING ROOM, Crystal was lost in her sad thoughts, whiling away yet another day in her painful life. It was another of her specialties, a seascape during a ravaging storm. Waves, close together, were pounding the dunes. The only man-made object in the scene was a battered and twisted snow-fence that had been part of a feeble attempt to save the sand from being swept away. She painted another dark stroke and then she heard a totally unfamiliar sound. A car pulled into her small driveway. She looked out the window. It was the last person in the world who she wanted to see. Lawrence Parker.

He opened the small white gate to her fence and walked up the crushed shell sidewalk as if he was coming home for dinner. It was too late for her to close the drapes and pretend she wasn't at home, which she had time to do when he tried to stop by several weeks before. No, this time she was trapped.

"Well, can I come in or not?" Lawrence asked as she opened the door and guarded the threshold. "It's been a while, Crystal. Thought I'd stop by."

"Come in." She made a point to sit in a corner chair, away from the sofa where he flopped down while looking swiftly around her small living room with a visible sign of contempt.

"How on earth do you live in a place like this? And in this neighborhood? You're still the hottest woman on the Outer Banks and this is where you choose to live?"

"I love it here. It's peaceful."

"Yeah, well, whatever. Anyway, I'm here to see if you want to go to a party with me. Down on Hatteras next week. I've got tickets."

"Well, shouldn't you be taking Leeann? Or are you to no longer together?"

"Oh, yeah, sort of. But I was hoping you would go with me. Okay, maybe not as a date. But as…well, I need your help on something."

"Figures."

"You see, maybe you've heard about this dude. He's some foreigner or something. Some kind of count. I don't know exactly, but he's tearing up the real estate market around here like you wouldn't believe. Apparently the guy's liquid assets are unlimited. You may have heard about him. Van Zant or Van Sant. Something like that. Anyway, I need to meet the dude. Now I've got a big deal that's really going to pay off here pretty soon, but until it goes through I want to do some business with him. But I can't get anywhere near him. I even went to his hotel complex which they spent all winter and spring fixing up. They say he lives there, but I couldn't even get past the front desk. Neither he nor any of his people ever returned any of my calls. Imagine that and I'm the smartest businessman on the whole coast!"

"If you say so."

"Oh, I am, honey. Just you wait until this deal goes through I've got lined up in Corolla. Carova and Knotts Island, actually. Gonna make millions. Gonna burn some fences, but heck, the world's over-populated and nothing can stop the rush, so I may as well cash in, right?"

"Listen, I don't want to go to any party. I've got a lot of work to do here, so if you..."

"What are you talking about, work? This isn't work. You paint. You sell a few a year and you live off that little pension of yours, right? You oughta cash that thing in and invest that money with me on the project I've got going. I'll let you buy a couple of percentage points. In just a couple of months, you'll be pulling in three or four times what you're pulling in now."

"Not interested. Beside, my money is in an irrevocable trust. Can't touch it. I don't want to touch it. I love my life the way it is now, thank you."

"You've got to be kidding me. With your looks, you could still hook up again with some money. In fact, you know I've been waiting for you a long time."

"No thanks. I've seen how people turn out after they've been close to you."

"If that's supposed to be a zing, doesn't work, honey. I've got the touch and I've got the money. Leeann is on her way out with me anyway. Gonna need someone to take her place. You'd be perfect. I've always wanted you. You wouldn't have to live like this."

"Listen, it's time for you to go."

"Hold on, hold on. Forget about all that. What I really need is for you to go to the party with me. It's a big fundraiser that this dude is holding at his hotel. The tickets are $250 each. Here. Here's yours. I just need you to show up with me or at least show up and hang with me while I'm there to get the attention of this guy. I hear he's single. Who knows, maybe he'll come after you. Even you wouldn't be able to turn away from that kind of money. I just need a good lead-in to him. I've got some properties I'm stuck with and he would be the perfect guy to unload them on. But I need your help."

"You know, Lawrence, you are the most disgusting individual I have ever met."

"You won't be saying that when my deal goes through. So you'd better get onboard while you can. I could go buy some hot young chick. All day long I could sweep them off."

"Okay, it's really time for you to leave."

"Hey, calm down. You know I say these things because I'm so in awe of you. Come on, give me a break. If for no other reason, just for old time's sake, come to this party. I'm making a donation to the fundraiser, too. Gonna give them two grand. Mental health or spousal abuse or something like that, I don't know. I know the newspaper will be there. Already lined up a photo of me and the donation. How can I be so bad if I donate money to charity? So come on. Go to the party. You don't have to go with me. Just when I get there, we hang together until I get to meet with this count guy. That's all I'm asking. Nothing more."

"Your asking — and conning — never ends. So, let me see you to the door. I've got work to do."

"Oh, my asking for you will never end, that's for sure. Remember, when you hear about my deal, you're going to be the one calling me."

"Won't happen."

"Hey, so you're not going to go? I paid $250 for that ticket for you. You need to get out of here. You need to mingle again. This would be perfect. How many people you know down Hatteras anyway? A couple, if any. You could meet new people. They wouldn't know about your past. So, come on, do me this favor. I won't bother you again if you at least show up and act nice to me. I'll make it up to you. I'll let you in on my deal. You can borrow against that trust."

She finally managed to get him out the door onto her tiny porch. The wind chimes, even on the windy day, seem to angrily lay still at his presence. "Good-bye, Lawrence."

"So, you're not coming?"

"Probably not."

"Well, if you're not then give me back the…"

She closed the door in his face and then clicked the dead bolt hard. As he drove off in a tire-screeching huff, she walked back to the corner of her living room where her painting was waiting. Crystal stared at the dark, foaming waves striking the empty beach, the Hatteras lighthouse vaguely in the background, not yet finished being painted. She looked over at the ticket on the small coffee table and it appeared as if it was staring back at her, waiting for an answer.

Crystal uncharacteristically smiled and then said aloud, "Maybe."

CHAPTER 39

"Well, did you get the ticket?"

"I sure did."

Leeann was ecstatic and yelped a sigh of excitement tinged with relief. She was one of the last in the middle Outer Banks to hear about the fundraiser in Hatteras and by that time all the tickets had been sold. Actually, half of the three hundred tickets were sold and the other half were given away to natives of Hatteras and Ocracoke islands. Patti, a friend and a fellow broker who often worked the southern beaches, got an extra one from a resident who would be off the Outer Banks that day. Leeann met Patti at a restaurant in Manteo to pick up the ticket, but also to grill her for as much information as she could about the mysterious Count Van Sant.

"So, where on earth did he come from? Have you met him?"

"Have no idea! And, no, I haven't actually met him, but I have seen him. He was on a boat heading out from the marina one day. He goes scuba diving a lot."

"What does he look like?"

"Well, he looks about forty, medium height and he has almost white hair. Closely cropped. Thin, but you know, muscular thin. Not gaudy like, but like…well…like a leopard, I suppose."

"That sounds good, but he's bound to have a wife or girlfriend. What's the deal on that?"

"From all that I've heard, he spends most of his time hidden away. He goes diving a lot and I even heard he spends a lot of time at Bluewater, taking those military courses, you know. I even heard he goes somewhere once a week to skydive. The rest of the time he stays hidden away in a section of the hotel he bought. Actually in a couple of homes that's been enclosed on the property. They're very hard to get to see. You literally have to be a special guest to get into that part of the place, but I hear the courtyard of it, which is huge, is where the party is going to be."

"You didn't answer me! Does he have a wife? Girlfriend?"

"We don't know. Really. He's only been here since last fall. I'm pretty sure he doesn't have a wife, but don't know about a girlfriend or not. I did hear that the other day on the docks he really gave the eye-over to a couple of girls walking by to another boat. So, at least it appears he's looking."

"Where did he get his money? Is he as rich as they say?"

"Richer! There's this old fisherman named Mabley down there whose boat engine went out a week before the season's first charter. Well, the Count sent over some of his people for a look and they ended up bringing in an entire new engine the next day. Came in at dawn on a tractor trailer and the boat had been put in dry dock that night. Cost way over a hundred thousand dollars is what I heard. And you know what? The Count wouldn't take a dime. Told the man that he could take him out diving someday if it would make him feel any better."

"Wow! So, he makes friends okay?"

"He seems to keep to himself and his close friends and associates, so I don't really know. But some of the watermen down there seem to like him. Respect him, too, and that's a hard thing for any outsider to get from those folks."

"Tell me more about his money. It must be old money. From his family overseas or wherever or something."

"I don't know. From what I saw he looks a little too rugged and tough for being any kind of heir. He…I don't know how to explain it, but he doesn't look like the type who has ever set foot on a golf course. But, then again, I really didn't get all that close and I only saw him for a minute or two. You'll recognize him right off. His hair is white. Don't know where that came from."

"The money! The money! I want to know more about the money!"

"All I know he's got plenty of it. You heard about all the places he's bought. And he's not throwing money around. Every purchase is shrewd and smart and thought-out. What isn't working, he plows the money in to make the changes. That old hotel he bought was a train wreck, not on a low-budget, but on a no-budget. He made that thing almost overnight into the top hotel on the entire Outer Banks. It's amazing, just wait until you see."

"What kind of car does he drive?"

"Heavens…I don't know. There's a fleet of four-wheel drive Suburbans, all black with tinted windows. That's all you see that stays there full time."

"So, nobody really knows where he came from?"

"You hear everything. Hungary, New York, even California. The best guess I've heard is that his descendants came from a family caught up in the aftermath of World War II. Like a stateless citizen. One whose money is global, yet roots are nowhere. I mean, why not come to the Outer Banks? He obviously loves the sea. He must love scuba diving. Perfect place for him to settle down, I guess."

"He just came out of nowhere? That's odd."

"Not when you think about it. After all, this is the Outer Banks. People come here from all over. Always been like that."

"Yeah, but this seems different."

"No, just that he has so much money and instead of throwing it around, he's picking and choosing and being smart. People like that, as you know, are the ones who last. Not the high-flyers and hard-fallers. I've tried my best to sell his company some homes, but they come in, do a massive amount of due diligence and then they go, telling you they may call back. Haven't heard back from them yet."

"Yeah, they sound smart all right."

"I'm surprised Lawrence is not hooked up with him. He always seems to get hooked up with all the big-time operators."

"Yeah, I suppose. But not this time. In fact, he's mad that he hasn't been able to even get in the door with them. I'm hoping he doesn't get wind of this party. I don't want him there."

"You two not getting along again?"

"What do you mean again? Like we've had a good period before?

Nope, not with him. The ego the size of mountain, the manhood the size of a sand flea. No, same old Lawrence."

"Ha! Yeah, so often the case."

"Worse still, he's really been going through some bad times. Now, he's got that big deal set up for Carova, but he's struggling hand-to-mouth to make it to closing. Hard times for all of us right now, as you know."

"Ain't that the truth."

"Yeah, I just don't want him there. I want to enjoy myself. I don't get to go to Hatteras very often, so it'll be a real treat, especially without him."

"Oh, I get you! You think you're going to be able to go down there and sweep that Count off his feet and get into some of that serious money, now don't you?"

"Oh, no, not at all. Not me. He's certainly out of my league and I'm sure he's got all the younger girls he could possibly want."

On the way home from the restaurant, Leeann's mind was racing as fast as she was plowing through traffic on the 158 By-Pass. She would first have to make an appointment with the dentist about getting her teeth whitened. Then, another botox treatment. She'd watch what she ate for the next two weeks before the party and then work out as much as she could. Her hair would have to be done and for that she'd go to Raleigh. Find some more clothes. Everything needed to be perfect for this meeting.

She was still stunning, many said the most beautiful woman her age around the middle Outer Banks, especially with Crystal being a hermit and out of the scene. Perhaps she didn't have Crystal's exotic beauty, but she did have tons of personality and drive. That would make the difference. Even if this Count was already in a relationship, she would still get his attention, she assured herself.

Time to make a change, she reflected. Time to get down to business.

CHAPTER 40

THE THIRD STORY LIVING ROOM of Brent's spacious living quarters had an impressive view due west to the horizon of the Pamlico Sound. A few channel markers, some small fishing boats and a couple of pelicans could be seen along the sparkling water. But on this late afternoon, Brent's attention was downwards, into the large courtyard that separated his dwelling from the water. To the hundreds of guests below.

He stood alone at the large picture window which was not only a one-way glass, but also bullet proof. The entire complex, in fact, was as secure as any on the Outer Banks. Under the pretense of being made "hurricane-proof" the building where Brent lived also held three other highly secure and private living quarters for high-end guests and was virtually impregnable. There were steel plates inside all the walls, floors, and ceilings and the security system was the best in eastern North Carolina. After all, it was put into place and maintained by a security firm that Brent started that was run by Frank and several friends of his who were experts in the field.

As he stood next to the window, watching Lawrence Parker working the crowd, he thought of the irony involved. The only person he hated, the person who stole fifteen years of his life, was now happily inside his compound. *Spiders didn't make webs as elaborate and menacing as this*, Brent reflected with a smile.

He turned towards the north side of the room which was essentially an entertainment center, but to him, battle stations would have been the better term. There were two large screen plasma television monitors on the wall. One was tuned to a business channel and the other was playing a DVD from a wildlife series. On the large desk in front was an iMac that was hooked into his currency trading operation that was conducted from New York, London, and Dubai.

He sat down and studied several new e-mails, smiling at one

that listed a $187,000 profit in just two days. Indeed, Ray would have been proud of how he managed the estate he was given. Despite the amount of money that he had spent, his net worth was now above the $200 million mark due to his pessimistic nature and how he had shorted the right things at the right time, just as he had been taught. His various operations had generated enough profits since noon to more than pay for the lavish fundraiser that he was giving that evening.

Brent stood up and walked back to the window when his attention was taken by the television monitor showing the wildlife video. His eyes approvingly gazed at a Peregrine Falcon swooping down into a flock of bats, grabbing a meal. It was about time for him to join the party.

A buzzer sounded off and Brent walked over to the window seal and clicked a small remote. Heavy dead bolts in the door and door jamb sounded and the okay was passed on to Frank for him to enter. He joined Brent at the window and began his briefing.

"Everything's going well. Politicians and judges are here and local law enforcement. Most of our watermen friends are here, too. They're mainly congregating over at the bar," he added with a smile. "When I came up to them, they were setting up a betting pool as to what time you would want to leave and go do a night dive to get away from all the people."

Brent laughed. "Well, I'd put ten bucks on nine o'clock, if I were you."

"Oh, and your buddy is here. He's been driving the local newspaper photographer crazy about getting his photo taken. He's donating two grand and, get this, it's a pledge, not even a check. Says he'll pay by the first of July."

"If he's even around by then."

"Right. Anyway, the clown was waiting for you to show up so you can be in the photo with him. Apparently, he gets a big kick out of being in the newspaper. I told him you wouldn't be in any media photos. He looked kinda bummed. And you're giving an additional hundred grand to the charity that he or none of these folks will never even know about."

"What was your overall impression of him?"

"Just a grating little turd. Kind of basic, you know. Trying to get as much attention to satisfy his obvious insecurities, that's all. A nobody really. We'll figure a way to get around that hedge fund deal. Then, he'll be all ours."

"Hmmm...," Brent responded softly.

"And that woman, Leeann, his wife. Your girlfriend. Pretty funny, there. Apparently neither knew the other was coming. Kinda testy scene when they bumped into each other. Our plants in the crowd have some amusing tidbits for you on that. Again, pretty funny. But I can see why you fell for her back in your earlier life. She is very attractive. Full of personality. I don't think she's the person you knew back then. She's on the prowl. One of the plants struck up a conversation with her and you were all she asked about. So, just remember that, okay?"

"I will. She must still be over at the dining area. I haven't seen her in the courtyard here."

"She is. She thinks that you'll be arriving through the main entrance, so that's where she kind of camped out."

Brent's eyes swept over the crowd below and both men again silently surveyed the people. Frank saw that he was ready to go down to the party and he spoke into the tiny microphone in his sleeve to the rest of the hidden and blended security detail. "Okay, coming down."

They both glanced at the monitor as yet another falcon expertly dove into a flock of bats for food. "Remember, Brent, that guy you're going after down there is not a harmless bat, he's...."

"Yeah," the Count of Cape Hatteras interrupted. "He's a snake."

CHAPTER 41

LAWRENCE, AFTER WORKING THE CROWD for over an hour, finally caught sight of his target: the mysterious Count Van Sant. Overhearing several people saying, "There he is!" and nodding towards one of the small bars, Lawrence spotted the man about thirty feet away. He was facing away from him and laughing with a group of local salty and sun-drenched boat captains and first mates. He was dressed simply in jeans but with a very expensive white silk shirt. His hair was cut medium short, but its whiteness contrasted with his dark tan. There was a hard edge to both his appearance and his mannerisms. Quickly, Lawrence could see that this was certainly not the typical multi-millionaire he knew.

Lawrence started to walk straight towards the Count, but all of a sudden felt two gentle, yet authoritative fingers on his arm, causing him to immediately stop. "Sir, don't approach him now. He hasn't finished talking with his friends." Lawrence looked over, then around, realizing that he was surrounded by several extremely low-key, yet obvious security personnel. Confused and even a bit shocked, Lawrence did what he was told and nodded at the polite but firm agent who remained slightly behind him.

A minute later, the Count shared a final laugh with the watermen, then turned around slowly. For the first split second, Lawrence's head jerked back slightly in surprise. There was a quick sense of familiarity, which he shrugged off as possibly having met the man at some business gathering or perhaps had even read about him in the financial journals. The eyes were penetrating blue and the smile he gave well-wishers was kind and genuine, but surrounded by small wrinkles that seemed to add muscle to his face rather than age. He seemed to blend in just as smoothly with a group of wealthy Nags Head businessmen who now had his attention, as he had with the seasoned watermen just before.

Lawrence didn't see the nod that Frank gave to the Count. A

few seconds later, the Count started walking towards Lawrence, who was looking around uncomfortably, as if seeking permission from the security staff to move. Lawrence noticed they had dropped back a bit and blended in with the rest of the crowd. But, of course, he knew they were still nearby.

The Count walked squarely up to him and looked down with a smile that Lawrence could not fathom. It was genuine all right, but not like the one he saw when the man greeted the people just seconds before. The usually rapid talker, Lawrence was now totally speechless as he stared at the man, still with a faint sense of having seen him before.

"Welcome to our party, Mr. Parker. How good of you to support our fundraiser."

"How...how did you know...."

"Oh, it's my standard policy of not only doing business, but in my personal life as well. I know all about anybody who happens to enter my sphere of influence."

Lawrence really didn't know what to think. He started to speak again, but the surprise and the realization that he was in front of someone who could only scoff at him was a bit unnerving. After all, that was how he, himself, had treated everyone else in his life. At least up until the last thirty seconds.

"You are Lawrence Parker. Attorney. Real estate developer. Going through a bit of rough patch right now as are most of your colleagues. Tapped out now, but you have a surprisingly ingenious deal that is about to close in a few weeks. Married to a mortgage broker and you have a step-daughter, eleven years old. Hmmm... Corvette, typical mid-life crisis compensator. You have a history of ups and downs, but then again...," and the Count paused for several seconds while glaring into his eyes, "We all do."

The sudden glare and coldness disappeared, but the Count remained staring at him. It took a couple of awkward seconds before Lawrence finally managed to speak. "It's nice meeting you, sir. I'm sorry, but you just kind of caught me off guard there. Yes, it's pretty tough times now, but you're right, I've got one of the best deals lined up that the Outer Banks has ever seen. Financing is solid and I've got the votes with the partnership. So…"

"What would your uncle have thought about you building the the hotel and resort complex on Knotts Island and Carova? I thought he wanted all that land donated to a wildlife group."

"How? How did you…"

"Oh, your plans can't be kept from me. I have — let's say, friends — who keep me abreast on things. Especially on regional business matters."

"But, the deal…he…"

"Oh, don't worry. You don't have to be sly with me. In fact, you couldn't if you tried. Just suffice it to say that I know he would have been pretty angry at your greed."

"Sir! You…"

"Don't think I'm criticizing you. I'm not. Merely stating fact and solid conjecture. I'm rather greedy at times, too. After all, this is business and you and I are businessmen. Sun Tzu. 'Every battle is won or lost before it begins.' It seems you have this one all but won. That hedge fund is bottomless. Good choice, too. Contrarians who are wiping up betting against the banks. Around July, they'll be scooping up all the financials at bargain rates and your real estate deal with them will be tiny in comparison."

Lawrence remained speechless, as well as in shock. He thought his plans were totally unknown by anybody outside the tight circle of his backers. This man before him was not what he had envisioned at all. He suddenly felt that his mission here to try to tap into the Count's financial resources had drastically changed. That was over. Lawrence now had a startling sensation that his main mission was simply to…escape this Count…this Count of Cape Hatteras.

CHAPTER 42

TWICE ALREADY LEEANN attempted to introduce herself to Count Van Sant. When she first spotted him, she began to walk over, but then her husband got there first. She was perturbed about him attending the event, almost as much as he was for her being there. Why they didn't tell each other ahead of time about the trip would be a topic of discussion they would have later. If, in fact, they even bothered to speak to one another upon their return "home."

After her husband left the Count — and rather meekly and stunned it appeared to her — she tried to approach the Count, but in an instance he was surrounded by several couples who were obviously and immediately charmed by the mysterious new visitor to the Outer Banks. Though she was at least fifty feet away, Leeann did have a strange premonition that he had been to the North Carolina coast before. She shook that thought off as soon as she spotted two developers she knew, hoping for a chance to unload some property on them.

Leeann was in too dire a financial predicament to linger too long over small talk. As soon as she started bringing up some "wonderful" property she owned, the developers quickly glanced at each other, then politely found a reason to walk away. Leeann frowned, her mind racing to conclusions of her financial stress when all of a sudden she felt a slight tap on her bare shoulder. She turned around and involuntarily gasped.

"Well, I believe I do have the honor of meeting Mrs. Leeann Parker, one of the leading mortgage brokers in the community. Thank you very much for attending our little fundraiser here this evening."

She was speechless. Her hand even went to her mouth and her eyes were wide in a level of concern that bordered fright. She found that her senses had locked up, unable to communicate or even move at all.

"I'm sorry if I startled you, but I do make it a habit to introduce myself to all my worthy guests, most especially the ones who are as beautiful as you."

Slowly, her senses were returning. She was looking directly into the Count's pale blue eyes and could not look away, as if she was staring at someone not quite human, not quite real. A ghost, perhaps. Up close, he was oddly familiar, but she had no earthly idea why she thought she had seen him somewhere before. Perhaps, with as much money as he had, she had seen him in a business magazine or a trade journal. At any rate, she finally managed to sweep away her surprise and fascination just enough to speak.

"Why, thank you. I'm sure you've said that to about a dozen women here today already."

"No, just you."

She looked at him more closely. He had a free spirit about him, he was obviously very well-bred judging by his perfect teeth and impeccable manner. There was a look of extreme intelligence and confidence as well, but without any need to flaunt such powers. In fact, the way he kept looking at her so approvingly, Leeann all of a sudden felt the pangs of growing success on her part. Perhaps, this wealthy stranger would not be so difficult to catch as she had thought.

"So, do you ever make it up the Nags Head way, Mr.... Count...."

"Matt would be fine for our purposes. Never have given that much importance to names or titles. They change quite often, you know."

"Oh, believe me, I do know. Matt, then."

"But, yes, sometimes I do go north. I go through there when I'm traveling to Louisburg. That's where I skydive."

"What a silly sport. You should try something safer. I like to play golf."

"Hmmm…golf. No danger. No physical exertion. Plus, fashion plays a part. Sorry, no thanks. Golf is one of God's ways of telling you to get a life."

"You do speak your mind…Matt."

"That I do. Otherwise, people wouldn't speak theirs. I'm a very tolerant person, but dishonesty, shallowness, and vagueness are not qualities I allow in my presence."

"Then you probably have very few friends."

"Quite the contrary. I have many friends. True friends. People I totally trust. People who risk their lives for me and people I would risk my life for. I have — if I may be so confident — the best friends anyone could possibly hope for."

"That's…very good. I'm happy for you."

"And you, Leeann? How many friends do you trust? I mean, totally."

She didn't like the direction in which the conversation was headed. First and foremost, she wasn't in control. This was the sort of person who probably had never been controlled. She quickly imagined him coming from some castle on a huge estate somewhere deep and hidden in Eastern Europe, growing up with a bevy of servants and with closets of gold and silver.

"Well…I have…there's…"

"See, there you go. You have no true friends. Just a lot of acquaintances who you may suspect talk badly about you behind your back. Or people who you wouldn't trust, whether it be with money or boyfriends. Despite all your acquaintances, you still probably often feel alone. Is that fair to suggest?"

She looked down at the ground, trying to formulate how she would respond. He indeed had a bluntness that he obviously loved to project. He was just a little too confident for her, even though she could tell that attending parties was not his first choice of a way to spend an evening. Yes, he looked like he was well-educated, sophisticated, and worldly, but strangely, there was a hardness, a coldness, that managed to seep through his exterior. Leeann remained perplexed, not knowing the extent of how he was attracted to her, changing her earlier assumption that he would be easily catchable.

"Well, either way, it shouldn't matter. You have your husband who I met a short while ago. And your daughter. That should compensate."

"Yes, I love my daughter very much."

"And your husband? I couldn't help but notice that you two haven't been near each other and my associates tell me that you arrived in different vehicles."

"Do you always know so much?"

"As much as the expertise my money can gain for me pertaining to anything that immediately surrounds me. Not just with people. Anything that may concern me. I put global commodities and currency markets in that category, too, by the way."

"Then, if you know so much, you probably know that my husband and I have been having some difficulties. But that's quite common. We'll work things out."

"I'm sure you will. Now, please tell me about your daughter. His stepdaughter, right?"

"Oh, my daughter is fantastic! She's a bit too nerdy for me, but I just take that as natural rebelling. If I was nerdy, then I'm sure she would be the wildest and most glam little thing on the Outer Banks. But, no, she's at that stage where she wants to grow up to be a marine biologist."

"Maybe she will."

"Oh, yeah, right. I was at that stage once, too. She'll learn how tough, how unpredictable life can be. She'll become me someday, whether she likes it or not."

"That sounds like you have some negative feelings about yourself. How could you? You're very beautiful, you seem very bright, you have a good career, and you have a cherished daughter. What's the problem?"

"Oh, maybe you're right. The marriage thing is kind of depressing and I shouldn't be saying such things to a total stranger. But, after all, you are the epitome of frankness. And after today I probably won't see you again anyway, so…"

"We'll see each other again. Now, tell me more about your daughter."

"Oh, she's great. She's just a little confused right now. She's really gotten into sea turtles. That's what consumes her now. Weird, I know. But she's eleven and still a little girl. Thank Heavens she's too young for the boy thing. Especially this year. It's just too much going on right now for me to deal with that. And you? Do you have kids? A wife? Ex-wife?"

"No, none of the above. Having no children is the one big regret in my life. Now, back to your daughter. Does she go out on turtle watches?"

"Yes! I had to go with her on one! Never again for me, I'll tell you that. Boring!"

"But she had a wonderful time, I'll bet."

"Yes, she did. Suzanne really is a smart little kid. I'm proud of her. Her father was a surfer. Died surfing…at least…well, anyway, her father was just so into anything to do with the water. I think that's coming out in her genes. I try to get her interested in other things, fashion, music, you know. But she just studies her books and DVDs about wildlife and has no concern about being fashionable at all. Very sad."

"Well, you do know that fashion is just a camouflaged word for moving merchandise, don't you?"

"Why…well…I don't believe that. I don't believe you believe that either. Look at the clothes you're wearing. That shirt is very expensive and very stylish."

"That's because I pay people to do that for me. Actually very seldom do I dress up this much, even though this is what I was told was called *casual elegance.*"

"Well, anyway, my daughter keeps asking for one of those new iPhones. And after I gave her a color-coordinated set of cell phones that go with all the clothes I buy her. Says she needs all the features and doesn't care what it looks like. Hmmph, hopefully she'll get over that. Let's see her when she gets to be my age not to care about appearances."

"Let her enjoy this time of innocence, especially when she has the gumption not to conform to standards dictated by others. Let her enjoy studying about turtles. In fact, she needs to swim with truly wild turtles. That would be a thrill for her."

"She would die for that. Isn't she silly?"

"Not at all. I do it all the time myself. In fact, that would be a splendid way to capture your presence for yet another meeting. You can bring Suzanne down here and we'll find a shipwreck offshore where there's turtles. I'll have a dive buddy of mine film the entire episode. She's too young for scuba and to actually go on the wrecks, but she can snorkel at the surface. The turtles sometimes hang right next to the boat. We'll watch over her. She could use the film and the insight for a school project."

Leeann fought from smiling too blatantly, not wanting him to grasp the joy she had in being able to see him again. Here she thought she had one in a thousand chance at lassoing the obvious catch of the year on the entire Outer Banks. Now she believed she had him all but hooked.

"You know, that would be interesting. I've always been in favor of finding ways she can excel at school. Let me think about it and I'll call and let you know."

"By all means."

"Is cell the best way to reach you?"

"No, I don't have a cell phone. Had one for a couple of weeks, but found out I didn't need it."

"You don't have a cell phone?"

"I have a lot of cell phone stock if that counts for anything."

"Well, how do people get in touch with you?"

"I'll have one of my associates exchange contact information with you and we can go from there."

"Splendid."

Leeann was undoubtedly buoyed by what had transpired. She knew well enough from her long history of manipulating the opposite sex that she was now past the point where she needed to quit while she was ahead. Leave him wondering, make him feel there's other places she could be. But there was one final thought that was lingering ever since she saw him from across the courtyard and especially when she finally saw him up close. She fought with herself, knowing she would have at least the better part of a day with him on his boat to go see the turtles. Should she ask now or wait? Finally, she decided with confidence that she already had him hooked enough to press a little further during this, their first meeting.

"You know, there's something I must tell you. Ever since I first saw you today…"

"Yes? What is that?"

"You really remind me of someone I knew a very long time ago. You have some of his features. But, you're also very different, of course…just a coincidence, I suppose."

"Was he someone special to you?"

"Yes. But I was very young then. Something happened."

"What?"

"Nothing really. Just one of those things. He's part of my past. And that past and everything with it is dead."

"Things from the past sometimes have an eery way of returning to the future, wouldn't you say?"

"No, the past is the past. It's all final. Besides, let's stop dwelling on the past. You're going to take my daughter and me on a turtle expedition. She is going to be so thrilled!"

"As will I."

CHAPTER 43

THE PARTY WENT RATHER WELL, Brent thought, as he made his way back to his suite and changed into a pair of worn shorts and an old t-shirt. Virtually everybody had left and a team of workers were all but finished in the process of cleaning up and returning the hotel back to its original state. Even the tents that had been brought in were already taken down and on their way back to Virginia Beach. It was time to rest a bit, mull over the events of the day, then get a good night's sleep to prepare for the next morning's dive.

Leeann had indeed changed in many ways. The old spark was there, not dimmed from the many years that he had been away. For some reason he had this notion that she would somehow see through his facade and realize that he had not been killed in that fire after all. He wasn't that disappointed when she didn't. It was close. But she didn't.

Leeann was still certainly very attractive, but there was a hardened edge on her that he hadn't envisioned. He was prepared for the effects of the smoking, alcohol, and drugs. It was the mental shallowness that even her beautiful smile couldn't disguise that bothered him. All of the people in his inner circle had warned him about this, but of course, he swept those honest sentiments and concerns away with the notion that some things just had to be overlooked, given the circumstances of his mysterious departure from his past life. After all — he kept trying to convince himself — if he hadn't disappeared like he did, she would still be the *real* Leeann.

He had both of his television monitors on, but he scarcely even saw the stock readings running at the bottom of the screen, nor the graphs of commodities from the day's tradings. He wasn't even eating any of the fresh backfin crab meat that he had brought in with him. He had done so much meeting and greeting at the party that he had neglected to enjoy any of the food. But now he wasn't hungry. He blankly stared at the screen, thinking about Leeann and what the future could possibly hold for them. Brent also thought about her daughter and how fun it would be to take the young girl, who apparently loved the sea as much as he did, to find some wild sea turtles.

The special phone in his room suddenly chirped and the unfamiliar sound of it snapped Brent back to reality. That phone line was connected only on-premise and only his most trusted staff were allowed to interrupt him in his special haven. It was only to be used in emergencies and when you were as wealthy and as connected as the Count of Cape Hatteras, seldom did matters ever rise to that level.

"Brent, it is something here you need to see," Anna's hushed and serious tone advised. "We're in the security control room. Please come as soon as possible."

Two minutes later, Brent walked into the room and both Anna and Frank were standing next to a large monitor, their faces still awash in surprise and concern. "We have something for you to see," she said, as Frank pulled back a chair in front of the screen and offered it to his boss.

"Okay..." mused the Count, as he sat down.

Frank clicked a remote and a foyer that separated the main hotel structure from the cottage and suite section came into view. One or two people hurriedly walked through, passing several local paintings of seascapes that were on both sides of the room. Brent could see from the moving time line at the bottom of the screen that this sequence had taken place almost at the very end of the day's party.

About fifteen seconds went by without anyone in view. Then, Anna whispered, "Here...here she comes."

She was sleek, with long rich brown hair that was tied and almost hidden with a large sash. Oversized sunglasses hid a lot of her face, but not enough to keep Brent from experiencing a sense of familiarity. He leaned forward in his chair, watching her slow and elegant movements as she looked at each of the paintings on display. She stopped in front of the largest one and stared at it for almost half a minute.

It was a beach scene of the Cape Hatteras lighthouse before it had been moved from its prior position of dominance, almost in the sea. A painting she had just finished a few days before and had put on sale on Gallery Row. Barely visible in the fray of an incoming hurricane, the lighthouse's distinctive markings could easily be recognized, despite its location in the distant background of the painting. In the immediate foreground, there was a battered and coiled up stretch of snow fence that had given up trying to save the bit of beach that it was guarding. Within minutes — the painting seem to suggest — the wired-together fence would be swept off to sea to return perhaps, or be lost in the approaching abyss that was now only a few feet away.

Suddenly, the woman backed off from the painting and turned around, her hidden eyes sweeping the rest of the room. They settled directly at the wall-mounted security camera and then a slight, but genuine smile broke out across her exotic face. She walked closer to the camera and stopped, staring at it for a few more seconds.

Then, her tanned hand moved to her face and took off the sunglasses. She looked directly into the camera — the smile diminishing a bit, but still there — and suddenly Brent realized that it was Crystal.

Her dark eyes were still totally captivating even from the vantage point of a security monitor. Then, just before returning the sunglasses to her face and turning on her heels to leave, she whispered, "Welcome home, Brent."

CHAPTER 44

ON THE FIRST PASS, Brent missed the Nags Head side street he was looking for. Then almost once again when he finally saw the street sign that was nearly hidden by the sweeping branches of a nearby live oak. He made his way down the narrow roadway tucked on the western side of the 158 By-Pass and even passed completely by Crystal's house before realizing he missed it. She had no visible numbers on the side of the house and for a split second he marveled how she was apparently even more difficult to find than himself.

He pulled into her little driveway with his battered 1998 Dodge Dakota pickup truck, his personal vehicle of choice for the few times he had ever left his Hatteras compound without his bodyguards. Today was one of those times. It would be a meeting that needed no one else but himself and the one person from his former life, other than his father, who knew his true identity.

Brent had barely walked half the short distance from his truck to her tiny porch when the door opened and Crystal appeared. She was as elegant and captivating as ever, a bit older, but even more stunning than she had been decades ago. Her hair was still long and dark, piled up on top of her head and wrapped in a loose bun. She had virtually no makeup on at all, but her flawless, naturally dark skin framed her rich brown eyes, which by the way, were shining with delight, something they hadn't done in years.

"Hello, Brent."

"Hello, Crystal."

They briefly hugged on the front porch and she expected him to at least kiss her cheek, but he seemed hesitant and unsure. He followed her inside and sat down on the offered sofa, while she brought glasses of iced tea.

"So, how did you know?"

Crystal smiled as she handed him the glass, then sat next to him, near an unfinished painting of another seascape. "Oh, I knew the second I saw your face. I'm an artist...I know faces. I never forget faces."

"Yes, but it seems all your paintings lack people. There's just the sea, the beach, sunsets, wild horses, things like that. No people."

Crystal took a sip from her glass and stared silently out the window for a few seconds before answering. She shifted and then turned her huge eyes back onto Brent. "People haven't been part of my life for a long, long time. That trip to your party was one of the few times I've even left the house, if you don't count the grocery store or the art galleries."

"I know all about what happened to your family. I'm sorry. Truly."

"Thank you. I had a beautiful little daughter and a husband who didn't deserve what happened. I had a wonderful life before I knew how wonderful it was."

"I know the feeling."

"You must. So tell me about it. What happened down there?"

"It's a long story, but you know as well as anyone since we all used to hang out together that I never did any cocaine. I was set up in Rogotha by Lawrence. Simple as that."

"Yeah, I never could believe those stories about you being arrested on drug charges. I remember back then you were saving all your money to start a diving business. Everybody else was buying short boards and you were buying scuba gear."

"Yep. I probably had all of about $250 saved for my business."

"Obviously that's changed. I was really impressed with your hotel. You fixed that old place up magnificently. But how?"

"I was fortunate to have had a cell mate the last year or so of my incarceration who I escaped with during that big hurricane down there last year. We made our way back here to the Outer Banks on a freighter, but he was lost at sea on our trip in. We hit a squall and he drowned. Part of his fortune that he had stuffed away was given to me. He gave me a new identity and access to a lot of money. He was very well-connected, let's just say. A world class expert on creating new identities. Sadly, he didn't make the last few miles where he could have lived in the luxury that I do now."

"Goes back to what we know all about. You can't appreciate anything until it's gone."

"Sadly, that's often true. But he was always in high spirits and humor even when we were in that old prison. He never wasted his time and enjoyed every second like he was a billionaire and free."

"Then he probably already knew that money wasn't everything."

"True."

"That's what I learned. I had to learn it the hard way." Again, she wistfully looked out her front window, as if she was patiently waiting the arrival of her daughter on a bicycle, coming home from school.

"So, are you ever going to go back?" he asked. "I mean, start getting out in public more?"

"No, I don't foresee that any time soon. I would have to be — the only way I could do it — would be to hide my feelings. To be…shallow. To pretend like I wasn't still hurt about my family. I'm all through with pretending. So, no, I won't be going anywhere anytime soon."

"I can't say I blame you much. Unless you have family, there's not a lot out there. I suppose that's one reason why I spend so much time diving."

"But, tell me this. I thought you had died in a fire. They buried somebody here."

"That was probably the remains of some poor inmate who they sent up here to get everyone thrown off track. That was before DNA. I helped save some people in the fire and that's why they put me away in a deeper prison, rather than kill me like Lawrence intended…paid for, as well."

"I guess you probably know all the rumors that he had Leeann's first husband, Scott, killed. They say he gave him an incredible amount of coke during a day of surfing. Just the two of them out there. Even the police suspected, but what could they do? There wasn't enough evidence. Besides, Lawrence is from a wealthy family. He had great lawyers."

"Lawyers and police are not going to save him from me."

"So you escaped back here with great wealth and it's payback time for those who hurt you. I sure hope I'm not on your list."

"Not at all. Even though I was hurt, I'm glad you dumped me when you did before it got too serious. I really would have been hurt."

"That's when I was so stupid and all I thought about was money. How ironic. Now you have all the money in the world and it doesn't matter. Back then, I would have owned you. I was such a horrible person."

"Stop that. That goes on all the time. From the beginning of time to the end. At least you're one of the few who got past that."

"I guess if it wasn't for the loss of my husband and daughter, I would indeed be truly happy. I mean, I'm happy just the way I am. I just miss my family."

"We all have lost. It's part of life."

"Are you going to take Leeann back? I was at your party only for a few minutes. When I saw you, you were talking to her. I knew it was you as soon as I saw your face. You always looked at her like that."

"Wonder why she didn't know."

"She was probably a little coked up when she got there. But she got over things differently than you and I. When things are over with her, they're over. She has no deep feelings. She now just goes where the money and convenience happens to be. She can easily forget the past."

"Then she's definitely different from me."

"Me as well."

They were silent for a few long minutes, their eyes drifting downwards and lost in their mental versions of what could have been. Crystal took another sip of her tea, then looked into Brent's eyes. "You didn't answer. Are you going to take her back?"

"I don't know yet. She's changed quite a bit. She still looks great and she has that personality. But, you see, I had the best detectives on the East Coast go through the people in my past life. That was one of the very first things I did when I returned. You, too, sorry about that. But I always considered you as a great friend. You'll always be one of the people who I couldn't imagine life without. You're home to me, still. But, I really don't know about her. She would have to change. The best wrecks are offshore in deeper water. The most uncomfortable ones are in the shallows. Like people."

"I agree wholeheartedly. Give me someone with true and deep feelings over money and shallowness any day."

"But I'm the one to blame for how Leeann turned out. If I hadn't been so bull-headed and gone down there in the first place, nothing would have happened to me and she and I would have been happy together. I'm the one who made her the way she is, so how can I hold that against her?"

"If she is truly like you thought…I mean before what happened."

"That's true. I was very naive back then. Without question. That's why I have to see if she can change. Maybe when she finally learns who I really am, then she'll go back to how we were back then."

"Could happen, of course. Either way, I'm rooting for whatever will make you happy. What Lawrence did was inexcusable. I'm not a violent person, but he truly deserves whatever horrible future that comes his way."

"Oh, that's being worked on, don't worry about that."

"He still comes by here every once in a while. He wants sex with me, but that won't happen. I think he's the most disgusting individual I have ever met. He really is a snake."

"Hey, you're giving snakes a bad name."

They both laughed. Brent looked at her more closely and realized that past her exceptional looks, there was a person of incredible intellect and sensibilities. There was great concern in her and he knew that even though she had turned out to be a tortured individual, she was still one with a good heart.

"How did you even get to the party anyway? I thought they said you were living in near-poverty. The tickets were $250."

"Of all people, Lawrence stopped by and left me a ticket. I only went because I heard from the gallery that the designer at your hotel had bought four of my works and that they were on display together. That's really the only reason I went. Lawrence wanted me to be seen with him in order for him to be able to meet you. Isn't that hysterical?"

"Well, he managed to and he didn't know who I was anymore than Leeann. I think all he could see when he looked at me were dollar signs."

"Same went for Leeann, I'll bet."

"Probably so."

"Then, they're made for each other."

"Unless one of them goes broke."

"Brent, you're positively evil," she said with a laugh. "Well, not evil, but...well..."

"Oh, I'll admit there's a budding evil side of me now. Something I never had before. I don't know if it could be called pure evil.... Let's just say I've been honing my skills at rectifying past injustices. Now that sounds better than evil, doesn't it?"

"God will do all of that for you. You do know that, don't you?"

"Yes, I do. But unfortunately, I'm just a tad bit impatient."

CHAPTER 45

THE TWO GO-FAST BOATS were moored together — one yellow and red and one yellow and blue — drifting in the slight current about three miles off the coast of Hatteras Island. Other than the color schemes, the boats were identical. Two Fountain Executioner 42s, each sporting the older but hardy twin supercharged Lightning 502 engines. Ten years before they would probably have been sitting here in the middle of the night with loads of coke or pot, manned by crusty ocean mules of highly-questionable means. But today, their mission was much different. An eleven-year-old girl was going to swim with wild sea turtles.

Brent was in the water with Suzanne, as her mother anxiously watched from the aft deck, as if expecting a school of sharks to swoop in any second. She didn't realize that Frank was underneath both vessels with a bang stick in the unlikely case that such an encounter would occur. Stuart McCloud was watching from the other boat, while his wife, Monica, was donned in snorkel gear and swimming on the opposite of Suzanne from Brent. Despite the natural tendency for a mother to be worried about her child, in this particular situation and with these particular people, Suzanne was as safe as if she were back home.

The boats were staged there as virtually every fishing and dive charter boat that docked in the area were each scouting out previously assigned sections of the *Graveyard of the Atlantic*, looking for the appearance of sea turtles. Brent had friends on the boats that went to shipwrecks to make "bounce dives" to see if any turtles were on the bottom. It was already ten in the morning and none had been sighted. "They'll find them," Brent reassured Suzanne. "You will swim with turtles today."

In the meantime, Brent and Monica were helping the little girl adjust to the snorkeling gear and swimming in the offshore water. Monica, a noted marine biologist and a veteran North Carolina wreck diver, was a vital part of the little girl's great adventure. They could not see the bottom, since they were still relatively close to land and the water was a little murky. But the moving light show of sunlight twinkling underneath the surface was proving a complete joy for Suzanne.

Only a couple of times did her snorkel accidently dip into the water. She popped up sputtering just a little bit. Not enough to scare her, but definitely enough to bother her mother. Even the most self-absorbed of parents could be bothered by the potential of the sea.

Stuart reached for his cell phone, listened for a second and then leaned overboard waiting for Brent to re-surface. When he returned, Stuart said loudly, "Yo! Count! There's a big group over the *Manuela!*"

Brent popped his head above the water, pulled his mask on the top of his head and motioned with his hand underwater for Suzanne to surface. She looked up at him and saw the biggest smile she had seen from the man since the short time they had met. "Well, Suzanne, we're off to see some sea turtles."

Two minutes later, everyone was aboard both vessels and geared down for the trip to the *Manuela*, which was more than thirty miles further offshore. The soft sounds of the sea were quickly replaced by the high-powered displacement of the Executioners. Normally it would take hours to get there, but with these boats, it would be minutes. Stuart was at the controls of one vessel and Frank was on the other. In the respective boats, Monica and Brent manned the throttles in case a wave or swell would jack the boat from the water. There was barely one to two foot seas that day and with the lack of wind, having to throttle back when airborne would probably not be necessary.

Brent took the cell phone offered by Frank and again his face broke into a big smile. It was Captain Mabley of the *Third Avenger* on the other line and he was delighted to inform Brent there were four sea turtles lounging around his anchored boat, otherwise alone over the sunken tanker. The venerable old Outer Banks waterman began throwing pieces of lettuce overboard to try to convince the turtles to stay on the surface until the two go-fast boats arrived.

Twenty minutes later, Stuart shut down the engines on the first Fountain. He coasted alongside Captain Mabley's vessel, while the first mate dropped several foam cushions between the hulls. Frank did the same, drifting onto the opposite side of the *Third Avenger*. Suzanne was hopping up and down excitedly on the boat as Monica helped with her snorkeling gear. She could see one of the turtles' head poking above the surface about fifty feet to starboard, gazing at the new visitors.

"Now, remember, stay near me, just a little bit behind and follow my lead and my speed," Brent told Suzanne. "We don't want to spook them back down to the wreck, but if we do, watch how they tuck in their fins and glide on downwards." She looked up at him and her eyes were glistening as brightly as the sun hitting the tops of small waves off the stern. He looked back with what Monica later told everybody was the proud look of a father, happily teaching his daughter about the natural wonders of the sea.

Brent and Suzanne slipped softly into the water first. They slowly made their way towards where the four sea turtles were, while Frank and Monica put on scuba gear and gently lowered themselves into the clear and deep blue water. Stuart handed Monica an underwater video camera, while Frank cleared his ears, descended rapidly to about fifty feet and swam quickly and directly to a spot underneath the turtles. The one who was still on the surface poked its head up to look at the activity on the surface, then looked below the surface at Frank. His presence was not menacing since sea turtles in the *Graveyard of the Atlantic* were accustomed to divers. But Frank did serve as a sort of underwater herder, keeping the turtles from diving to the wreck until Suzanne had a chance to see them up close.

Suzanne was indeed an extremely smart young lady, one who inherently loved the ocean from the very first day when she was brought home from the hospital and her surfer dad had taken her out onto the beach. She did not have to be told again to keep her fins underwater, as Brent had instructed when they were in the water the first time back near Hatteras.

She carefully swam alongside Brent, as she had seen so many nature films showing young whales staying close to their parents. She found herself breathing deeply, though not from the exertion of the swim. Instead, it was from the sudden grasp of what she was now witnessing. She was less than ten feet from two wild sea turtles who were watching them with expressions of mild curiosity, mingled with a just a small bit of concern that these human creatures would try to hold onto the rear of their shells and be given a ride. Brent had told her how some divers did that and how he never did. They stopped about six feet away and the turtles continued their gentle, sweeping, and circular movements, keeping in easy view of their guests.

The interaction with the turtles lasted for almost twenty minutes. Monica, with her elaborate underwater video set-up, swam slow wide circles around them, making sure she had great shots from up close and at wide angle. She even caught the period when one of the turtles seemed to drift a little towards Suzanne, as if as curious about the little girl as the little girl was about the turtle.

Monica also caught the exit that — one by one — the turtles made when they finally decided to return to the shipwreck. It was so clear that the standing bulkheads of the *Manuela* could just barely be seen from the surface, 170 feet down. The bright and clear day combined with the clarity of the far offshore water made the turtles' descent both mesmerizing and magical.

Brent and Suzanne floated motionlessly on the surface, looking straight downwards, while Frank moved laterally, clearing a path for the turtles. One by one, they pulled their fins inward, then drifted downwards in long, sweeping circles. One of the turtles — upon reaching where Frank was watching at about the sixty foot level — pointed its fins outwards, braking its descent. It expertly stopped just a few feet from Frank and after giving him a close once-over, the turtle again reined in its fins and headed downwards. Frank looked up towards Suzanne to make sure she had seen what happened. She exchanged a vibrant thumbs-up sign with the diver.

After swimming back to the boat, Suzanne's first words upon taking off her mask and climbing upon the transom on the stern were loud and joyous. "Momma! Momma! I have got to take scuba lessons! I've got to take scuba lessons!"

"See what you've done, Matt," she said to Brent, trying to cover up a smile of thankfulness that finally a man in her life other than her first husband had taken a true interest in her daughter. "You've created a little Jacque Cousteau."

"Oh, I think that feeling for the sea has always been there," he responded with a proud smile. "What do you think, Suzanne?"

"Oh yes, yes! Momma! That was the best time I've ever had in my whole life! That was so awesome!"

On the way back to shore, it was hard to figure who was the happiest, as an unusual paternal feeling of discovery had overcome Brent, just as the sea turtles had overcome the little girl. They had chosen to return on Captain Mabley's boat, since Suzanne had a million questions for Brent and Monica about diving in the *Graveyard of the Atlantic*. Frank and Stuart headed to shore in the go-fast boats. Leeann had found a spot on the old Sportfisherman where she could work on her tan, while all of her daughter's questions were being answered. Monica also ran back most of the digital footage she retrieved from her camera on a laptop. The three of them huddled together watching the event that was now saved for life.

A couple of hours later as they neared the coastline, Suzanne started to show signs of exhaustion from what was such an exciting day. She still had her big smile and the light of excitement in her eyes and before she headed back into the cabin where her mother was sleeping, Brent and Monica came over with a small, waterproof box that was sealed with O-rings. At first, Suzanne thought it was another piece of camera gear from Monica's bag, but this time, the small box was handed to her by Brent.

Suzanne popped the clamps and slowly opened the box. Immediately she was wide awake and she looked up at Brent with thankful eyes, complete with tears. Inside was the latest version of the iPhone. Her second dream had come true in just one day.

"We've already programmed our numbers in there for you," Brent pointed out. "If you ever have any question about the sea, you call Monica. If you're ever in danger…you call me."

CHAPTER 46

"Okay, I know this is the millionth time we've asked this, but are you *sure* there's no other outstanding votes, shareholders, options, anything along those lines on that property? Our lawyers say there's not, but we're asking you. We mean, absolutely sure."

"Absolutely," answered Lawrence, his game face betraying no doubt.

The three visiting members of the hedge fund that was preparing to close the deal simultaneously sat back in their chairs. They looked silently at one another as if choosing what to believe and when to believe it. They had flown down that morning from New York and met Lawrence in his law office in what he thought was a final courtesy call prior to closing. Instead, the hour-long meeting seemed more like an inquisition.

"Listen, I've laid out the deal of a lifetime down here. You're going to get one of the most unique properties left on the East Coast. It'll be a mecca for those wanting to get away from city sprawl. But it'll be an hour closer to the airport than the rest of the Outer Banks and nowhere near as built up. I'm handing you a gem on a silver platter."

They listened with frowns on their faces and again their eyes met one another as if making notes for discussions they would have on the private jet back to the City.

"I'd develop that property myself if I had the money," Lawrence continued. "That's what you have, plenty of it. I've got control of the location. I'm going to pass it off to you and you're going to make a great deal of money on this deal. It's solid."

Perhaps being so skeptical was a necessity for investment bankers, but Lawrence was still a bit unnerved by the meeting. It ended in a matter of minutes. It was enough to cause Lawrence to soothe himself in the best way he knew how, even as their vehicle was pulling from the parking lot.

He shut his door after telling his secretary that he would be unavailable for the rest of the day. A minute later he had two long lines of coke spread out on the glass surface of his desk and that would be only the beginning. He snorted both lines, stood quickly while absorbing the first strong rush, then walked over to where he kept his bourbon. He soon felt better.

Just why were those guys so hard core? he wondered. The deal was all but done. Despite the opposition from the attorneys of his uncle's estate, he still controlled 51 percent of the vote. There was nothing anyone could do now to stand in the way of the project. *Done deal!*

Just in the proverbial nick of time, too, his scattered mind admitted. His wife and stepdaughter were spending a lot of time down on Hatteras Island with that mysterious Count. All Suzanne talked about was the Count this, the Count that. Lawrence didn't care much about Leeann as she had become what he considered a burden to him anyway. But he just didn't like the idea of this guy swooping down on the Outer Banks with all of his money. This was, after all, Lawrence's home. What right did this outsider have in coming here and stealing all of his respect and acclaim? Well, the new deal that was all ready to go would change that. Two weeks from now and he would score big time. Maybe not the kind of money the Count had, but enough to vault him to the level where the question arises of, "So, when's enough enough?"

Besides, while Leeann and Suzanne were going down there twice a week, he had his little personal deal going on as well. Leeann wasn't the only one who could run around. He had impressed a gorgeous lady all right. After all, she was poor and his current cash flow problems could doubtlessly not be understood from her vantage point. She saw the Corvette, the watch, and that was obviously enough to impress her.

Thinking of her and how he just had to have her began to eat into his coke and bourbon buzz. He kept thinking about the adamant manner in which he was questioned for the last time by the investment bankers. It was almost like they knew something. Like how he even offered the girl a chance to buy into his project. Even signed a little note saying that she would have the right to buy a couple percentage points. It was more a joke for him than anything else. Brought about under the influence of a wild coke spree that made him say and do many crazy things. Anyway, it wouldn't come to reality since he demanded $200,000 for the two points. That girl was lucky enough to pay her phone bill, much less have $200,000, but at least it made her finally submit to his desires. Besides, he thought he remembered tearing the note up before he left.

He went back to his desk and spread out two more lines, bigger than the first ones. He felt better now. The reality of what he had set up and how it was only a couple of weeks away began to pound into his feelings as strongly as the coke. He would be more than really wealthy. He would regain all of the respect that he had managed to lose over the years with the elite business people along the Outer Banks. He wouldn't have to "buy" affection — or sex for that matter — any more. They would come to him instead of him having to go beg to them.

He snorted the line really fast and the reaction caused him to throw back his head. He stood motionless for a few seconds then reached for his glass of bourbon. *Yeah, this time I've got everything covered*, he thought. *I won't have to lie again, work again, beg again.* He took the second line and sat down in his chair. He started smiling as he imagined what it would be like to hold such a massive check that was quickly coming his way. *And I won't even have to kill again.*

CHAPTER 47

PERHAPS IT WAS ONLY INEVITABLE that two people of vastly different backgrounds gradually drifted together into a romantic relationship. Frank, the former Marine and Bluewater operative and Anna, the young Russian business major working in the United States on a student visa found themselves in love. Even though they had known one another for the entire summer they worked in Corolla, it was their busy and complicated stint with the Count that finally brought them together.

This surprised many people around them because quite often during the moments between the rapid building of the Count's empire, they were seen on the verge of arguments. Not over policy or financial concerns between their separate entities, but instead, on global politics, history, and economic discussions. As they gradually sorted things out during the months they worked together, they finally realized much of their philosophical interpretations of life were very much in common. Thus began a relationship that drifted into a warm love and mutual respect, despite the vast and opposing outlooks they were each brought up with.

The love fostered slowly and of course, cautiously, because they were not sure what the Count would make of it. They knew him to be a ruthless, unrelenting businessman, but they also knew him as a kind man of simple tastes. They had worked hard to kindle their boss into meeting women and perhaps forming a relationship himself, but he was just too focused and too driven to succumb to worldly passions —hopefully they reflected — for the moment.

One day, even the extremely busy Count of Cape Hatteras noticed Frank and Anna huddled closely together at lunch on one of the viewing docks of the hotel's pier. He reacted only with a smile. They saw him and smiled back, happily realizing they had his blessing.

Yes, indeed it was a relationship that was one in millions. Two very different people from opposites sides of the world who had evolved into being — deep inside — two people perfectly suited for one another.

It was to be the most improbable and unpredictable relationship on the Outer Banks...until the arrival at the Inlet Inn of a very unusual guest.

PART V

CHAPTER 48

MEGHAN BROWN happened to be the epitome of the young, clean-cut, American actress. She had no tattoos, didn't do drugs, never been in rehab, didn't smoke cigarettes and definitely didn't do the clubbing beat with a different date every night. Instead, she enjoyed spending her small amount of free time time with her family and her close friends. Meghan worked extremely hard on her acting career and all of the business ramifications that grew from her celebrity status. But having just turned twenty six, she encountered her first big nightmare.

Her problem was certainly not of material comfort. Instead, it was being cast in life as someone she truly didn't feel she happened to be. Nor who she wanted to be. She was called the most natural, wholesome beauty in Hollywood, which was a place she seldom visited other than to work on movies or for business meetings with agents, producers, or designers. She still thought of herself as the average little girl from Missouri who just happened to be plucked out of obscurity and thrown into the global raging storm of mass media celebrity status.

She had long blonde hair, wide-apart rich blue eyes and a healthy gathering of freckles that drifted across her captivating nose. Millions of pre-teen girls had idolized her a few years before. Her current following fell off with the older set who seemed to gravitate more towards anyone *but* someone who symbolized a clean-cut style of living. Meghan still had a solid following in all age categories, as she came across on camera as a person anyone would love. But each day that passed she felt more and more out of touch with herself.

Despite such a fortunate circumstance of fame and money, Meghan was at a stage in her life when it all seemed like the proverbial house of cards. She was definitely at a crossroads, not just professionally, but personal as well. She had just ditched her long-time boyfriend after finding out he had been cheating on her.

Johnny Johnson, a wannabee actor with only several small television roles to his credit, beat her to the starting line in the public relations game. His own publicist quickly released statements about how he was so hurt and how Meghan had someone new in her life and had been cheating on him. Without the talent to fall back on, he wasn't about to be the bad guy in the breakup, so he reversed the tables on Meghan from the get-go. Cheating on Meghan Brown would had been the death knell of his stumbling career and he and his agent knew it. Now he could get the "sympathy" vote and perhaps even a role.

Meghan was also torn between maintaining her image as America's last remaining squeaky-clean heart throb or taking an enticing new role that had been offered to her in an upcoming film. It would be the first time she would play a "bad girl" and she needed to fully reflect and focus upon the potentially career changing decision. Coming at a point when the tabloids were accusing her of causing the nasty breakup with her boyfriend complicated things even more. To many of her fans, it would be like admitting her "guilt." But she knew the role in a film backed by the best in producers, writers, and director would be *the* pivotal point in her evolving career.

So, during the week that she sheltered herself in her Malibu mansion, deeply hurt over her ex-boyfriend's actions both before and after their breakup and her career up in the air, Meghan decided that she needed some place very private to sustain her retreat. The barrier of paparazzi and tabloid reporters were literally camped outside and maintained their vigil twenty four hours a day. Helicopters often swooped over, hoping to spot her on the second story "private" deck. On the third day she was betrayed to the media by one of her so-called close friends, who no doubt picked up a nice tabloid paycheck for her observations. Meghan needed to leave town and she needed to do so in a hurry and with no one in tow.

Three days before, she had confided to the people she trusted the most in life, her parents. She told them to please find her a place where she could escape for a week or two. Otherwise, she told them, she'd go crazy. There was no worry of the typical acts of desperation so well known from other stars going through similar circumstances. She would not be showing her crotch to the photographers, they would not be filming her snorting cocaine and she would not allow herself to be swept up in one of those "caught in the car trying to pull away" incidents. She just needed a place that was totally secure and virtually unknown, where she could hang for a week or so and begin to rebuild her emotions.

She peeped outside through the one-way glass window from the third story of her home and saw dozens of reporters and photographers waiting for just the slightest glance. Thankfully, at that very instance, her father called. He may have found the perfect place.

CHAPTER 49

"Okay, John, I want to hear the full report."

The manager of Meghan Brown sat in a chair which he drew up to a large sofa that overlooked the Los Angeles skyline. The parents of his most important client — arguably one of the most popular actresses in the United States — stared at him patiently with looks of deep concern on their faces. He began.

"Well, first off, this place and the people who run it come with the highest recommendation you could imagine. From someone we know who's based in Washington. I ran everything by him and he gave it his blessing. Secondly, you two are going to have to trust me on this, as from what we've seen recently, actually over the past year or so, there are people very close to Meghan who we can't trust.

"The owner of this hotel facility also owns a high-tech security agency and both the hotel and his security business have some of the most experienced, respected, and trusted people in the business. Many of them are former military and Bluewater operatives who have guarded people in extremely dangerous circumstances all over the world. The hotel has the equivalent of a stealth army and the private investigator I sent in to check the place out says it is impregnable.

"Now, as for her suite itself, Meghan would have sole occupancy of a suite that would be as hard to get into as the White House itself. It's unbelievable from what I've heard and the photos I've been shown. Not only that, but it's as luxurious as any suite you'll find here in LA or Vegas for that matter. It's something like 2,500 square feet not counting an open area in the middle that is essentially a courtyard with a retractable roof. It's one-way glass and can be pulled back with the press of a button, so even a satellite in space wouldn't be able to spy down inside. She could sunbathe all she wants without even going to the beach.

"Don't worry about the accommodations. It has been furnished with nothing but the finest. The owner is someone who we've had great difficulty finding a whole lot of information on, but again, I fall back to someone I completely trust back in Washington. The man is a Count of some kind. Near as we can figure from a displaced family in Eastern Europe that had to flee the Nazis during World War II and the Russians, afterwards. That's what makes the personal background check so difficult.

"Anyway, he's extremely wealthy and we think he's in charge of the family fortune which has been described as worldwide, deep-seated, and very liquid. In fact, the suite where Meghan would spend her R&R was originally not supposed to be for rent. The Count built it for his father, who is an invalid and wheelchair-bound. Instead, the father expressed to his son that he wanted to be closer to the water, where he could watch the fishing boats come and go.

"You see, there's a huge barrier that now separates the two suites, one of which is supposed to be where the Count stays when he's there. And he isn't there often, from what we heard. He travels extensively, no doubt financial centers like New York, London, Dubai, and of course, the Caymans. So, for the lodging itself, I'm totally convinced that would be the place for her.

"Now, the other important piece to the success of her getaway is something I've gone over with several times with their head of security. He flew out here and in just a couple of days determined that her whereabouts have been betrayed by someone else in her close circle. Not just the one girl. That's why no one else but you two are in this meeting with me. He kept telling me that everything is on a 'need to know basis.' Which I understand completely. After all, no matter what we try, the paparazzi and press have always found her. They'll go all out with all the headlines involving that boyfriend. We have some suspects and we also believe a lot has to do with the security of her cell phone and her text messaging, but anyway, the chief of security there has told me that if we do want to use their services, we have to follow their guidelines.

"It's going to be kind of unusual to say the least, but you both have told me — and Meghan herself — that what she needs is total peace and quiet and privacy. The only way, according to this security guy, is that we follow their instructions exactly. In fact, the transition aspect — from here — to the hotel is something even we won't know. That's how thorough this operation is. That's also why I did such an extensive check on these people. Even the head of security was awarded a Silver Star in Iraq and had the highest security clearance that's obtainable by Special Operations type people. So, we can trust them. They're even going to confiscate all of her communications equipment and supply her with their own, which are scrambled and untraceable from what he explained to me.

"Something funny in all of this is that Meghan is not going to be able to bring her own clothes. This will eliminate the possibility of any of her staff planting homing devices in her things. This lie being told by that scumbag boyfriend of hers, ex-boyfriend, thank goodness, has brought all the press as you know, and they will resort to anything to get their stories. In order for Meghan to have time to repair from all this and to recuperate, then we simply have to follow their plan. Otherwise, they won't deal with us. That's what they told me. And even though it's going to be expensive, they don't seem to care if we say no. Business revenue doesn't seem to be a major concern with them. Which I think is a good thing in this case.

"So, are we onboard with this?"

The mother and father silently looked at one another for a few seconds, then nodded their heads ever so slightly at one another. The mom turned to the manager and asked, "Will we be able to be in touch with her at all times?"

"Yes."

"Will she be safe?" she continued softly, yet with a strong maternal force in her voice.

"Safer than she would be here. Or anywhere else for that matter."

The dad spoke up. "Who's to say this guy and this Count or any of his staff won't be on the hook to the press any less than all the folks around here?"

"Well, for one thing, he runs a tight ship with an iron fist from what I've been told. And, like I also said, they obviously don't need any tabloid money. Besides, once she's spirited away and taken to her suite, she will see absolutely no one without her own permission. Meghan told me that she just wants to lock herself up somewhere completely secluded and safe and not see a soul."

"I guess we need to do this for her," her mom pointed out, while her husband nodded in agreement.

"But, what about the people there and this Count guy himself?" the father asked after a few more seconds of thought. "With Meghan Brown at his hotel, who's to say he or his people won't be star struck?"

"Actually, I wondered about that, too. I even asked his security chief about that and he said his boss probably has no idea who Meghan is."

"That's ridiculous!" the father responded. "Only someone in a dungeon for the past decade wouldn't have heard of our daughter."

"Yeah, you're probably right."

CHAPTER 50

THE OVERRIDING SENSATION that Meghan felt was not relief or even joy that she had escaped the media. Instead, her excitement came from feeling like she was actually living a part in a movie...not as a role, but for real.

The moment she entered a private hanger at the airport in Riverside, she was swept up in a swift and orchestrated transition. It began with her bags loaded onto a Lear jet and orders to change into a set of clothes that had been provided to her by one of her new "bodyguards." Before she could change in a small restroom nestled next to a tiny interior office, she heard the engine of a tug fire up. She opened the door and watched as her bags were loaded onto the jet. A man motioned for her to close the door a bit, as the main doors to the hangar began to creak open. The jet was towed out and in another few seconds she heard the high pitch of its engines began to whine. The doors closed just as the jet began to taxi towards the runway.

"Ma'am, you can come out now."

Meghan appeared in a set of blue jeans and a long-sleeved, plain white shirt and looked quizzically at her new handlers. One motioned towards a beat up king cab pickup truck that was parked in the corner. Another man held open the door and motioned for her to climb into the rear seat. She had already been warned that her trip would be unlike any she had ever taken before and — with the confidence given to her by her parents and her manager — she did as she was told.

Two of the serious-looking men climbed into the front seat and she listened as one spoke into a phone unlike she had ever seen before. Meghan realized it was some sort of scrambling device and it gave her a sense that for once she was finally surrounded by professional people who truly knew what they were doing.

"Frank, are we clear?" the man asked. Then after a pause, he said, "Cool."

"Can you tell me what's going on?" Meghan asked.

"The paparazzi following us have left...they haven't cleared the airport yet, so we're gonna wait a while longer. There's also a straggler...probably the one who stayed behind just in case the jet was a decoy run. We're either gonna wait him out or Frank will take care of him."

"Who's Frank?"

"He's our boss."

Five silent minutes later, the phone rang and the driver listened to the ongoing developments. "Okay, great. We're ready to head out when you say so."

"So, what's up now?" she asked.

"The one dude that was left behind took off. Some of our guys are searching to make sure there are no others, then we'll get the word to move."

"Where are we going?"

"Not to Hawaii, where that jet and your baggage is going."

The all-clear was given and the door opened just enough for the truck to pull away. Meghan was instructed to lay down on the rear seat underneath a blanket. Only when they were half an hour away from the airport was she allowed to rise. "We're pulling into this other airport in about twenty minutes. That's where we'll take our jet."

Five hours later, she found herself at a rural airport between Wilmington and Greenville, North Carolina. The plane taxied up to another hangar and let her off right at the door that was open and waiting for her. She was whisked inside, despite the fact that the men had already been told that the paparazzi were on flights headed for Honolulu, no doubt following the homing device someone planted in her baggage.

Inside the new hangar, her jaw literally dropped as she saw her next mode of transportation. A new sea plane, with the pilot already inside waiting for her. Under instructions, she climbed into the rear seat, as one of the other bodyguards and Frank also boarded. The doors of the hangar opened and the plane taxied out for takeoff. Less than half an hour later, it made a long, banked turn after the men spotted a particular vessel sitting in the middle of the southern Pamlico Sound, southwest of Hatteras and Ocracoke islands.

Upon the approach, Meghan had her face up to the small rear window like a kid who was flying for the very first time. Frank smiled and advised her to back her face away just a bit from the window, politely explaining about the unpredictable landings that occur on water. She did so and noticed that she was thrilled with how the unusual day had evolved. Then she realized, just as the plane came in for a quick, relatively soft landing, that she was experiencing a real adventure. Not words from a script with a double brought in whenever anything mildly exciting had to take place. But something, *for real*.

The plane moved right up to what she knew as a cigarette boat, a beautiful yellow and blue painted craft that had *Grafton* painted on the stern, right over *Hatteras, N.C.* Wow, she thought. A long ways from the North Shore of Hawaii.

With no land and not even any other boats visible, they climbed aboard and roared away, as the seaplane left in the opposite direction. Twenty minutes later, land came into view and Frank instructed Meghan to go into the small stateroom located towards the bow. Sadly, she did so, wanting to see where she was headed. But, she quickly remembered the turmoil that her known presence always created, so she went below and waited for the arrival to the mysterious destination.

Minutes later, the echo of the engines became loud even though they were now barely coasting. Voices could be heard, as well as the sound of a rope that was thrown over and slid along the deck above her head. She noticed things had gotten darker, and then Frank came down the short flight of steps to tell her that she could now come out.

They were inside a two-boat bay that had a low-ceiling, narrow catwalks on both sides and doors that were being electronically shut.

She heard the crackle and squawk of several radios and then the engine suddenly died. When she climbed onto the aft deck, she saw only the men who had been with her for the day's travels. None held any awe for her and they politely treated her without the slightest bit of deference that so many people gave her. Meghan liked the treatment and she felt safe and secluded, as she and her parents had been promised.

"Ma'am, this way, please," Frank said. He spoke quickly into a microphone connected to his collar, got the "all-clear" that he needed, then unlocked the door. She walked through a deserted but well-manicured courtyard, following Frank to yet another locked doorway.

"Here's your card," he said. "There's another one on the table in the entrance hall. The bedroom is stocked with all the clothes and bathroom items you need. Your mom gave us the list...you know, sizes and what you use and all of that. The phone in there is secure. You may call your parents or anybody else whenever you want. Just don't tell any friends where you are. That would defeat the purpose of all that we've done today. Anything you need, you just pick up the blue phone. We have staff on duty just for you."

She unlocked the door and walked into a split-level entrance way that led to a lavish parlor and bedroom suite that even she had never imagined. Blue sky could be seen above the huge middle section and the first of many stars became visible in the dying light. "Wow," she said out loud.

As Frank was leaving, pulling the door behind him, he said, "Welcome to Hatteras."

Meghan smiled and waved a thanks, then turned around again to view her new surroundings. She felt a nearly-forgotten sense of being unnoticed and alone. Stillness and joy. Safe and completely hidden. *No*, she reflected. *Welcome to Paradise.*

CHAPTER 51

IT WAS THE FOURTH DAY of her visit to Hatteras Island and the movie star and global celebrity Meghan Brown was beginning to feel like someone else: Meghan Brown, the little girl from Truesdale, Missouri with a big smile, freckles, and an innocent outlook on life. She ventured out for the first time that morning to a small book store in Buxton where no one recognized her. She returned safely under the hidden eyes of the hotel's security team. Nestled on the huge sofa which was directly underneath the one-way glass ceiling over the interior court-yard, Meghan smiled to herself. This was exactly what she needed.

She already learned to stay away from the Internet sites that streamed with celebrity "news." For the first couple of days, she often checked out the sites, horrified to find out that she was still being portrayed as the one who instigated the breakup by cheating on her boyfriend. It infuriated her to no end how he was constantly on all the entertainment shows, talking about how heartbroken and surprised he was at her "infidelities." And all the while, he was the guilty one. But in the entire world, only she and her parents seemed to know that. Maybe they and her manager had been right. Maybe she should have come out to the press immediately to set the record straight. But she had grown so tired of that nonsensical world that she just decided to leave.

She put the magazines and books she bought that day on the glass-topped coffee table in front of her and she leaned back in the lushness of the sofa, staring above. How crazy her life had become. How unfair. How different she was from how she was being portrayed in the press. Yeah, she probably should have come out and denied it publicly herself, rather than releasing such a bland press release. With him constantly on the media attack, lying so convincingly to the cameras, she was outgunned. If only he could act that well in films, she thought. Then, maybe his career actually would have gone somewhere without her help.

Meghan should have taken those explicit films off his computer she had found of her boyfriend and his girlfriend that they had obviously taken while she was on the road working. *In her own home*, she angrily thought. Oh, how she could have had a good time dispelling all the rumors with those videos if she had just thought to retrieve them. Now, he would just deny they existed and even challenge her to produce them. Not being able to do so, she would be seen as even more unsavory. She was truly trapped as the world shook their heads in disgust at the All-American Sweetheart who was no longer.

At least the very few people she came into contact with at the hotel — mainly security and the charming woman named Annie who brought her meals — couldn't have cared less about who she happened to be. They only said "ma'am" and smiled, but not evasive at all. After a couple of days of that treatment, she really began to relax and even began to strike up small talk conversations with them. Yes, she was beginning to feel like they were her family.

One thing she did enjoy checking each day were the paparazzi and entertainment press who remained camped out in front of an exclusive hotel in Hawaii. They talked about how she was secluded, lonely and embarrassed. The security people connected to the Inlet Inn had been right after all. Someone inside her camp had been keeping the press abreast of things. The decoy and the illusion worked perfectly and in her new surroundings she was finally able to relax.

With that relaxation boredom eventually arose. So she started to become friends with Annie and whenever she brought a meal, she got her to sit down and talk for a while and they quickly became close. Meghan would ask her about all sorts of things, from her favorite way of cooking shrimp or crab meat and how she got along with the other guests who were back in the main and public part of the complex. That morning she even asked about the person who owned the place.

"Oh, I can't really talk about him," Annie pointed out. "He's just a really fine, nice man, that's all."

"Oh, come on, Annie. What's he like as a person? What does he look like? What does he do when he's here?"

"He just goes out on one of his boats and does that scuba diving thing. He likes to spend time with his dad. And he likes to go over all those financial papers he has around. I guess that's how he got so rich to fix up this place and go all the places and do all the things he does."

"Is there anyway I could meet him?" Meghan asked. "I just want to thank him for having such a great place to stay and for all that his company did to get me away from that commotion back in LA."

"He ain't real social, if that's what you're thinking, dear. He's kinda quiet, 'cept when he's with me when I bring him his meals. He always asks about how I'm doing and how my husband — that's Webster, you know him — is doing, too. He and I laugh about things 'bout every day that he's here."

"Like what things?"

"Oh, like things…well, like I always get on him about jumping out of those airplanes. Or swimming with those sharks out there. I tell him he's crazy."

"Yes, I have to agree with you. Does he have any girlfriends? Do they come here, too?"

"Now, dear, that's getting to where I'm not supposed to talk about such things. He's real private, you know."

"Oh, come on, Annie. Just between you and me. I just wonder, you know I can't help it. This mysterious Count thing and all."

"Well, we all tried to set him up a time or two. We got him introduced to some fine women, I'd say. But he just seems too busy on other things. He really liked one of them…a school teacher…but she was already engaged to be married. She went out scuba diving with him. They seemed to like each other when she was here. But like I said, he's got a whole lot going on right now. He'll find somebody. He's just the busiest man I ever saw."

Hours later, Meghan was still reflecting over that conversation. Her curiosity was roaming on that aspect of her stay, the hidden man who seemed to have his own private army. She gradually got it out of her mind as she put her feet up on the sofa and pulled up a Nicholas Sparks novel which she had already read several times before. She read for a while, then put the book down. Stretching out on the sofa in the sunlight, she drifted off into a comfortable nap, caused by staying up to the early morning hours the night before watching old movies.

Two hours later, she heard some voices through the thick walls from the courtyard, mainly a little girl laughing with excitement. Meghan walked over to the two security monitors which were mounted near the door and flicked them on. They each showed close up views of the patio and entrance way that led to the first exterior wall that insulated her suite from the rest of the hotel complex.

There was a family, it appeared, all but one situated around a laptop with a video playing. There was the little girl standing up, frequently jumping up and down with joy, as she watched divers swimming with sea turtles. There was a man, extremely fit and with premature white hair, standing behind her and a woman who kept pointing out various aspects of the video to the little girl. Nearby sat another woman who was probably the wife and mom, flipping through a tabloid styled magazine, obviously bored with the occasion.

Meghan watched them for several minutes until the one woman clicked off the video and folded up the laptop. The little girl hugged the man, who must had been her father, Meghan thought, then hugged the woman with the laptop. The other woman quickly stood to her feet and motioned for the little girl to follow her. Meghan smiled and thought to herself about how innocent and lucky the little girl happened to be. Like she had been so many years ago. She was with her family at the beach, was probably getting ready to go out to eat at a local restaurant or maybe even a walk to the nearby docks. Didn't have the baggage of being a celebrity in a mass media world. Meghan missed such a peaceful, quiet, yet exciting existence.

She was just getting ready to turn off the security monitors when she noticed something strange. The rest of the family were strolling down the brick walkway that led to the pier, but the man turned around on his heels and walked towards the first wall that contained the set of private suites. She watched in surprise as he inserted a card into the security system, then walked into the interior courtyard towards the second door that led to his suite.

He had a look of happiness across his tanned face and piercing eyes. He was thin, but muscular in a cat-like manner, or perhaps more accurately to these parts, like a barracuda. He had a look of confidence, but also a look of…what she quickly had to determine was pain, or maybe subdued anger. Either way, Meghan knew two things. This man was an extremely complicated person.

And…he was the Count of Cape Hatteras.

CHAPTER 52

THE *GRAFTON*, WITH BRENT at the controls, meandered over the waves through the inlet, then puttered along slowly for a hundred yards into the relative smooth waters. Then he pushed the throttle forward, fast and far, as the sleek go-fast boat roared towards a rendezvous with the *Offshore Roamer*, twenty nautical miles to the southwest. Meanwhile, Stuart and Monica were already doing surface interval time after completing their morning dive on the *Proteus*.

Brent lately began the habit of staying awake deep into the night, immersing himself into such intricacies of life as the global financial markets and even works of fiction. A pile of DVDs that Anna bought for him remained pretty much untouched, even though he did frequently watch his favorite set, *The World at War* series on World War II. Waking up mid-morning instead of his usual five a.m., Brent utilized his Fountain Executioners to help make up for lost time to the dive sites.

Frank peered though binoculars on the eastern horizon as he sat in the passenger seat looking for other vessels to try to gauge who was headed out and where. He also enjoyed looking for schools of dolphin or shad and they would frequently veer off course to look at such spectacles close-up. They were both men of the sea and they were truly appreciative of the time and equipment that was at their disposal. Each man knew that for a split second of action or inaction here or there in their past lives, they would not even be alive anyway. That tasting of "the sweetness of the grape" always magnified their appreciation of the sea they loved so well.

About a mile to the northeast, Frank spotted a large flock of seagulls and as he studied them through his binoculars, he saw several of then straighten up and swoop into deep dives that penetrated the water's surface. He pointed the scene out to Brent, who veered the vessel to port and shot towards the gathering. A minute later, the engines were off and Brent and Frank were staring over the side into clear water that was being colored by a vast, sweeping cloud of bait fish. Here and there were also glints of the sides of mackerel or drum feeding on the school. Suddenly the sound of steps came from the hatchway to the stateroom and faster than a barracuda, Frank withdrew his SIG Sauer P225, pointing it at the emerging figure.

"Wow, is that for real?" she asked, looking at the weapon and climbing onto the main deck, her eyes slit from the sudden brightness of the sun.

"Who are you?" the Count demanded.

"Wow, you just don't know how happy I am to hear that phrase."

Frank quickly put the pistol back into its holster, which was hidden underneath his shirttails. He turned towards Brent and saw that he was quite angry, not so much at the girl, but because such a potentially dangerous breech of security had taken place. "Hey, sorry, man," Frank said. "She's okay, she's a guest at the hotel. In the suite next to yours. The one we told you about."

"Hey, it's my fault," Meghan pointed out. "Of course you wouldn't think anybody would be in the boat because it's in that private dock house next to our rooms. But I figured this would be the only way I could meet the host and...so, here I am."

"Yeah, okay," Brent said softly. "But you shouldn't be here. We'll take you back."

"Awwww...come on. I won't be in the way. I just wanted to get out. I want to come out and see all the diving that you do all day out here. I won't be a burden."

"But...you..." the Count stammered.

"Hey, come on. I'm a paying customer. I know this isn't part of the deal, and I know I wasn't invited along, but let me stay. Out here is private. I like that probably even more than you. So let me stay with y'all, puh-leeze."

The Count looked closely at her, then turned his attention to Frank, who nodded silently at him. "Okay, young lady, you can stay today. But try not to get in the way. We don't need you to get hurt or anything. I think you're the one that Frank here and Anna said needed to be kept safe and sound. Now again, who are you?"

Meghan broke into her huge famous smile, closed her eyes and sweetly demanded, "Please, say that one more time."

"Brent, she's Meghan Brown. She the most famous actress in America."

"Hey, no, I'm not. I get pretty good box office, but who's counting? Certainly not me. They love midwestern style girls. But, no, I'm not the most famous. If you asked my so-called peers, they'll tell you that I'm untalented, shallow, goofy, and politically incorrect. I don't really fit in with them at all. Hey, I don't even have a tattoo. So that's one of the reasons I'm here on the Outer Banks, hiding from all that nonsense."

"Well, I'm sure you're not all that. But we're going way off shore. There's ocean swells out here coming up and you may get seasick. If you do, you're going to have to just ride it out. We're not coming back early."

"Awesome! You don't know anything about me, do you? You can't believe how that feels. I feel…like an average person. Here I've only known you for two minutes and you've already made my fondest dream come true."

"But…"

"No buts about it. Listen, if you had seen any of my films, you would know that I have been at sea many times. I lived on a yacht off the Catalinas for a week during a shoot. I've shot films on the Great Barrier Reef…the Mediterranean even. I know my way around and I'm not going to get seasick."

"Yeah, but we…"

"Hey, if you have some extra gear, I'll go down myself. I'm a certified open water diver. I've been many times."

"But these are offshore wreck dives in the *Graveyard of the Atlantic*. This isn't reef diving in the Caribbean."

"Okay, I've done a little research. You're going to what wreck?"

"The *Proteus*."

"Okay…yeah, that's the one that's just a quarter mile away from the sub…the *Tarpon*, right?"

"Errr…yes.

"Lessee…about 150 feet deep, right? My dive computer is back in LA, but I'm going to guess that I can do about thirty minutes bottom time, then three decompression stops on the anchor line. I should stop at thirty feet for ten minutes, another ten minutes at twenty just to be conservative, hang as long as I can at ten feet, then head to the boat when my pressure gauge says five hundred PSI? Does that sound about right?"

Brent looked at her and smiled, a feeling of warmth and respect overpowering his initial anger at the situation. "Yeah, that's about right."

"So, hey, you *really* don't know who I am, do you?"

"No, I'm sorry."

"Don't be sorry," she said, again flashing him that million dollar…or rather twenty million dollar smile. "Let's just get going. There's diving to be done."

CHAPTER 53

THEY BOTH SAW IT. A shooting star that crossed the recessed roof area of Meghan's suite. "Okay, let me make a wish," she said, tightly closing her eyes. "Okay, done!"

"What did you wish for?" Brent asked.

"Can't tell or it wouldn't come true."

"Oh, yeah, that's right."

The two days since they met on the boat had gone by rapidly for them both. Brent's close circle of friends were quite amazed at the situation, especially after he canceled a day of sky diving. That was a definite signal that the Count of Cape Hatteras was indeed more-than-just-interested in "America's sweetheart." Despite those hopes for him to finally have a real relationship, both Brent and Meghan had already set the parameters for the relationship only a few hours after they returned to shore when they first met.

The Count insisted that he was too old for her, being fourteen years her senior. She disagreed, but countered that — despite her current recluse status — would sooner or later be swept back into the mass media limelight anyway. A place where the Count would never tread. With everything understood, they allowed themselves to drift into a close relationship, one that would perhaps last no longer than a few more days.

Brent and Meghan were on two separate lounge chairs stretched out underneath the skies, surrounded by the luxuriousness and safety of her suite. They shared a bottle of white wine, she on her second glass and him having only taken a quick sip. They had spent two days diving together and now they were on their second night of talking. The first evening was casual and humorous, while the second night, things began to turn very personal.

"Okay, Brent, I'll tell you my biggest secret, if you tell me yours. Seeing how you obviously never pay any attention to the magazine covers at the grocery store. But, of course, I guess you've never gone grocery shopping. I'm sure you have people for that."

"Not at all. I walk over to the Red and White all the time."

"And you haven't seen my photo? It's always there, unfortunately on those magazines at the counters."

"Nope, all those faces look the same to me. I really don't pay it any mind."

"That's another thing I like about you. Well, anyway, like I've already told you, I'm here to escape the press that seems to have convicted me as America's sexy sweetheart gone bad. But my secret? I'm going to tell you something about my ex-boy friend. The tabloids would offer so much money for such information. I just have to clam up and it's simply driving me crazy. Especially since all my fans, especially the young girls, think I've let them down. In a world seeming to hang on by a thread of decency, I seem to have been the one to cut that last bit of thread.

"Anyway, my ex-boyfriend left his computer on one day last week and he was still logged in. Now, I'm not a snoop. I never was, but instead of logging him out and then logging back on, I was just looking for the weather forecast and I was clicking around and all of a sudden I came to a folder. Well, inside were several files that he was saving. I thought, 'how cute, how romantic.' They would be of us. Well, they were of him and this girl who works at a bistro near my home. And they were taken at *my* home. That louse can barely find work. The only roles he's gotten recently was because of my fame. He hated that. But that wasn't my fault. I don't like the fame game. I'd rather be completely unknown. I'd like to be a clerk in a small book store somewhere. But I'm not and what am I supposed to do? Walk away from all this money?

"So, I confront him about the videos. He has a fit. I storm out. He leaves a while later and the very next day, I get calls from my manager and my agent and parents about how he's all over the entertainment news talking about how I dumped him and she's a slut and all of this. I rush in to get the film files and they'd been deleted or downloaded and moved. Surprise, right? He got the first jump with the press and when I said it wasn't true, all it did was make me look out to be a two-timer *and* a liar. He checkmated me perfectly. Everybody feels so sorry for him and they hate me because I let them down. Or something like that. I know, I know. It must seem strange to you, but that's how the game works.

"Plus, there's this role I've been waiting for all my career, a really bad girl role. A girl who breaks her boyfriend's heart so badly that he commits suicide. Well, now if I take that role, people will say that's because all the things were true after all. Even my best fans won't forgive me. I went from America's Sweetheart to America's Heart-breaker, America's Two-timer. At the very time I needed to push my career to a higher level, zoom. I'm trapped."

"Who cares what anybody thinks? Even in your world. You're bound to have plenty of money set aside. So what if they think you dumped him? What's the big deal about that? Happens all the time. Why worry?"

"Well, I do worry. And if you want to bring money into it, I'm on the verge of losing my fragrance line which — and I know you have no clue about this — is based on a "nice" girl's perfume. He completely shot my entire image and with the sympathy vote, he's already managed to get the attention and probably the roles he needs. And he's the slut!"

"If that's the darkest secret you're holding, then I wouldn't feel too badly."

"Yeah, right, thanks. It's more serious than you think. It's my reputation. Suppose somebody made false claims about your hotel? And nobody wanted to come back. It's like that. But I'm glad I told you. I admit I do feel better now. That bastard! Well, thanks. I trust you to keep this quiet. Now, you have to tell me your secret."

"I will. Because I trust you, too. Besides, when you leave here, the last thing you need is to be in any way remotely connected to me. You see, I have this little vendetta to take care of and it could escalate further than any level you've come across."

"Wow. Sounds exciting."

"But first I have to speak to Frank about something. If you'll give me a few minutes."

"Sure."

Five minutes later, Frank appeared at the end of the dock where the Count was waiting. "Hey, Brent what gives?"

"I've got a little mission for you."

CHAPTER 54

Two hours into their day of kayaking, Hatteras and Ocracoke islands disappeared over the horizon. Brent and Meghan had left the docks at dawn, heading southwest with the intention of going as far as they could. The day was bright, cloudless and the sun lit up the sand in the shallow waters as if they were in the Bahamas. It was a great day to kayak and for these two, an even greater day to further delve into each other's lives.

"The last couple of nights have been so amazing," Meghan said. "I still can't believe you were in that prison for all those years."

"Oh, I can, all right."

"And here I am alone with you way out here. My parents would think I'm crazy. They'd have a fit!"

"We're not alone. There's a boat way over there. See that tiny dot on the horizon?"

"Great. I thought we had the Pamlico Sound all to ourselves."

"Well, out here, we kinda do. They're not fishermen. That's a couple of my bodyguards. One can't be too careful, you know."

"Oh yeah, you're telling me?" she laughed. "I let my boyfriend ruin my career."

"You'll just have to be more careful next time."

"You betcha."

They continued paddling, watching the various bird life that drifted by. Every once in a while, they'd see flashes of schools of small fish, dotting across the sandy bottom. Then, about a mile ahead, they each saw an amazing sight so far from either shore. A tiny sandbar.

"Hey, look!" Meghan shouted. "Our own little island!"

"That's going to be your island. You saw it first, so you can name it. Just remember, it probably won't be here by the next tide."

"Cool! Let me see…I know! I'm going to name it 'Our Island.'"

"Then it's fitting that it's temporary."

"Oh, I don't know about that. I think we're going to end up being the best of friends. Who knows? I may fool you and never go back. Seeing how my career is shot."

"Don't give up on that. Amazing things can happen. Directly or indirectly, everything's in God's hands."

"Hmmm, I'll reflect upon that later."

They reached the sand bar that protruded about a foot above the water level and was no more than ten feet long and about five feet wide. Two sea gulls flew off when they were about fifty yards away, relinquishing their rest stop to the two visitors. Meghan climbed from her kayak and pulled the vessel onto the sand. "I hereby claim this island for…the Countess of Pamlico!"

Brent laughed out loud, with the sound rumbling across the water. "I love it! Perfect!"

They both secured their kayaks and Brent then withdrew a beach towel from his kayak's storage compartment. He spread it out as Meghan turned slowly on her heels, breathing in a sweeping view of both beauty and emptiness. Only the skiff with the bodyguards could be seen and they were like tiny specks, a couple of miles away. "Well, now I see why you chose to escape to the Outer Banks."

"Wherever you are, life can be beautiful."

"That's right. I still love ole' Truesdale. I was as happy there as I've been anywhere, looking back on things. I think the freedom I have right now here with you is the best! I know I have to go back soon and I know you have the big ordeal you're getting ready to tackle. But for just you and I today, right here. I mean, you just can't find that too often. Especially after all the talking we did last night. Which, Mister, reminds me of something. You haven't even tried to kiss me good night! I'm mortified."

"Sure you are," he said with another loud laugh. "Besides, I told you before. You're too young for me."

"Twenty-six? Oh, I've been kissed before, all right. But I gotta admit it is kinda refreshing. Here I am, Hollywood star…well, ex-

Hollywood star…and I meet a perfect gentleman…one who just spent sixteen years in a dungeon. And I don't even get a kiss!"

"It's just…that…"

"Well, that's something we can talk about. That's something I can actually help you out with a bit, for a change. Now, you told me about everything last night. When you left, I stayed awake for a long time. I thought over everything you said. And you know what? I see that you are still carrying a torch."

"Not for Leeann, I'm not."

"Oh, definitely not. That was the big letdown, huh? You have your girl taken away from you. In a manner that causes you to be locked away for a long time. You come back rich and powerful. And one would expect that you'd both run into each other's arms like some old movie. Well, life didn't work out that way, did it?"

"Not in my case. So, what can you do? You idolize a woman every second of every day for all that time and then I come back and see that she's not who or what I thought she was. So, no. I'm not carrying a torch for her."

"Oh, I don't know about her specifically. I guess I'm not an expert going by my experience with my ex-boyfriend. Or maybe I am because I now can see through the fog. But I can tell you have feelings there for someone. Maybe that teacher."

"She was fantastic, no question about that. But she was engaged. She's married by now. Doesn't matter now anyway."

"It's not that beautiful little Russian girl, is it? So smart and so charming."

"No, but she's the daughter I never had. What a great person. She and Frank are going to be perfect together. When that wedding takes place, you need to come. I'm going to pay for all of it. It's going to be the wedding of the decade down here. After all, those two saved me that day on the beach."

"I'll be there, all right. Where is Frank, anyway? I haven't seen him in two days. But forget about everybody else. Let's get back to you. Okay, but there is someone. I can tell."

"No, I don't think so. I'm in a holding pattern, I guess. Everything is focused on what's coming up. I don't have time for any relationship anyway. I have to focus. Anyone who I really like, I'll push away, just for their own good."

"You know, you worry me about that. I want you to be careful, okay?"

"Oh, I think you know I'm as guarded, protected, and prepared as I can be."

"Well, speaking of prepared, this sun out here is really starting to get hot. I'm a Midwestern blonde with freckles and fair skin, so if you don't mind, can you put this sun block on me? What I put on this morning doesn't seem to be doing any good now."

"Yes, and I can do even better than that. I have a lean-to that I can set up for you. It'll give you some shade. Out here, that's the best protection you'll have."

She watched him unbuckle the storage compartment of his kayak and withdraw a set of retractable poles and a zippered pouch that contained a waterproof covering. He stuck the poles deeply into the sand, then connected the brass hooks to the fasteners at the top of the poles. Then he withdrew three spikes, inserting them into the brass rings on the bottom side of the material. Meghan moved her towel into the welcome shade, facing away from his bodyguards. She then stretched out, smiling up at Brent with her famous blue eyes.

"Oh, this is great," she purred. "But I still need that lotion."

Five minutes later, she looked over her shoulder and said, "That was very nice, but pretty much mechanical. You can do better than that."

He silently put the top back on the bottle of sun block, then looked towards the south.

"Oh, come on, Brent, today is *your* day. We expelled all my demons already. I'm the actress who ran against every style in Hollywood. The goody two shoes who frowned upon wild behavior, then I'm portrayed as the ultimate Hollywood hypocrite. I'm sure my dealings with the fragrance line are being terminated as we speak.

I'll probably be on the celebrity reality show circuit next. But what's saving me is realizing what you've gone through and what you're facing. Which far overshadows any problems I have.

"You're still upset over the death of the man you served time with and who brought you this vast fortune. You're jaded after the love of your life turned out to be the norm of our times. You feel like you're too old to start a family and you miss not having a daughter like the little Suzanne girl you're so fond of. You have old-fashioned values that are long gone in this day and age and we've both become victims of that in different ways. We're two fish out of water — no pun intended — looking around at this location, but we will go on."

"You're right."

"Of course, I am. Maybe this is God's way of making me move on. To make me take my career to the next level instead of staying where I'm situated and comfortable. Maybe it'll be for the best. Unjust as things are."

"Could be. That's probably true for both of us."

"Yeah, but after listening to you last night, I saw just how puny my problems are. I've been good with my money. I'm not one of those fashion divas. I don't have the full-time stylists...all of that. Me or my family will never have to work again, so what am I crying about? I'm really being hypocritical now. I've berated so many peers for so many years about how self-absorbed they are and then wham! Here I am. You made me see that.

"I don't know what you're going to do about that guy who took your girl and set you up. I don't want to know. Like you keep saying, it's on 'a need to know basis.' But even I can surmise that you may not be so worried about him as you are about repercussions that it may bring from others. I know you're not telling me everything for my own good. Anyway, we know what directions we must follow and we'll do so.

"What I'm talking about...right here and now...is the two of us. Just for today. Tonight. Tomorrow. And then we go our separate ways. You need this. So do I." She slowly turned over onto her back, stared straight into his eyes, and invitingly curved a finger at him. "So, if you don't mind...my front needs some lotion."

CHAPTER 55

BRENT AND MEGHAN WATCHED not only the sunset from the little sand bar that was getting eaten away with each passing second, but also the intense afterglow of the vanished sun. The bright yellows shifted to rich reds, then to dark purples. It was an experience that was as breath-taking and as powerful as their last few hours hidden beneath the canopy. Then, knowing how tricky the tide could be, Brent used the small emergency beeper stowed in his kayak and instantly they heard the firing up of the bodyguards' skiff far in the distance.

An hour later, the skiff and the towed kayaks made their way into the private boat house. Standing on the dock was Annie with a huge smile aimed straight for Meghan. "I told you, girl, that everything'd work out, now didn't I?"

"Wha…?"

"We're all so excited for you. We knew that boy was full of crap. Well, you'll see, they're frying his sorry butt right now and everybody is all sorry they got on you."

"Annie, what on earth are you talking about?"

"Honey, you don't know?"

"Know what?"

"I'll let you go in and find out for yourself. Just look on any of those websites with entertainment news. You'll see. But first just let me hug you for being able to take all this so good."

She embraced Meghan and gave her a quick smile. Meghan then went inside with a look of concern and confusion on her face. She turned to Brent and asked him to follow. Frank was standing next to the door and unlocked it with his card. Brent smiled at Frank as they passed and he nodded his head at his boss with a wink.

Meghan rushed to the home entertainment section of the suite, turning on the television and the computer one after the other. She impatiently waited for the computer to warm up. She logged on quickly but before she could make it to the first website, the television channel she clicked on passed on the news:

"Word is a-buzzing about the steamy videos of former Meghan Brown boyfriend Johnny Johnson and an unknown female that appeared overnight on several websites. The really astonishing thing is that the videos were obviously made weeks and even months ago and some were even taken inside Meghan's home. Due to their adult nature we can't show you much of it here, but perhaps most shocking is this sequence that we can show, with Johnson making obscene gestures to the living room portrait of Meghan.

"Contacted briefly early this morning was Johnson himself. He apparently was unaware about the videos being released and denied they even existed, despite the fact they had already been on-line for over two hours. Meghan Brown was unavailable for comment and is still believed to be in seclusion in a luxury hotel in Hawaii.

"We do have this statement from her manager, 'Meghan Brown was completely innocent in this entire ordeal and was emotionally devastated at how she was treated by her former boyfriend as well as having the majority of the press unjustly convict her on the spot. She is still emotionally recuperating from this ordeal and wishes to express to her true fans and friends who stood by her these last two weeks, her sincere thanks and appreciation. She also looks forward to returning to work as soon as possible.'

"There is no information on how or why the videos were uploaded. Further details are expected as we have several teams in the field searching for additional information."

Meghan leaped into Brent's arms and shouted with glee. She started to grab the scrambler phone to call her parents, but first rushed outside to find Annie who was still at the docks with a big smile and outstretched arms.

Brent followed her outside, then walked over to Frank. "Hey, man, great job."

"The least I could do after that security lapse with the boat that day."

"Hey, who better to break security than someone like her?"

"Yeah, you're right."

"Oh, and Frank. How the heck did you do it? You said the girl-friend turned down a quarter of a million from that big tabloid. How'd you get her to break?"

"It was a little difficult," he said with a grin. "But it didn't quite get to the point where any sharks were needed."

CHAPTER 56

THE LARGEST BED in the largest bedroom on the entire Outer Banks belonged to the Count of Cape Hatteras. But on their last night together before they parted ways, Brent and Meghan couldn't have been any closer together.

"I am soooo going to miss you," she purred, snuggling up to his chest. "This has been the wildest period of my life. Not that I've led a wild life. Just a busy one."

"Well, err, thanks."

"Oh, you know what I mean. I think you're my very first real man. The rest have been boys. And as we know, I got your second virginity." They both laughed and held each other even closer.

"Thank you for that," he said. "It took someone like you to bring me back to this point. It's been a long time for sure."

"Thank *you*."

"I'm really going to miss you, too. But you have to go. You've got your entire career and millions of people waiting for you. With the way you came through that thing with the ex-boyfriend, you should have no trouble changing your style of roles, if you choose. The public owes you that for the way they gave up on you."

"You know, what happened is still amazing to me. Why on earth would she have uploaded those videos? How did they find out she did? She should have known it would have ruined Johnny's career. Strange is all I can say, but you just wouldn't believe the mentality out there. There's some weird people and fame and money can really take its toll."

"I have no doubt about that."

"Actually, it's amazing you've stayed like you are. Some people in your circumstances would just go, as we say back in Missouri, hog-wild."

"In some ways I have. My financials are really, well, hog wild. Not really, I suppose. Very organized and geared for the big downfall that's going to happen in a matter of months. A negative savings rates, people walking away from their mortgages, and the most spoiled population on earth. Credit card debt. Immediate gratification finally catching up. There's going to be a reckoning and we've prepared for it."

"My advisors have done pretty much the same. We have a lot of cash sitting there waiting. But you. You could be a modern day Rhett Butler and the only personal vehicle I've seen of yours is that beat-up old truck. And the clothes you wear are...well, not in style."

"Hey, I love my truck. Besides something like that is invisible. That's what you need when you go back to your world. An invisible vehicle. As for Rhett Butler, that I could never be. Too much the dandy for my tastes. Though he was right about a lot of things. 'There's as much money to be made from the wreckage of a civilization as there is to its building' or something like that. He's right there."

"Yeah, I see your point. Besides, I like you fine just the way you are. It would be fun, though, to be in a serious relationship with you and to show you my world. Dress you up a bit, take you to some restaurants I know in LA, New York, Toronto...that would be something."

"Nice thoughts, but I'm afraid the ways things may go, we'll never be able to see each other again."

"We better and you promised you'd be safe."

"Oh, my personal safety is a given. I have the best people in the world around me. It's the fog of war and the blurred lines that could be a problem. I'm not worried so much about the first guy. It's the people that will lose when he loses. That's our big worry. For the time being, I don't want you to have any visible connection with me. For your own good. Find somebody decent in your world."

"Yeah, right. Anyway, I know how angry you are and I've touched on this a little before, but let me raise this a little more bluntly this time. Do you *really* have to do this? Is it worth it to you to destroy him? You've got all the money in the world. I'll be yours forever just for the asking. What about that little girl you're so fond of? Suzanne. Do you want to risk everything when you could be her, what, unofficial godfather? Is revenge against someone even so despicable as him really worth jeopardizing all of that?"

Brent was silent for a minute. Staring upwards through the retractable roof, watching dark bursts of clouds rushing by the brightly visible stars.

"Come on, Brent, answer my question."

"First, I am too old for you…"

"No, you're not."

"Secondly, the epitome of your job is being as visible and social as possible while the epitome of my job is to be as hidden and camouflaged as possible. We would never work out. Then, I have money put aside for Suzanne in case anything happens to me. In such a way that her mother would not be able to touch it. Besides, Leeann won't bring her down here anymore. She didn't think for a moment that her daughter and I would build up such a bond. She had her own plans and they didn't materialize. So, this way, she gets back at me. About the only chance I'll have to see her is at her school's awards banquet next week. Did you know she won first place in the science department for her presentation on swimming with the sea turtles? She put the video on YouTube and can you believe it's gotten several hundred thousand hits already?"

"That's awesome!"

"Yeah, it brought the school a lot of recognition, but all the local hype is on some retired professional baseball player who's handing out the awards. The guest speaker of the event. Typical America. Sports comes before science."

"Who cares? I'll bet she won't. It's a shame I couldn't meet her. And you…you're being so cute right now."

"What…what are you talking about?"

"Look at you. You're mad because some other kids will get more recognition that your little unofficial godchild. Wow, I can't wait for you to be a real parent. All your money, power, mysteriousness, and intelligence and you're still gonna be just another proud American parent. I love it!"

"Hah! You've got me there. But that may never happen…"

"Oh, yes it will. Let me look into my crystal ball…if I never convince you that you're not to old for me…lessee…I see you meeting someone really special when you're…yeah, say, forty-five. It won't be like when you were struggling, unsuccessfully trying to establish yourself back before your nightmare began. And the mood swings that probably brought. You'll be financially secure. You'll have all this revenge business behind you. You'll be able to relax with the woman you fall for — one who will seemingly come out of nowhere — and the dire circumstances won't be there to divert you from being what you're truly destined to be: a great husband and a great father…yeah, that's what I see."

"I hope that's the case. I hope I don't screw things up."

"You'd better not. Now, okay, let's get to the revenge factor. Think about it. Do you really need it?"

"Having said what I've told you already, yes. I was destined to ruin him just as he ruined me. I don't think I'll be able to be that 'great husband and great father' until I do. I'm sorry. That's set in stone. They say people like him live their entire lives and never get their due. Well, that won't be the case with him. So, let's just change the subject."

"Agreed, I don't want our last night together to end on a negative note."

"And it won't. This has been a great experience for me. And to think I never paid any attention to those magazine covers when I went over to the Red&White."

"Tell you what, Brent. I have a lot of clout with some of those magazines and I'll do this. In a couple of months, you'll see a cover shot of me and I'm going to be winking. That wink will be aimed only at you."

CHAPTER 57

A WEEK LATER, the Count of Cape Hatteras sat on the very back row of the school auditorium and remained in the shadows. Monica and Stuart were seated next to him. While they all seemed a bit out of place, they were as excited as any parent or student at the end-of-the-year awards presentation. On the Count's part, perhaps even more so.

Leeann had cordially, but rather stiffly, greeted them before the event as family, teachers, and students were mingling in the large hallway. She thanked them all for their help with Suzanne's project, as the little girl looked up at the Count and said, "Did you see how many hits we got on YouTube? It's nearly three hundred thousand!"

"I'm so proud of you," he said, with both Monica and Stuart nodding in agreement.

"But it was all of us," Suzanne said. "We all deserve this award." Leeann silently steamed as it was quite obvious from the little girl that she wasn't included.

When it came time for the presentations, Leeann shepherded Suzanne off, regaining control of the situation. Brent went to the back row. He was joined by Monica and Stuart, while Frank sat in the far rear on one side and another bodyguard sat on the opposite side. Since they were in Manteo, Brent was a little concerned that there may be someone there, perhaps an older teacher or neighbor who could recognize him, despite all the past years. In addition to his regular security concerns.

The principle opened with remarks about how all the fields of study were equally important before drifting off into a detailed summary of the guest speaker's baseball highlights. The speaker, with a ruddy, drinking man's complexion and the proverbial cap that hid his baldness was roundly applauded and an impromptu standing ovation occurred when he appeared from stage left. After twenty minutes of old ball game stories, he again received a round of applause and remained standing with the principal to awkwardly make each presentation to the honored students.

Meanwhile, a muffled noise could be heard from behind the stage curtains. Frank and his fellow bodyguard were the very first in the audience to notice. A teacher standing to stage right suddenly put her hand to her mouth, then tried to casually walk behind the curtain to the opposite side of the stage. The noise from behind-the-scenes grew a bit stronger, enough so that the principal himself sternly gave the eye to an assistant principal, who went backstage to see what was going on. Frank, meanwhile, drifted over to where the Count was sitting and slowly put his hand inside his coat. The other bodyguard casually walked down the aisle towards the stage, forming the first perimeter of defense.

Finally, the principal took over the microphone and advised the audience to "please hang on for a second." He motioned for the former athlete to have a seat, and then went backstage himself, after a quick and urgent wave from the assistant principal.

Less than a minute later he reappeared, so flustered that he momentarily got tangled in the curtails, which brought a fit of laughter from every child and most of the parents. His eyes were wide open and his face was flushed. He was smiling but more in a state of awe than anything else.

"Parents, students, faculty, and other guests, please allow me to make a change in today's program," he gasped. "We have a surprise guest who just arrived and has asked to be able to present the science award to our very own Suzanne Smith. Ladies and gentlemen, I'm in as great as shock as you surely will be, but allow me to introduce…from Hollywood, the very talented and beautiful actress, Meghan Brown!"

Meghan, in all her style and beauty, walked out on stage with her huge smile, big blue eyes, freckles, and the God-given ability to make people feel as if she had known them all their lives. She waved to the crowd, then shook hands with the principal while nodding at the former baseball player. Before she walked up to the microphone she spotted Brent and winked.

"I'm sorry for coming in unannounced and uninvited," she began. She was forced to pause by the continued frantic cheering and applause. "I happen to be on the way to New York for a photo shoot and some interviews when I first saw that fantastic video that Suzanne did on YouTube. I sooo love sea turtles and I watched it so many times, that I just felt like I had to make a quick detour and come down here and make this presentation myself. I hope y'all don't mind the interruption."

Again, the crowd roared their approval with shouts of "We love you!" coming from all sides of the room. Monica and Stuart looked at Brent and each one of them were totally surprised and full of pride. Brent was just shaking his head in wonder and respect at someone he knew far transcended any normal concept of goodness.

"Thank you, thank you so very much. You know, I've been reading those Nicholas Sparks novels for years about the Outer Banks and I'm so happy to finally come down here and see this place for myself. I've had so many people tell me that those novels are silly old-fashioned love ballads, but you know what? I believe love stories like that are for real. And from what I can imagine, I'll bet you can find more *real* romance and love down here than you can in all of California, no matter what they say."

Again the room was overcome with cheers and applause.

"Unfortunately, I have to go straight to New York from here, but I want you all to know that as soon as things settle down a bit in my life and (as she stared directly at Brent) to those close to me…I'm going to hopefully have the opportunity to return and learn to love this place for myself. With that, please allow me to do the honor of presenting the top science award for 2008 to Suzanne Smith. And let me be the first tonight to say that I love her video! Keep up the good work."

Suzanne walked over with a huge look of awe, but not enough to overshadow her joy at seeing the science award plaque. Meghan, all decked up — as if she was on one of those magazine covers at the Red&White, as Brent would say — appeared every bit the glamorous movie star she happened to be. She jointly held the plaque with Suzanne and leaned downwards enough so they were both on an even level. A steady array of camera flashes went off and it took more than a minute for the photo opportunity to conclude.

Meanwhile, Leeann was standing near the front row, her hand to her mouth in shock and disbelief, mesmerized herself at the surprising presence of such a star. She wanted to walk closer, but she was in such shock her feet were as if in concrete.

"Before I go I want to congratulate each and every student here tonight and I want you to know how proud I am of all of you for studying so hard and achieving so much. Keep up the good work, all of you.

"And, one last thing, if y'all don't mind." Meghan put her arm around Suzanne, drew her close to her side and looked toward the crowd, but actually straight into Brent's tear-filled eyes. "Someday, I hope to have such a precious little kid myself just like Suzanne."

PART VI

CHAPTER 58

LAWRENCE PARKER WAS BEAMING with joy, grandiose and pride. He was also greatly relieved that in about an hour's time, he would go from a negative net worth of five million dollars to a positive net worth of several million dollars. Not to mention, he would be able to call off the pack of killers from Rogotha who happened to be his main creditor. With such an awareness, his most notable trait surfaced as he gazed across the table in the bank's meeting room: cockiness.

"So, Count, I'm not surprised that you bought the minority stake in this venture, but I'm kinda surprised you're not going to vote with us. You could make even more money if you go along with us, you know."

Brent, seated between Anna and his main attorney, just stared at Lawrence in silence, letting him continue.

"Yeah, man. When you have 49 percent, you may as well have one percent, except for the money you'll make. But why on earth are you opposed to this deal? I mean, look at these guys. This is serious money."

"All money is serious," the Count replied.

"Well, this is *real* serious money. Hedge fund guys from New York. You think you're going to be able to find some kind of way to stop all this from happening? No, you're going to get your check today for your share and you're going to leave and that's that. You won't be able to give us any more trouble."

The two representatives from the hedge fund stirred uncomfortably in their seats, as did the two attorneys who sat with them on the same side of the conference table with Lawrence. One started to speak, but was interrupted by Lawrence.

"Yeah, you think you're something, huh? You all of a sudden appear on the Outer Banks and you think you're going to buy into this deal in order to torpedo it? Oh, you're gonna have to take the money. We're not going to stand and let you have any shares of this project. You're out, dude."

The Count remained silent.

"Listen, Mr....Count," one of the hedge fund managers said. "He really doesn't speak for us. Lawrence, here, is a little loose and free for our tastes. We agree with him and the concept of the business plan and he's right about one issue. You may be playing us to hold out for more money, but we're not going to give in. We'll vote to create a special class of shares. After that, you'll get virtually no voting rights at all and much less cash. You'll even be at the bottom of the pecking order, if, God forbid, something goes wrong. We're going to give you the amount that we told you and you're going to leave us alone. We've got 51 percent of the votes and that's that."

Still, the Count remained silent.

"Yeah, Count, that's how it's gonna be..."

"That's enough," the hedge fund manager said to Lawrence, before turning his attention back to Brent. "Now, let's be reasonable. You're not going to get your way on this one. We've checked you out. You're worth, what? Just over $200 million? Well, my portion of my family's trust fund is double that. And this hedge fund has $1.7 billion in assets. We've got our money invested with Bernie Madoff. We're connected and we know what we're doing. Access to the finest lawyers in the world. We are truly the very definition of 'connected.' You're not going to mess with us, you do understand that, don't you?"

The door opened and in walked the bank president and a secretary. He walked to the head of the table and said, "Gentlemen and young lady, it is now ten a.m. and I would officially like to open this meeting. We are here today for the vote of transferring these properties. We have one hundred percent of the voting stock present and now if..."

Suddenly, there was a quick series of knocks on the door and then it opened abruptly. The branch bank vice-president rushed in, his face flush with concern. "John, sorry for the intrusion, but we have someone else here who claims to be a shareholder. She's..."

As she walked into the room and stood at the door, Lawrence's face went completely white and for a second or two, it looked as if he was going to faint. The Count turned around and he, too, was extremely surprised, though not in an obvious state of fright as was Lawrence.

The visitor was Crystal.

CHAPTER 59

CRYSTAL, ACCOMPANIED BY AN ATTORNEY, walked to the opposite end of the table from the banker. She warmly gazed at Brent for a second or two, then turned her attention to Lawrence who was still in such a state of shock that he was silent and motionless. Crystal's attorney broke the silence.

"I'm here today representing Crystal Watlington. I'm from Raleigh and I've left my credentials and contact information with your receptionist. We would like a moment to address this meeting."

"Granted," the banker said, himself deeply curious about the intrusion.

"I have in my hand copies of a signed, notarized, and legally binding agreement between Lawrence Parker and Crystal Watlington. For the agreed sum of $200,000 which I have here in the form of a certified bank draft, Ms. Watlington is due two percent ownership of this LLC and also to have two percent voting rights in the issue that is being decided today. I ask that this be immediately formalized and if not, I want this meeting and vote postponed until the matter is decided either by the participants or in a court of law."

"What the hell is this all about, Parker?" shouted the lead hedge fund manager, springing up so rapidly that his chair fell over. "What has your dumb ass done now?"

"It...I..."

Anna looked at Brent, but he gently shook his head to convey that he had nothing to do with the sudden turn of events. They quickly turned their attention back to the melee in the making.

"Parker, you..." the hedge fund rep said. "You swore there were no other people in on this. What the hell is going on here? Never mind. We'll handle this ourselves. This meeting is closed."

"However, before you close this meeting, let me be the one to answer some of the questions you may have," Crystal's attorney firmly said. "First off, the documents I bring are airtight and solid. The witness to the signed agreement was Roger Frantelli, a neighbor of Ms. Watlington's who happens to be a retired New York City police captain who has lived in Nags Head for the past ten years. He has an impeccable reputation and even serves on the local police advisory committee."

"You! You're behind this!" Lawrence spat, pointing his finger at the Count. "You gave Crystal the money. You…"

"If you'll allow me to continue," her lawyer cooly interrupted. "Count Van Sant has absolutely nothing to do with this transaction or agreement and also has no prior knowledge whatsoever of what has taken place between Ms. Watlington and Mr. Parker. Furthermore, and to save you people some time in the meetings you're obviously going to have, Ms. Watlington will vote her two percent as a nay in terms of selling the property to the hedge fund. Now, I'm going to assume that the Count, from what we've been told, is also voting no, so that means the deal will not go through on a 51 to 49 percent vote."

The other hedge fund manager leaped out of his chair and pounced on Lawrence, with both of them going to the floor. He stood up and overtop of the still-in-shock Lawrence, then violently jerked him to his feet. "You dumb son of a bitch…what were you thinking? What the hell…"

"Oh, it was quite simple, sir," Crystal softly spoke. "Your partner here promised that he would give me a warrant to buy two percent of the stock if I would sleep with him."

"But…but…she didn't have the money," Lawrence stammered. "I checked. All she had was a hundred thousand that couldn't be touched! Just the interest…"

"Well, she got it somehow, you idiot!" Then he threw Lawrence back to the floor.

The Count stood up and sadly looked at Crystal. He was extremely grateful for what she had done, but was hurt for how she went about it. He, too, wondered how she obtained the money.

CHAPTER 60

IT WAS CRYSTAL'S SUGGESTION they drive the short distance to the old Nags Head pier where they could talk about what just occurred. Frank made a quick sweep of the pier, walking to its end and studying the handful of people who were there. He returned to Brent and Crystal who were waiting in the parking lot and gave them the "okay." He assigned another bodyguard to accompany them to the pier, with yet another stationed in the parking lot. Frank then moved on to a task that he and Brent decided needed to be taken. To find Leeann and her daughter and bring them to a safe house until the ordeal came to a close.

They walked along the middle of the pier, passing a couple of middle-aged fishermen peering over the side at their lines. The body-guard stayed a distance of about fifty feet away. There was a mother and father, showing their two young kids how to bait a hook with some cut-up shrimp, which made both Brent and Crystal smile. After reaching the end of the pier, they turned around and walked back for a few yards, staying out of earshot of a grizzled old fisherman who was intently staring into the water below at the pier's end.

"Crystal..." Brent said, then stopped before saying anything else.

She looked absolutely charming, easily one of the most beautiful women to ever grace the Outer Banks. She leaned against the old battered boards of the railing, her long, dark hair drifting over her shoulder with the slight breeze. She still had her natural tan and her green eyes reflected the blueness of the sea, creating a color that was like Crystal herself, mysterious and indescribable.

"Are you going to ask why I did it?"

"No...well, yes, that, too," Brent stammered, still amazed at what had happened.

"I did it for several reasons. One of which is, of course, I did it for you."

"Well, thank you. But I was hoping you wouldn't say that. I feel badly about it. Given time, I could have taken care of him myself, but I'm sorry you had to do…what you had…"

"Oh, that's all right. Disgusting, yes. I just knew, though, that it was one of those rare occasions where a lot of different things could be made…maybe not right…but changed for the better, let's say. He always wanted to have sex with me. No matter what. At any price. Well, he got his wish, sort of. Besides, he was so stupid and egotistical, he was bound to finally have such a downfall. I was glad I could be part of it."

"Oh, this is going to be more than just a downfall. He's in very serious trouble. Those angry hedge fund managers who are going to sue him are the least of his worries."

"He deserves whatever level of evil and anger comes his way. I'd like to see him go to prison. You know how he's always been so claustrophobic. How fitting to see him put in a tiny cell."

"I don't think he's going to even make it to a cell."

"I can't say I feel the slightest bit of pity for him. What a despicable person. Ruining others while making himself look like the hero. Finally, he's going down."

"He'll be going down, all right."

"So, how's everything at your hotel? Are my paintings still there?"

"But of course. We've even bought some new ones. We're gradually going to have them in most of the deluxe rooms. It's going to be a virtual Crystal Watlington museum."

"That's sweet of you. Something to remember me by."

"Well, I was hoping that when this mess is finally over, we could…see each other more often. You could even move down to Hatteras if you like."

"I haven't given it that much thought. Things have happened so fast these last few days. I would love seeing you. But I wouldn't want to be in your way. I'm sure the mysterious 'Count of Cape Hatteras' has anyone he wants at his beck and call."

"It's not like that at all. I'm not like that, you know that."

"Oh, of course you're not. I'm just teasing. We've known each other forever. But, yes, I would enjoy seeing you. You know where I live. You can come by in that old pickup of yours."

"Yes, but seriously, you should think about moving down to Hatteras. A lot of artists are down there and on Ocracoke. You could make some really good friends there."

"That may not be in the cards for me. I'm still real leery about going out. There's just been too much hurt in my life. I still go through it. And there is no way that I can overcome what has happened in my past. My daughter is gone. My husband is gone. I was so…so selfish and self-centered for so many years. I'm still in the process of trying to forgive myself. Sometimes, I really envy you. Not about your money and your power, but about your ability to have re-invented yourself. To become somebody so totally different. You were able to start over with a clean slate. That is my one true wish."

"It is refreshing, my circumstances, but I really haven't changed that much, when I think about it. I can be nice, but like in the case with Lawrence, nothing would have stopped me from getting my revenge. Who knew that revenge would be obtained for me by the first girl I fell in love with…so many years ago."

"That's sweet. But I hurt you so much back then. And look at all the other guys. I just broke hearts like it was nothing. I'm still ashamed about that."

"You shouldn't be. Look at all those great years that Leeann and I had together."

"Oh, yeah, right. What? Two years? Then you disappeared."

"Well…"

"Anyway, thanks for the offer. I haven't really decided what I want to do. I could go anywhere, I suppose. I haven't decided. I'm just happy that if I did leave, that I was responsible for bringing down one of the worst human beings who ever set foot on the Outer Banks. I think of what he did to you. What he did to Scott. And so many others. He was always a parasite and I don't think anybody'll have to worry about him again."

"That's for sure."

"I'm also so sorry you haven't had kids yet. You would have been such a great father. You can't fool me. I know you were behind that surprise appearance at the school by Meghan Brown. That had you written all over it. That's who you should marry."

"That was her idea, really. As for marriage, that would be crazy. She and I are total opposites."

"That's not what I read. After that thing with her ex-boyfriend, she told the press that someday she would just drop everything and hide out in seclusion for the rest of her life. Hmmm, where better than at your hotel?"

"That wouldn't happen. Besides, she's too young for me."

"She could have loads of kids."

"Well, you still have time. You could, too."

Crystal instantly became quiet, a sad and pained expression shot across her face and she looked far out to sea.

"I'm sorry, Crystal. I shouldn't have brought that up."

"That's okay. Besides, you're right. I could still have a child. I just don't think I could handle it though. I would just worry too much. It would also bring back so many memories…"

"Well, let's just change the subject, okay? I'm really curious as to how you knew all about the deal. I thought it was pretty much kept quiet. There was not even any overtures to the planning commission yet. They were going to own the land free and clear before anything. That hedge fund bunch is pretty serious. Lawrence wasn't supposed to have told anybody."

"Well, there you go. Lawrence. Tried to impress me, I guess. Anyway, from what I was told, all those hedge fund people are living on borrowed time, no pun intended. There's a reckoning for them coming up. At least that's what I heard."

"That's right. I've positioned myself for a huge sell-off. It's going to be a disaster there, all right."

"Well, it won't matter to me. I don't need lots of money. I see through all that glamour and style. Don't need it, don't want it."

"Basically, I agree with you, but I was given a fortune to help me though life and throwing it away would not honor the past. Which reminds me of something else. Not that it is any business of mine. But, you didn't cash in your trust. So, how on earth did you come up with a quarter million dollars to pay to Lawrence? Again, it's none of my business, of course. I'm just curious."

"Well, I'm glad you asked," she said with a huge smile, one Brent hadn't seen from her since they knew one another back in high school. "A friend of mine. Like an uncle figure that I never had. In fact, that's really why we're here today on the pier. He wanted to see you."

Brent looked around, saw no one coming their way and then turned back to a still-smiling Crystal. "Is he your new boyfriend?"

"No, of course not. You know I'm not ready for that. If I was, you and I would probably be married with a child on the way by now."

Brent studied her and felt a huge warmth rushing over him. He felt — looking into her eyes — that he was almost…home. "Well, where is this benefactor? I'd like to meet him and thank him for what you two did today."

"Oh, you already know him," she said, sweeping her eyes towards the end of the pier, while turning around slowly.

The scraggly old fisherman put down the fishing pole, took off his weathered hat, and raised his arms up for a bear's embrace. He shouted, loud enough to echo across the water far below. "Dude!"

It was Ray.

Chapter 61

Where can I go? That was Lawrence's first thought as he spun the tires of his red Corvette on his way from the bank. Everything was completely torn away in his life. A couple of hours before, he walked into the bank as if he was the ruler of the universe. Now, he was a hunted man and not just by lawsuits that were probably already being drawn up. He was a hunted man by the Rogothans and all he could hope for from them would be a quick and painless execution. But he knew from experience they would not be so kind.

He couldn't go back to his office. That's where his remaining bit of cash happened to be. About eight thousand dollars in a locked drawer in his office. Luckily, he suddenly realized, he brought along his remaining bag of coke which he planned on celebrating with even before returning to his office. Lawrence stared into his rear view mirror, trying to see if he was being followed. Several cars looked suspicious, but he needed a snort. A huge one.

The best and quickest place he could find was the parking lot of a strip mall. He stopped on the lot's edge next to a delivery truck that was advertising the wares of the nearby store. Leaning down in his seat, he quickly cut out two long, thick lines on the center console. After two violent snorts, he shook his head, leaned back and peered around to see if anybody had noticed. As the first powerful rush came over him, his eyes glared at the empty truck, imagining that someone could be inside, waiting to jump him. He threw the car in reverse and pulled away swiftly, not even bothering to choose which direction.

Several miles south and into lower Nags Head, he started to agonize over something that he had dismissed several times before. The Count. He was so familiar. He reminded him more and more of Brent Williams and the thought grew in intensity as much as the cocaine buzz that was egging on such sentiments. *It couldn't possibly be*, he thought. He had seen the burnt remains himself. He had seen the bag of personal items that the Rogothan government had sent. There was no way he could be Brent. *No way. Just no way.*

Again dismissing the idea as absurd, he shifted around in his seat, watching his hand meander over to the bag of remaining coke. He needed some more. And quickly. Things were starting to unwind, not just in his life, but in his mind. Tangents were shooting far and wide, shifting from thoughts of who the Count really happened to be, along with images of how he would be killed. Tortured, no less, by a group who he knew were both experts and addicts of inflicting pain to those who screwed them over.

Lawrence needed to escape. To fly off somewhere. Drive off. To start over. Completely change his identity. To find some small town in the middle of nowhere and start over. To hide. To live. But where? And with what? He knew that a return to his office would be too dangerous. They were probably already waiting there for him. Surely, there were men also at his home. Now, he couldn't go to either. He even needed to ditch the Corvette. Too obvious. But what would he drive? How could he move on?

Panic burst in and his body violently shook, enough to make the right side tires hit the curbing. He jerked the wheel back and looked into the rearview mirror, seeing the puff of tire smoke he left behind. His mind raced. He looked around to make sure a cop hadn't seen his erratic driving. He slowed down and focused on the road ahead. He didn't need to draw attention. Jail would also be a death sentence for him. They'd get to him there as well. He looked into the rear view mirror and shouted in terror. For a brief instance, he saw Brent staring at him. His eyes hard and cool, glaring at him with a smile. The car hit the curb again and he looked back, this time seeing just an empty mirror, but another puff of smoke. Like a ghost.

Lawrence ditched into the parking lot of a grocery store, parking towards the side opposite from the 158 by-pass. He leaned down and set up two more big lines of coke. This time, elation hit him. He realized he was still alive. He had been in fixes before and gotten out. This was just another one. More serious, of course, but somehow he would be able to talk his way out of everything. He'd get them the money. Somehow.

Three million dollars for the Rogothans! How? His mind lurched back and forth from hope to agony. From confidence to fear. He drove away and as the buzz intensified, building upon the first lines, so too did his loss of reality. Or perhaps, such a loss was bringing him back to something much worse. Realizing just exactly the level of trouble he was in. If he was found, he was going to be killed…and all because of that Count Van Sant fellow setting him up through Crystal. *Yeah, that's exactly what happened.* He looked into the rear view mirror and there was Brent's face again, silently taunting him. Lawrence spun around in his seat and saw no one. A cold chill came over him and his mind continued its wave of uncertainty.

Lawrence completely drove through Nags Head and rounded the bend towards the causeway towards Manteo as if he was on a set of rails and not in control of the vehicle at all. He would find out what happened, all right. Before he left the Outer Banks and North Carolina for good, he was going to get to the bottom of his demise. Crystal was just a pawn. It was that Count who did him in. *But why did he look so much like Brent?*

Suddenly he laughed out loud. He knew what would happen first. The Rogothans would go after his wife. *Yeah, that's right.* They would kidnap her and Suzanne. That would give him enough time to head out. He laughed out loud, thinking the gang would be dumb enough to think that he actually cared about either one of them. They could die. He didn't need them. They would be excess baggage where he was going anyway.

Yeah, maybe he could call his secretary to bring him his eight thousand. He needed that if he was going to head out. But no, she would probably rat on him just as Crystal had done. *What the hell am I gonna do?*

The first thing, he finally decided, was to find out once and for all who that Count happened to be. He needed to know so when he got back on his feet, he was going to come after him. *Yeah, that's what I'll do.* Who knows? It could be Brent after all. The more he thought about it, the more he accepted the fact that somehow he had been screwed over once again by those close to him. Yeah, Manuel hadn't had him killed like they were supposed to have done. And he paid them! *That's what I get in return! Everybody's out to get me!*

He made the decision to drive to the family farm over on the mainland. The home where many years ago, he had told Leeann that's where they would retire. They fixed it up after his father had died. Early in their marriage and when they were at the peak of their wealth, he had even gone along with Leeann's desire to move Brent's body from the Colington cemetery to the farm. At the time, Lawrence thought it was funny. She had not yet been corrupted by living the good life and here, he would be able to walk outside and down a path leading away from the farmhouse to see where Brent was trapped. Many times he walked down there and drank bourbon or smoked a joint over the grave. Certainly not in mourning. More like gloating over the man who attracted both of the girls he had wanted for himself.

Yeah, it was time to look into things there. He pulled off Highway 64 after he passed over Roanoke Island and onto the mainland. There was still plenty of coke left. He indulged yet again. He started giggling. He started raving. He started hollering to himself. *Yeah, I'll find out once and for all! I'm going to take a look at that body! And if it's not him…I'm going to find that Count.* Whether he's a real Count or Brent, or even Brent's ghost, he would destroy him. Then he would make his escape.

Or so his lost mind told him.

CHAPTER 62

"WHA...?"

"Yeah, man, it's me!"

Brent and Ray embraced in such a wild bear hug that bodyguards from both camps thought they would fall over the side of the pier. Crystal was clapping, an uncommon broad smile shooting across her face. Brent's bodyguards moved in, checking out the situation. Meanwhile, the two middle-aged fishermen had put their rigs to the side and waved at them.

"That's okay, they're with me," Ray said, as Brent signaled to his own bodyguards that everything was fine. "Hey, you've got former Special Ops and Bluewater dudes, I have former SAS. We're all safe as can be right here."

"How on earth?"

"Oh, it was easy. I woke up as I was coming up on the beach, right here in Nags Head, believe it or not. I felt my feet touch the bottom and then, boom! I was wide awake! It was dawn and some young surfer dudes found me. I told them I'd spent a night of heavy drinking and needed to get to a phone. Yep, made a couple of calls and you know my identity system worked like a charm. An hour later I was at an ATM machine. I took those guys to a surf shop here and replaced their cheap ass Chinese boards with some locally made ones and that was it. Home free!"

"Yeah, but why didn't you get in touch with me?"

"Well, I didn't know you survived until a week or so later. I had to be careful, too, you know. Couldn't check up on that identity and cash hoard I had for you until I was firmly in place myself. By that time, I could tell you were setting up a pretty good organization yourself, so I just stayed in the background. Besides, I had a lot of catching up to do myself. I bet I've eaten a billion spiced shrimp since I then."

"Man, I can't believe it. I am so glad you're okay. I'll turn everything over to you."

"Like hell you will! You did a great job. Oh, I've been keeping track of you all right. The hotel is fantastic. Been by it a few times and some of my people have even stayed there. Besides, you just got a fourth of what I had. I've got the rest. So, keep it. After all, if you hadn't gotten me out of that prison and over that mountain range, I wouldn't be here right now."

"Well, I can't tell you how much I appreciate it. Everything. All those things you taught me back in Rogotha."

"Hey, thank *you*. You made that time worthwhile. You're the son I never had. Kinda late for me, but what the heck. Couldn't have asked for a better son. Anyway, you were right about something. Crystal here *is* the most beautiful woman on the Outer Banks... in fact, just about anywhere I'd say and I've been to a whole lot of places all over the world."

Crystal rolled her eyes with a smile at both of them. Her dark skin and brilliant eyes shown with independence and charm. "That's not true, but thank you."

"So how did you find..."

"It was easy," Crystal explained. "Ray came to me late last year to see if I was okay. He didn't tell me exactly who he was or how he knew of me until a couple of weeks ago. I thought he was an art dealer. Anyway, when he told me the gravity of the situation, I told him what I could do and well, we made a deal."

"But, Crystal, you didn't need to do that. I could have ruined him, given time."

"It needed to be done long ago and I also did it for Scott just as much as I did it for you. And for anyone else in the future that Lawrence would have used and abused. Let's just leave it at that."

"Okay."

"Anyway, he's done for now," Ray pointed out. "All you have to do, Brent, is to just sit back and enjoy yourself. He'll be taken care of in no time. There's a hit squad from Rogotha already here."

"This is where I'm going to leave you two gentlemen alone," Crystal said. "They're issues that I can't be a part of. 'A need to know basis' is what Ray told me, so if you don't mind, I'm going home to catch up on some painting."

"I'll send some guys over to watch over you," Brent said. "The dust hasn't settled yet."

"Don't worry, I've already got that taken care of," Ray said. "She'll be safe."

"Crystal…again, thanks so much."

"Don't mention it, Brent. I was glad I could do something… good for a change. I feel better."

"Great, then I'll see you, okay? It may be a couple of days."

She looked at him with that long striking face, with the slight sprinkle of freckles across the bridge of her fine nose, and after a long pause, said, "Sure, okay."

CHAPTER 63

"THE FIRST THING WE DID was to try to find Leeann and her daughter," Ray explained. "To put them under protection. But they haven't been seen or heard of for two days. We even had a homing device in her car. That showed up at the airport in Norfolk. We got there ten minutes later. But no record of them flying anywhere."

"We've been looking for them, too. So, this isn't a good sign."

"Could be they were just getting away from Lawrence."

"I doubt it," Brent said. "I'm sure he'd sworn that he was coming into the big money on that deal today, so knowing Leeann, she wouldn't have left that behind."

"Yeah, you're right. We knew that, too, but we're still hoping for the best. I do have another device on his car. We're tracking him now."

"Same here."

"Man, that dude has got everybody after him."

"Yeah, I just want to get to him first."

"And well you should," Ray said. "My guys will just be the free safety in all this, just in case he gets by somehow."

"Oh, he won't get by. Whatever's left, the Rogthoans can have."

"That's the spirit. I'll just focus on trying to find his wife and stepdaughter. Take that from your mind and concentrate on Lawrence. Give him what he deserves."

They both looked to the east at the calm seas and the clouds that nestled softly over the horizon. They were silent, leaning against the railings at the end of the pier. The sun was well on its way downwards to their backs and they both just relaxed, while looking at the sea that instead of killing them had miraculously brought them to safety.

"So, Ray, what are you going to do? What about the cartel that was after you?"

"Oh, them? No problem. Made a deal with 'em. Gave them $100

million, plus I had to do two last identities for them. Believe it or not, a son and daughter-in-law of a cartel head who wanted out of the family business. Kinda cool. But, yeah, I'm fine with them and have no intention of working for them again. In fact, I know this sounds crazy, but I think I may go back to the agency. I think they need me and...well, I miss them."

"Wow."

"Yep, saw a movie when I got out...man, I cried like a baby, you believe that? About Charlie Wilson, the congressman. Man, I remember those days. And I got to thinking, what the heck am I doing? Why do I need all this money? I was just as happy an hour ago when I caught a whiting off here than I would in any fancy party in New York or LA. You know, money, lots of money is not what it's about. Being able to buy anything you want is fine, I guess. I'm just more impressed at not having to do things I don't wanta, rather than doing things that's supposed to be so impressive. Am I making any sense here?"

"Yes, you are. I'd rather drive my old pickup than I would any new sports car. And you know what, one couldn't find a more beautiful woman in the world than Crystal. All she could care about now would be having money enough to buy paints and brushes."

"Yeah, only the truly rich — down to earth people like you and me — are able to make those distinctions. That's one of the things I always tried to instill in you back in prison. I'm glad you still see things like this."

"Me, too."

"Hey, by the way. How'd you like Meghan Brown? You know I helped set that up for you. I passed on the recommendation to her parents and agent. Well, not directly, but through an old friend of mine in Washington. I figured with that focus of yours, only a movie star like that could get your attention back down to the basics of life. You two hit it off or what?"

"Yes...yes we did. I guess. Man, you're amazing."

"I figured you two did...after hearing that she came to that school awards show and all. What a fantastic person. She deserves better than that celebrity life. I'll bet she even knows that."

"Yep, she does. Just hanging in there for the money, I believe, then I think she'll walk away and have a passel of kids. Hope so anyway."

"Son, now that's who you should be going after. I can't steer much better than that to you, you know."

"Oh, too young for me and too different. But she's definitely a great person."

"Yeah, well, you'll have plenty of time for worrying about such things in the future. And don't forget Crystal. Someday's she's gonna work through her problems. Keep her in your heart. Nice choice to have, though."

"Yep."

"Hey, by the way. Was I not kidding about how this country has become? Nobody wants to do manual labor any more. That's just for immigrants and then those couch potatoes sit back and complain about foreigners coming in and taking their jobs. Lazy! Dumbed down! Overdosed on self-esteem. Man, times have changed. A negative savings rate. This country's economy is bound to implode. Teens don't even cut grass anymore. That's up to lawn services that come in for big bucks. Again, with immigrants. Times are surely different from when I was a teenager."

"Even when I was. People don't even want to walk across a parking lot. At the hotel, there's always people almost fighting to get the closest parking space to the entrance. Just so they won't have to walk a few extra yards. Then they'll sue you if they step on a sand spur."

"I told you all that. You probably didn't believe me. But that's going to change. A reckoning is headed our way just as sure as the hurricane they busted us out of that prison. A big financial storm. That might get the attention of some of those people. Hopefully anyway. And since we know it's coming, we can prepare for it. You have, haven't you?"

"Sure have."

"Oh, yeah, don't buy gold until halfway through it. Gold and silver gonna's be cheap at the most awful stretch. People are going to have to sell things they don't want. They'll be unloading gold in the midst of things, that's how bad it's gonna be. That's when you buy precious metals. And those hedge fund guys. Man, are they going to be in for it. Some of them are going to end up cutting other people's grass!"

"Hope those I saw today will."

"When all this is done, you're gonna hafta come visit me. Don't have a home yet. Got it narrowed down quite a bit. I would come visit you, but still all this dust has to settle. I'm just gonna sit back and see how you handle your buddy. That's gonna be interesting, for sure. I'm gonna see how much I taught you. This 'dad' thing is pretty cool. Sorry I didn't get into that until it was too late. Just let that be a lesson to you, all right? Get one of these girls, settle down and have some kids."

"Yeah, you're right as usual. But right now, my total focus is on handling Lawrence. Again, thanks for all you've done for me. I don't deserve any of this, but thanks. You'd had gotten out of that prison somehow on your own without my help."

"You're welcome."

Just as the sun was low enough in the west to hamper their vision back towards land, they each watched a silhouette approach. The man stopped and chatted with the assembled bodyguards from both camps who were now about halfway down the pier. A few seconds later he resumed his walk and Brent saw that it was Frank.

When he arrived, Frank nodded at them both and Ray was the first to speak. "Heard a great deal about you, son. Brent's lucky he hired you before I found out about you."

"Thank you, sir. I'm glad you made it. Brent was real upset about you when we found him." He then looked at Brent, received a silent okay that Ray could be trusted and then said, "Of all places, we've tracked Lawrence to his farm over on the mainland. Where we set up the...you know."

"Excellent! He's even dumber than I thought."

The Count of Cape Hatteras turned to his old friend, shook his hand, and then they both quickly embraced. "Ray, I'll see you in a couple of days. Keep us apprised about Leeann and Suzanne. Time for Brent Williams to have a little visit with his high school friend, Mr. Parker."

CHAPTER 64

As evening approached, a huge thunderstorm appeared from the southeast, directly striking the Rodanthe area and obviously headed across the sound to the mainland. In its path would soon be Lawrence Parker's family estate. Located on the mainland's coast, several miles south of Stumpy Point, the farm was about a hundred acres. As valuable as the land happened to be, it had already been mortgaged to the hilt by Lawrence in yet another attempt to keep himself afloat.

Tonight, however, he was frantically digging the last foot or so into the soil where Brent's "body" from the Colington cemetery had been moved. A back hoe Lawrence owned idled nearby. It had been scheduled to be repossessed, one of the many possessions that Lawrence had thought would be saved by the meeting earlier that day. Now he was furiously digging with a shovel through the remaining soil to the casket and vault. Twice he stopped the process to snort more cocaine, but now he was focused and fierce in his attempt to reach the body.

All I have to do is break into the coffin, grab some remains and have it go though a DNA test. Then I'll confront Brent and demand protection from the Rogothans and money enough to get back on my feet. In return I won't reveal Brent's true identity. Yeah, I'll put the test results in a safe deposit box with some of the remains. Even he won't be able to counter that. I'll be safe.

Such was his fantasy.

He finally heard a clunk as the blade of the shovel struck the vault. He hit it again to be sure. Then he angled the blade to scoop off dirt, starting at the head of the casket and then turning around to work his way towards the opposite end. Lawrence started to grin as beads of sweat dropped onto the exterior of the vault as he continued working. A nearby rumble of thunder temporarily drowned out the engine of the back hoe, as the storm steadily approached. He dug faster, throwing dirt upwards and laughing proudly at his plan.

So, the land deal didn't turn out like I planned. What can I do about it now? But if I can get some remains here, I know it will show the famed Count Van Sant is an impostor. How Brent had gotten all that money must have been illegal. Surely, he would need that cover intact. With evidence that was only a matter of inches away, I can bribe him and maybe even be part of his business. Yes, that's it. I'll work for him in return for my silence. I'll control real estate purchases. Assets that would dwarf even what I had going today! Yeah, I'll be back!

Then, as he stood up to rest his back for a brief second, Lawrence noticed something in the shadows. A strange shadow. One that was more of a silhouette. Yes, a person. Someone was watching him! He squinted through not only the darkness, but also his cocaine buzz. Surely, no one could be here. He had locked the gate to the farm behind him. There wasn't another home for a mile. He walked to the edge of the vault to climb out. He looked back up and the image was gone. Nothing was there. Lawrence peered yet again into the small clearing and saw nothing. Just the leaves starting to rustle and wave with the approaching storm. His eyes swept all around and he saw no one. He looked back to the clearing again and seeing nothing, he laughed out loud.

Wow! This coke was great or I've had entirely too much. Perhaps, not. Yeah, I better do a couple of more lines before the rain hits.

He cleaned off the dirt and sand from the blade of the shovel. He then leaned it against the side of the hole so that the blade was almost flat, as it rested on the exposed vault. Withdrawing the vial, he laid out two lines on the blade, then retrieved the rolled up dollar bill from another pocket. He snorted the coke, then threw his head back and the sight he saw almost stopped his heart.

Standing above the grave site at the hole's very edge was the silhouette, a thin and muscular figure cloaked in a long trench coat. It was motionless with the obscured head peering down directly at Lawrence.

Frightened and speechless, Lawrence stared upwards as the figure bent forward slightly, exposing his face. It was Brent Williams.

CHAPTER 65

LAWRENCE DROPPED THE SHOVEL and backed towards the opposite side of the grave. His jaw lowered and his eyes were wide with fright. He suddenly noticed two other figures on each side of the clearing, also dressed in dark trench coats with their faces hidden. A nearby thunderclap startled him further. The first drops of rain began to fall.

"Who...Brent..."

"Yes, it's me. Do you mind if I ask what you are searching for down there?"

Lawrence further backed away, pushing into the wall of the grave site. He knelt down a bit and cowered, remaining silent. Fear had taken over his senses.

"Let me surmise that you are looking for me. Well, here I am."

Tears of fright began to roll down Lawrence's cheeks. He opened his mouth to scream but no sound came out. The two other men edged closer from each side. Lawrence's head went back and forth, eyeing each of them as they slowly came closer.

"We're going to help you see into that coffin, Lawrence. Let you take one good look. How fitting that would be. The end of the road, all right."

Two of the men jumped into the hole, withdrawing tools that could break open the vault surrounding the casket. Lawrence cowered away from them and he was unable to look either man in the eye, even from just feet away. They were unreal to him.

"Maybe I'm not Brent, after all, Lawrence. Maybe we're ghosts. Do you believe in ghosts? Do you believe in demons?"

Lawrence managed only a whimper. The two men began working on the vault.

"You would be right with any of your guesses," Brent continued. "In a way, I am a ghost. I am a demon. I am Brent Williams. And I am the Count of Cape Hatteras. I'm also the end of your wretched day…your horrible life as you know it. I am all of the above to you."

A bolt of lightning touched down on the Pamlico Sound as strangely cold rain began pouring. The engine of the back hoe sputtered, then stopped, a last puff of white smoke shooting from the exhaust stack. Another thunderclap exploded almost overhead, yet the Count remained perfectly still. As if nature herself was watching in glee.

The two men managed to push aside the heavy cover to the casket. It fell over to one side and they propped it against one side of the hole. They turned their attention to opening the coffin itself, as a half-weeping, animalistic sound came from Lawrence's mouth. The lid was finally opened, but Lawrence shut his eyes tightly and moved his head from side to side, as another flash of lightning exposed his terror.

"Look inside, Lawrence," the Count ordered. "Who do you see?"

He refused.

"Look inside! Now!"

Lawrence peeled one eye open and looked downwards. Instantly, he turned away, the sight of the skeletal remains making him vomit.

Brent studied the skeleton and then shifted his attention to Lawrence. "What did you see?"

Lawrence whimpered hysterically and tried to scale the rear wall of the grave to escape the scene of horror. Quickly, the Count's bodyguards grabbed him and threw him back into the hole, causing one of his legs to stomp into the coffin which smashed part of the disintegrating remains.

"Well?"

Lawrence remained silent. His bloodshot eyes looked at the Count with all the pity they could muster, begging for the torture to stop.

"Oh, we haven't even started, Lawrence. You see, I remember

how claustophobic you are. Remember you couldn't take the diving lessons with me because even wearing a face mask bothered you? Perhaps you should have been with me. Locked up in a dungeon for all those years. Faraway from everything I loved and desired. You stole everything from me. You ruined so many lives. You killed Scott. You destroyed the personality of an angel, creating a Leeann who I never would have imagined. You, you…yes, you. That's what it's always been about, right? You!"

Lawrence began to cry. He balled like a little child in the midst of waking up from a nightmare.

"Now. Get in."

Lawrence looked at him with even more fright. With an unbelieving look of horror.

"I said get in! Now!"

He remained still, hoping that it was indeed a nightmare and he would wake up at any second. The Count nodded at his two bodyguards and they each grabbed Lawrence and pushed him down into the coffin, on top of the shattered remains. Lawrence began screaming, loud enough to almost match another roar of thunder. He tried to escape, but was thrown back down again. One of the men put his boot on Lawrence's neck and pinned him down.

The men pulled back and prepared to lower the lid. The Count stepped into the hole. He walked until he was over Lawrence's crazed face, with eyes so wide, fixed on the Count's rain-soaked snarl. He then stepped aside and nodded again. The men closed the lid. One checked his watch.

The muffled screaming could be heard for a minute or two. The Count stood on top of the coffin, holding the lid down. Fifteen minutes later — one minute for every year Brent spent in prison — he moved and the men opened the lid. Lawrence Parker was alive. But his eyes pointed upwards in a frozen gaze of permanent insanity.

Alive…vegetated…punished…forever destroyed.

CHAPTER 66

IT WAS THE THIRD MORNING of captivity and Suzanne knew what she had to do. She needed her book bag.

When she and her mother were suddenly car jacked while running errands and whisked away, the little girl realized how smooth and experienced the Spanish-speaking men happened to be. Even at her young age, she knew it had something to do with the shady dealings of her stepfather. Several times after their capture, her mother had mumbled such things, especially when she lapsed into a drunken stupor with liquor they supplied. Just to keep her quiet and relaxed, or in actuality, passed out for most of the time.

As soon as they were thrown into the back of the van, the men roughly frisked her mother and searched for any cell phones. They took her mom's pocketbook and dumped the contents onto the floor of the van. They quickly retrieved her cell, then took the other one Leeann had in her suit pocket. Then they turned to Suzanne and shouted several sentences in Spanish that she half understood.

The older man and apparent leader of the group asked politely in English if she had a cell phone. Suzanne shook her head, but was shouted at by her mother. "Give them the phone, Suzanne! Do what they say!"

She looked up at her mother, then at the man, and reached into her book bag. She handed over the bright pink phone as another man grabbed the book bag, turned it upside down and shook out the contents. Three books came out, a pen, and a spiral notebook. One book was her math textbook, one was on sea turtles, and the third had been given to her by the Count. It was entitled "The Island of the Lost." She had just finished reading it the night before. The men picked everything up and put the items back into their respective bags, then passed them up front.

Suzanne could tell they turned onto Route 12 south towards Hatteras. She also contemplated that since they hadn't been blindfolded, there was the possibility that their kidnappers would just kill them whenever they received their ransom. She may have only been eleven, but she had already read enough books and seen enough films to know how things would probably transpire.

Unlike her mother, she kept her wits throughout the ordeal and even made mental notes as to the location and description of the house where they were taken. It ended up being on the soundside on a stretch between Rodanthe and Salvo. They were hustled to a third floor room that apparently had been a large walk-in closet. There were no windows and only one door. Suzanne saw a hastily installed metal bar locking system on the outside of the door as they were pushed in. She also counted the number of people at the large home. The best she could determine was that fourteen people were there and they were all armed and very, very serious looking. She tried to have her book bag brought to her, but they simply ignored her requests.

Leeann had made so much noise the first night that the older man (who Suzanne noted was called Manuel) came in and threatened her if she didn't calm down. That worked for only a short while. But even after she was pushed to the floor and physically threatened again, the leader came in with a bucket of ice and a large bottle of bourbon. That finally managed to calm her down and by what Suzanne estimated was nightfall, her mother was completely passed out. The same thing occurred on the second night.

It was that third morning when food and water was brought to them that Suzanne demanded that she have her book bag returned. "I need to study! I want something to read!" The two guards laughed out loud and slammed the door behind them, but a short while later, the door opened. It was the man called Manuel and he held out the book bag. At the last second, he pulled it back, opened it, and dumped the contents on the floor. He looked inside the bag, then tossed it in the pile. "Now study and be silent," he ordered in English.

"Thank you," she responded, smiling at the back of the door as it locked into place.

Suzanne patiently waited until her mother drank enough of the new bottle of bourbon to pass out again. Then she put the sea turtle book down, looked at the doorway and then opened the book bag. She felt around and then unzipped the hidden compartment that was deep inside the bag.

She retrieved her iPhone. With a smile, she began to text message her new stepfather. The Count of Cape Hatteras.

CHAPTER 67

A RARE SENSE OF GLOOM dominated the Count of Cape Hatteras' suite. Sitting along the c-shaped sofa area were Ray, Frank and Anna. The Count himself was uncharacteristically pacing along the window section that overlooked the protected courtyard and the Pamlico Sound. He was silent as he walked back and forth, staring at the floor and often shaking his head from side to side.

That morning they received the expected call from Manuel. The Rogothans wanted three million dollars for the "safe" return of Leeann and Suzanne, plus another one million in what Manuel described as "pain-in-the-ass" money. The financial aspect of the matter didn't bother the Count. He gladly would have paid the money and then hunted Manuel and his entire crew down with a salivating vengeance after the two were returned safely. But in this case, Manuel said they would be released two days after the money changed hands.

To make matters even worse, Ray had utilized some contacts to have the phone call traced. It turned out to be a cell phone from a moving vehicle that bounced off two different repeaters in the Newport News area of Hampton Roads. It would be essentially impossible to track anyone down in that area within the thirty-six hour deadline and besides, there was no guarantee that Leeann and Suzanne were actually being held there. They could be anywhere. If, of course, they were even still alive.

"Okay, we're going to have to do something," Ray said, his normally good-natured spirit vastly subdued. "We pay the money. Heck, I'll pay the money out of my pocket since I should've had someone watching over them sooner than I did. We'll just pay the money and hope for the best. That's all we can do."

"That could be throwing the money away and our only chance to be able to bargain," Frank said. "We should still hold out for a sign of their safety or for the exchange to take place at one time."

"Normally, I'd agree with you, but in this specific case, I don't think that's going to work," Ray said. "They wouldn't budge on that. The money is not a lifesaver for them. Manuel Hernadez has high connections to the Rogothan government. He's plenty corrupt and rich already. Down there he would be reasonably well-protected. He'd have to lay low for a while, that's all. The money from us would be secondary. Sure, he wants it, but what he really wants is respect from the Mexican cartels. That's what I've been told by some reliable sources. If he can show that he can't be run over and that he's just as brutal as they can be, then that would buy him grudging respect with the Mexicans. They may even decide to partner up with him on some deals. After all, while Rogotha indeed has a crap hole government, its location is perfect in case the Mexican border gets any worse."

"This is really all my fault," Brent interrupted. "I should've had them under my watch for the past month. I should have known this would happen. I brought them into this and it's my fault."

Anna stood and walked over to him, stopping in his path and then hugging him. He held her and then backed away, his bloodshot eyes glinting a heartfelt thanks for her concern. Everybody's heads and eyes went back to the floor and the huge room became quiet, as a heavy sadness filled the chamber. The Count resumed his pacing.

Frank suddenly stirred, reaching in his pocket for his vibrating cell phone. He clicked it open and his eyes shot wide open and in a split second he was on his feet. He read quickly, then looked at the Count with a big smile.

"What is it?" Brent asked.

"It's a text message from…little Suzanne."

CHAPTER 68

"THIS IS SUZANNE. Where is Brent?"

"This is Anna. He is right here. Where are you?"

"LOL. I know he doesn't like cell phones."

"Right."

"My mother and I are being held in a big closet. At a house on the sound between Rodanthe and Waves."

"Are you okay?"

"Yes, but we need help. They are mean."

"Keep texting as much as you can. Don't let them see you doing so."

"I know that. That's why I'm texting. They may have some device to see if anyone is making a cell call. So I'm texting."

"You are one smart little girl."

"Thanks."

"Brent says hi and that he'll do everything he can to rescue you."

"I know he will."

"We need you to describe the house and where you are inside."

The house is pale blue. It is three stories and big. We are on the third floor. In a big closet. There are no windows."

"How is your mom?"

"She's passed out. They give her alcohol every night."

"How many people are there?"

"I counted fourteen. Maybe more."

"Do they have guns?"

"Yes. Many guns. Big guns."

"When do they check on you? Bring you food?"

"Every few hours or so. They feed us twice a day."

"Are there any wires or explosives near you or at the door to where you are?"

"No. I don't think so."

"What kind of vehicle were you in?"

"A black SUV. A big one."

"Who is the leader there?"

"I heard them call him Manuel."

"You are so smart. And so brave."

"That's because I know you all will rescue us."

"No, it's because you *are* brave and smart."

"Thank you."

"Where do most of the people stay?"

"I don't know. I have been in here since we got here."

"Which side of the house are you on?"

"We are on the side that is closer to the road. Not the sound."

"Are there any dogs there? Have you heard any barking?"

"No."

"Frank says to stay still, cooperate, and stay low when we send you a message."

"Is that when you will come rescue us?"

"Yes."

"It will be soon. At night. Tonight. Late."

"Good. Tell Brent and Frank to be careful."

"I will. Don't text again unless it is something really important. But keep a watch on your cell phone."

"It's the iPhone that Brent gave me. My mom doesn't know I have it."

"Thank God."

"Yes."

"Frank says that when you receive the code word 'turtle' on text you and your mom need to lay down on the floor and protect yourself as best as possible. If there is furniture in the room use it for cover. If a mattress, put in on the floor and then get on it."

"Yes, we will."

"Is there anything else you know that you can tell us?"

"No. I don't think so."

"You are very brave. Brent says that he loves you."

"Tell him I love him and that he is my real stepfather."

"He will love that."

"Can you ask him one more thing for me?"

"Yes."

"The code word. Instead of 'turtle.' Can it be 'sea turtle'?"

Brent looked at Anna with a huge smile and nodded his head. Anna sent the final text of, "Yes. Of course." She looked back at Brent who was still smiling and the gloom and doom that had permeated the room only minutes before had completely vanished.

"That's my little girl," he said as proudly as any real father. Then he turned to Frank, who was already near the doorway. "Okay, let's go."

CHAPTER 69

BY NINE O'CLOCK THAT NIGHT, the exact location of the home had been determined and studied and a plan of attack had been finalized. The finer details were still being discussed and debated and potential scenarios of change were still being brought up. A two-man sniper/observation team was already in place at a home just down and across the street from their objective.

Luckily, where Leeann and Suzanne were being held was a home under contract with the Count's security firm and Frank had installed the alarm system himself. Only one other house in the cul-de-sac was occupied and that greatly decreased the possibility of friendly fire or possible witnesses. Things were rapidly falling into place.

"You can use some of my men," Ray offered. "They're former SAS and they can help out."

"No, I'm going to do this with our crew," Brent responded. "You gave me the money and the knowledge to build an organization like this and I think we're fully capable of this mission. I'm responsible for this situation, so it's up to me anyway. But thanks though."

"Oh, I know you all are. I'm proud of you."

Yet again, the men huddled around the set of plans and the map. Two more of Frank's security team were there, both former SEALs and Bluewater operatives. They would be part of the assault/extraction crew and were still going over the methods that would be undertaken.

Anna walked over to the Count and whispered to him. "You'll be going in with Frank, so can you please promise me that you'll watch over him?"

"Anna, I think we all know that he's going to be watching over me. He's indestructible. So don't you worry. We're going to pull this off. We'll be back safe."

Frank came over and hugged Anna, then shook hands with the

Count. It was sort of like 'game day' for both men, though what they were going to do was anything but a game.

"Okay, you two," Anna chided. "I do not want anything to happen to either of you two, okay?"

"Nothing will," Frank said, embracing her yet again. "Beside, you need to stop worrying about us. You have your part in this operation as well, so focus on that."

"I will, but I have just a small part."

"There's no small part in this," the Count said. "We all play a vital, connected role and without each other, the entire mission could go wrong."

"I hope you're right. But what does cause me worry is that there are fourteen of them and it's only four of you going inside. Is that not right, Count?"

"Yes, that's correct, Anna."

"Well, that is what causes me to worry. There are so many of them and just four of you."

"We have a support crew all around the perimeter," Frank said. "We'll be fine."

"Yes, but I love you and I worry about you. Both of you."

"Yes, it's fourteen of them," Frank sadly responded. "Unfortunately, it's probably going to be a slaughter."

"But, then why…"

"No, Anna," the Count said with a cold glint in his eye. "He means *they* are going to be slaughtered."

CHAPTER 70

ANNA WAS HEADED NORTH on Highway 12 along a barren stretch between Rodanthe and Oregon Inlet. It was four in the morning and totally dark on the moonless night. She was driving only about thirty miles an hour when she saw headlights approaching from the north. That car was also driving rather slowly. It blinked its high-beam twice and she did likewise.

When they met, Anna had just enough time to brace hard on the steering wheel as the screech of metal sent a multitude of sparks upwards and between the two vehicles. They both stopped and after taking a deep breath, Anna made two cell phone calls. The first to Frank, the second to 911.

The driver of the other car walked up with a genuine look of concern on his face. She smiled and said she was okay. She noticed that he was trim and fit, young, perhaps only twenty-five or so. He was one of Frank's new employees. He certainly looked like one of the special operations people that were such an important part of the empire of the Count of Cape Hatteras.

Five minutes later, the first deputy arrived on the scene. He climbed from his patrol car which he parked to the rear of the man's car, threw a couple of flares on the roadway, then walked up to them both.

Anna lurched into a loud, spirited rant in Russian, waving her finger at the driver of the other car and then at her own, pointing at the dents and scratches along the side. She continued her rant until the law enforcement officer motioned for her to quiet down. "Ma'am, do you speak English?" he asked politely.

"Yes, yes, yes! Do you see what he did to my car?"

"Yes, ma'am."

He made the standard early morning hours technique of trying to detect the smell of alcohol on each of the drivers' breaths. He detected nothing and then asked if either of them had consumed any alcohol or drugs, which they said they didn't. The officer then shined his Mag-lite along the roadway, looking for telltale tire marks.

Anna again went into a loud verbal rage, all in Russian and still pointing at the driver.

"Ma'am, I'm going to ask you to calm down. Now, nobody's hurt, right? So just calm down so we can take care of the situation."

"Yes, yes, but my new car! It is so ruined! This imbecile!"

The law enforcement officer gave a slight nod and grin to the other driver, one of those "better-you-than-me" looks. He walked away from both of them, took the microphone off his shoulder and said, "Hey 16, what's your 10-20? I have a little fender bender down here on Highway 12, about a mile south of the bridge. No PI, but I could use a little help here. Driver's extremely upset."

After a pause, another deputy responded. "10-4, 31. I'm in Waves. I'll head north right now."

The officer on the scene walked a few paces further away from the two drivers and half whispered on the radio. "Any state unit. 604, are you on duty tonight? You should 10-20 my location. Beautiful Russian girl having a fit."

"I'll 10-4 that. I'm in Buxton. Headed your way."

Fifteen minutes later, all three police officers on duty on Hatteras Island were at the scene, ten miles away from the home where Leeann and Suzanne were being held captive. Anna was leaning against her car after subtly being kept away from the other driver until backup arrived. Anna winked at the driver who had sideswiped her car.

She hit a button on her cell phone and whispered softly, "Frank, it's a go."

CHAPTER 71

THE LOCATION OF THE HOME was easy to find, even easier from the air. At night, it was brilliantly lit up from all four directions. There was a small rock wall around three sides. The soundfront section was wide open along the bulkhead and pier that jutted out over the water. The enclosed garage held two vehicles and there were two more SUVs parked on the concrete driveway. The rest of the small, nearly-deserted neighborhood was dark. As Frank and Brent peered down from four thousand feet from the open side of the helicopter, they couldn't have asked for a better marker for their landing.

"Okay, remember, you really gotta flare when we're touching down," Frank said, despite going through the scenario more than a dozen times already. "I'll be covering us."

"Will do," responded the Count.

Frank checked their alignment for the drop one last time, then nodded at one of the crewmen. It was the signal for him to text message Suzanne with the words, "Sea Turtle." He also sent the message to troops on the ground. They both adjusted their latex gloves. The raid was on.

Set into a tandem chute rig, Frank and Brent dropped from the helicopter and free fell most of the way in. The security lights around the perimeter of the large home made it so easy to see. The third floor sunset viewing deck was a perfect target, much easier than the many bull eyes that Brent had aimed for in countless practice jumps. Frank threw the small chute that activated the main chute and their speed dropped dramatically. They drifted into a wide circle, then narrowed the arc down as they pinpointed their exact landing spot. It was coming up fast, but not too fast. Frank looked to the south, about half mile away and waited patiently for the second diversion of the night.

The set of fireworks shot into the sky from the backyard of another home that was also on the soundside, about a mile south.

They were beautiful arrangements of varying colors that went off about two hundred feet high. Frank didn't need to see firsthand where the guards below were looking. It was only natural for anyone to gaze at fireworks and in this particular case, they all did so, looking southward and away from the northward approach of the invaders.

From a hundred feet above, they both saw two guards stationed at the top deck. They were both looking to the south as Brent flared the chute and Frank withdrew an automatic pistol equipped with a silencer. Their feet touched down, the chute folded and dropped backwards, just as one of the guards turned around. He didn't have time to see the two men before Frank put a bullet in the middle of his forehead.

The second man turned around upon hearing the clunk of the falling body and he two was met with muffled gunfire. One bullet in his forehead and the other in the middle of his chest. "Two down," Frank whispered into a microphone in his sleeve.

After releasing the chute, they both tiptoed to opposite sides of the closed doorway that led inside the third floor. Frank put his ear to the door, heard nothing, then motioned for Brent to stay behind him as he moved forward. He opened the door slowly, peering in. Seeing no one, they entered and saw lights from a room on the west side of the home. The door was open. Frank edged up to the doorway, peeped in, then drew back. He hand-signaled to Brent that two men were inside. Frank silently stepped in the middle of the doorway and Brent watched as the pistol fired two more rounds. They both went inside. One body had fallen from the chair that was in front of a set of security monitors that showed four views of the yard's perimeter. The other man was sloped backwards in another chair, blood pouring from his head wound. Frank spoke softly into his sleeve microphone, saying, "Two more." He quickly scanned the monitors and saw that the remainder of the men were still unaware of their presence.

Frank took out his cell phone and quickly text messaged Suzanne. "Are you okay? Alone with Mom?"

Seconds later, he showed the display to Brent. It said, "Yes. Yes." They both smiled. Frank text messaged back, "We'll be there in a second."

The room was across the hall and about 15 feet away. There was a metal bar and bracket that had been hastily bolted into the door jamb. Frank pulled up the elbow steel rod and carefully touched it to the floor. He opened the door and there was Suzanne, standing up, with a huge smile upon seeing her two rescuers. Her mother was fast asleep, or rather passed out on a mattress on the floor behind her.

Brent stayed with Suzanne, who hugged him and silently nodded her head in thanks. He motioned towards Frank in a manner to show where the real credit was due. Frank just smiled at the little girl, then he went back to check on the other third story rooms. Brent motioned for her to stay down. He shut the door and then quickly joined Frank.

Both men stopped in their tracks as they saw the shadow of an approaching figure, walking up the angled stairwell. They drew back, Frank in the doorway closest to the top of the hallway and Brent on the opposite doorway, one room back. Frank gave Brent a look of, *Are you ready for this?* Brent nodded his head.

The man, carrying a machine gun, reached the top of the stairs heading towards the room where the security monitors were located. Brent let him get just past the doorway where Frank was hiding, then put a bullet squarely in the middle of his chest. Frank caught the body and the weapon, dragging him back inside the room.

"Five down," he whispered into the mic. Then he glanced at Brent to see if he was okay. He was met with a simple expression of *no problem.* Frank spoke softly again on his microphone. "Sniper team, what do you see?"

There was a five-second delay, then Frank received the reply in his earpiece. Three guards were smoking on the second floor deck, just below the walk-in closet where Suzanne and Leeann were kept. Frank said, "Green light. All three."

There was not even a sound that Frank or Brent could detect.

Then Frank listened to the message from the sniper team. He looked at Brent and smiled. "Three more."

They returned to the security room and scanned the monitors. Three guards were mingled together on the southwest corner of the grounds. That still left some more inside the dwelling, even if Suzanne's count was off. "Water team, get ready," Frank softly ordered.

Frank and Brent softly headed down the hallway to the steps. Frank looked over the rail at the step's midway turn and saw one guard sitting in a chair asleep. He was obviously guarding the doorway, which he assumed was Manuel's room. No one else could be seen. Frank motioned for Brent to remain as back up. He then calmly walked down the last few steps, up to the sleeping man, and shot him in the forehead. He caught the body and gently lowered it to the floor.

Brent was now at Frank's side and covering the rear. No one else seemed to be on that floor. Frank walked the hallway and found the room he needed. It was a storage room that also contained the main fuse box. He studied the box and chart and put his finger on the toggle switch he needed. "Water team, five seconds," he whispered into the microphone.

At the appointed time, he hit the switch and all the rear exterior lights extinguished. Unseen to them — but Frank could perfectly visualize — two of the former SEALs peeled over the bulkhead from the water and dropped all three of the assembled guards in a quick instant. They never even saw their killers.

Frank told Brent to return to the closet and wait for the team to bring Leeann and Suzanne down. As he disappeared up the stairs, Frank softly tried the doorknob to a bedroom next door to where they believed Manuel was sleeping. It was unlocked. He withdrew a second pistol from his web belt and opened the door quickly. He hit the lights and was met with two men suddenly sitting up in twin beds, their eyes blinking in confusion. Two muffled pops and they were gone.

"All teams, could be more than we thought. One inside upstairs bedroom. Should be some inside downstairs."

"Chief, two here," one of the water team over the radio.

"Situation?"

"They're history."

"Nice."

"10-4. One more? Need us?"

"Yep, third floor. Meet Number 1. Two parcels to go out."

"Going."

"Sniper Team. Head out. Special Boat Team. Wait for signal."

Barely before Brent could have a few seconds to tell Suzanne that everything would be okay, the water team was there. She blinked for a second, but then Brent just smiled and said, "Friends. Good friends. Go with them."

"But I want to stay with you."

"Not now. There's still some things to do. They're going to take you and your mom to safety. I'll see you in about an hour, okay?"

"Okay," she said, smiling. "Did I do a good job?"

"You did a *great* job! I'm proud of you."

Seconds later, one of the men had the still-passed out Leeann over his shoulder, and the other had Suzanne in his arms. Frank was waiting at the stairwell to protect their front and Brent fell in behind to cover the rear. Frank spoke into his mic, "Boat team, go."

When they made it downstairs and to the bulkhead at the rear of the property, two skiffs roared up, their hull registration numbers taped over and their lights off. Suzanne and Leeann were passed over and Suzanne happily noted that the boat captain named Stuart who had been on the sea turtle excursion was at the helm. Seconds later, they were off and away.

The two water team members went back inside and finished the room by room search, leaving the room on the second floor untouched. Frank guarded that one. He looked at his watch and thought, *eight minutes.* At best, the only police on duty were fifteen minutes away and were probably still overseeing Anna and her "dispute." He smiled at Brent as the team members determined that no one else was on the premises.

"Okay, bro," Frank said, nudging his head towards the room where Manuel was staying. "This one's gonna be all yours."

Chapter 72

THE TWO MEN WERE ON BOTH SIDES of Manuel's bed even before he had a chance to awaken. Frank, nearest to the overhead light switch next to the door, flicked it on. Manuel's eyes blinked rapidly and he sat up in a state of utter confusion, then shock.

"Hello, Manuel," Brent said. "Welcome to another beautiful day on the Outer Banks."

He blinked again, started yelling in Spanish for his crew and then instantly grew quiet when Frank stuffed the tip of his pistol into the man's mouth. "Shhhhssshh," Frank said, matter-of-factly. "Wait a minute. Come to think of it, you can make all the fuss you want. Every member of your crew is dead. Yes, you heard me. Wiped out."

"Yep, that's right, Manuel," Brent said. "Not only that, but a good friend of mine who also happened to have spent a little incarceration time in Rogotha has some Colombian friends of his down there to take care of your son. You know, your oldest who can't wait to see you dead, so he can become Numero Uno in your gang. Yeah, well, he won't last the week either, lemmee tell you. We don't like loose ends, you know."

"Yeah, loose ends suck," Frank agreed.

"Who…who are you?" Manual asked in halting English.

"Your worst nightmare. Demons from your past. Debt collectors who's finally coming back to haunt. You take your pick."

"Well," Frank said with a smile. "I'd say it's all of the above."

"Yeah, and then some."

"Wha…what are…"

"Let us explain," interrupted Brent. "Let me give you a little history lesson. A quick one, because we're not going to be the ones left here with over a dozen dead bodies when the police arrive. No, that'll be you."

"Oh, more than a dozen, all right. Should make national news, heck, international news," Frank pointed out.

"Yeah, he's right. Anyway, Manuel. I'm the dude you wanted the four million dollars from. I'm the dude who's unofficial stepdaughter you took hostage. And was even going to kill, because I know you don't like loose ends any more than we do."

Manuel's eyes had already made the vast transition from shock to fear. That no one had come to his rescue was proof that somehow these *gringos* had indeed taken out his entire crew. He felt cold and old and battered and defeated. All in the space of a few seconds. Undoubtedly like how many of his victims in the past had felt during their last few seconds of life.

"Wha…"

"Will you just listen? Thank you. As I was going to explain, a long time ago, over sixteen years ago, you took a five thousand dollar bribe to have me thrown into jail and to be killed. That money was from your buddy, Mr. Parker, who you also probably know is now paralyzed on half his body with a near fatal aneurysm and has gone completely stark-raving mad. As you probably know, he was always a wannabee anyway, right? Kinda half-assed drug dealer. He really wasn't like the three of us. He wasn't a…a…"

"A modern day pirate," Frank suggested.

"Awesome! That's exactly right. We're all three real pirates, that's exactly what we are. Oh, the times may have changed, methods of transportation, weapons, and the tactics have been altered a bit, of course. You know, brief cases and user i.d. and passwords. Things are a little more technical. But we're no different than our ancestors of the sea. Pirates. And you, my dear sir, are going into retirement.

"That's right. Now I'm sure Blackbeard, in these very same waters right here, would have whacked you with extreme prejudice. He'd probably even lit up that gun powder tied in his beard. But, no, that would be too good, too quick for you, my friend. Especially after I did manage to survive, thanks to some decent Rogothans who spirited me away. 'Course, you do have to answer for all those years I spent locked up, you understand."

"My son...my..."

"Your son? How dare you. Anyway, the report we have is that he completely loathes you anyway. Sign of the times...ahhh, the 'Entitlement Generation' so demanding so impatient. Besides, I probably would've had several children by now if I hadn't been locked away down there. So, let's just consider this a little balance, shall we say? You'll live today, but from this second on, your life is going to be hell right here on earth. Frank, if you will, please."

Frank withdrew an envelope from a pocket in his vest and handed it to Brent, his pistol remaining an inch away from Manuel's face. Brent opened it, withdrew the cash, and stuffed the empty envelope into his own pocket.

"Oh, we're real careful, Manuel. No DNA from the salvia that closed this envelope, no, sir," Brent pointed out. "The money, well that's five thousand dollars. Not the five grand you got from Lawrence all those years ago. Instead, this five grand came from that friend of mine who has some of the most amazing — and brutal — connections that even you couldn't imagine. Seems this money came from a drug deal gone bad that had money from a bank robbery as part of the proceeds. They couldn't spend it, of course. You know, being numbered, consecutive bills that could be traced to a fatal bank robbery up in Virginia."

Brent put the money in the top drawer of the night table, next to Manuel's wallet and Rolex. "Yep, when the police arrive and see all these bodies, the FBI'll be called in, the SBI, heck, everybody! They'll tie you in with that capital offense up in Virginia and of course, all the ones here. You'll be the last man standing. Big trouble for you. I can see the news trucks and their satellite dishes parked in that big cement drive way across the street now."

"I...."

"Will you please quit interrupting me? Now Frank will handle the next step."

Frank took the pistol he had been using, ejected the clip and left one round in the chamber. He placed it in Manuel's hand and then held his hand and pistol to the bed, while Brent held another pistol harshly against Manuel's cheek.

"Go ahead, fire the weapon, Manuel. Come now. You really have no choice."

Manuel tried to shake his head, but Brent just jammed his pistol harder against his face. Manuel's terrified eyes shot from Brent to Frank, and back and forth again.

"If you don't pull the trigger we're going to pull it for you. We have latex gloves on and the powder residue won't be left with us. So make things easier for yourself, while I'm in this good mood." A second later the pistol went off and it was immediately taken back by Frank.

"Good, good, Manuel," Brent said. "Now you're officially the killer of more than half of the people in this house. Frank, next step, please."

Frank drew his other pistol and shot Manuel once in the leg and once in the shoulder. He fell back onto the bed screaming in agony and bleeding profusely.

"Manuel, you see, you're going to prison just as I did. But remember, this is North Carolina. You're going to Death Row. And if you somehow escape Death Row here, that money in the drawer will trigger a death sentence up in Virginia. Now, they don't mess around. No Texas, grant you, but Virginia just doesn't cater to people like yourself. So, you'll have a little time in prison like I did, but with better food and housing though of course, the end result won't be quite so lavish as mine. But then again, I didn't ask for it anyway. I wasn't a pirate back then. I was just a worthless Outer Banks beach bum."

Manuel weakly slumped into the mattress, his body becoming limp and useless. Frank put the clip back into the weapon and nodded for Brent to finish up.

"Okay, old friend. Maybe I'll see you again," the Count whispered to Manuel. "You know, I'll be one of those anti-death penalty protesters hanging out the night of your execution. I'll wave at your casket when the hearse drives by. Oh, yeah, sweet dreams. The police and the world will be here in about an hour. I have to go now. There's my stepdaughter to check on and then there's a beautiful woman who needs me as much as I need her back in Nags Head…and *you've* wasted enough of my life already."

CHAPTER 73

BRENT WILLIAMS DROVE NORTHBOUND of Highway 12 in his old pickup truck. It had been quite a night. He finally got to sleep at nine in the morning, but nonetheless awoke at noon and was wide awake. There was someone he really needed to see. Crystal.

Earlier, Suzanne was excited to see him after his return to the Inlet Inn. Daybreak arrived while they had a long talk. The little girl knew the importance of not saying anything about what happened. She was far wiser to the world beyond her age and she was thankful that someone was in her life who truly cared about her. As for Leeann, she was awake no more than twenty minutes or so and was given a sedative to go back to sleep. All she knew was that she and her daughter had somehow ended up in the safety and security of the Count of Cape Hatteras. The hangover was staggering and she was thankful that the sedatives kicked in so quickly.

After Annie oversaw the process of feeding and bedding down the mother and daughter, Brent decided to head north to meet up with Crystal. How strange to go through the long ordeal and then find out that the one person perfect in his life was the woman he fell in love with first.

He reached the intersection of Highway 12 and the street that led to the cul-de-sac where last night's battle had taken place. Police were directing traffic and had the roadway blocked at its entrance. Several television news trucks were parked along the side of the road just off Highway 12. As Brent peered down the street when he drove by, he saw yet another group of police officers who were blocking traffic to the actual cul-de-sac. Locals and tourists alike were parked along Highway 12, some standing outside their cars, watching the ongoing spectacle.

He continued on, smiling to himself at the final act that occurred, an hour after he and Frank safely left the scene. It seemed from news reports that the "last standing man" Manuel died as well.

The initial reports stated that as officers arrived on the scene, they found a wounded suspect who managed to drag himself down to the rear door. When officers made their entry, he pointed the pistol at them and was immediately shot and killed. In a way, Brent was saddened. He felt almost cheated that Manuel would not spend many years on Death Row. But then he smiled again. Yet another demon in his life was gone for good.

As he reached the peak of the Bonner Bridge, Brent scanned as far north as he could, excited about the prospect of seeing Crystal. He imagined her sitting in her little living room, painting a beach scene or a ship at sea. Yes, they had broken up rather quickly back in high school, but they had always remained good friends. There had always probably been something there. She had overcome her materialistic outlook in life and became a mother. Then her entire life was taken away, as was his. But now they both had a chance for a renewal. He would help her get over the loss of her child. And they were still young enough to have one of their own. Suzanne needed a little brother or sister, he happily thought as he passed the turn to the Bodie Island Lighthouse with South Nags Head gradually coming into view.

Driving through the commercial section of Nags Head was different from the times he had been through since his return. He was now accustomed to all the homes and businesses that hadn't been there before. He looked at people and their kids, in cars with license plates from so many states. Pennsylvania, New York, South Carolina, Texas, Rhode Island. He saw kids peering out the windows, acquiring images of "the beach" that they would have for the rest of their lives, when they too would be bringing their own kids to the Outer Banks of North Carolina.

Meghan was a great young woman and virtually any man in America, or the world for that matter, would crave for her company. He appreciated the week or so he had with her, as she had reawakened him to what love and excitement could bring. But with Crystal, he could retrieve part of his past life. As could she. It was perfect. The bad times for them had finally passed.

He finally came upon the narrow little street that turned west from the 158 By-Pass. He drove down, took a right and his heart raced as soon as he saw Crystal's little car parked in the driveway, a faint streak of rust along the fender wells. Her life was now going to change, he thought, as he walked up to the door and knocked.

A few seconds later, he knocked again. Still no answer. He knocked yet again and then stepped off the tiny porch and looked into the living room window. The interior was completely barren. He rushed to a side window which also had no curtains. He peered in and again, saw nothing. Just barren floors and nothing else.

Crystal was gone.

Epilogue

It was thirty minutes before dawn, that point when the stars begin to fade from the approaching light of the sun. The Count of Cape Hatteras and several bodyguards were already present, parked at the bottom of Penny's Hill between Corolla and Swan Beach. They watched the headlights of an SUV power over the steep cut between the dune. It was Ray Dampier and several of his bodyguards.

"Hello, man," Ray said as he climbed from the vehicle and embraced his protege.

"Thanks for coming, Ray. Sorry to bother you."

The two men walked up Penny's Hill, the second largest sand dune on the Outer Banks, a hidden jewel that gave the most impressive view of the region. The bodyguards greeted, shook hands, laughed with one another, then fanned out around the perimeter of the dune.

Brent and Ray reached one of the plateaus, then walked a hundred feet to the northwest, stopping at the highest point of the dune. Both men scanned the entire horizon, marveling at the breadth and magnitude of the scenery. A faint pink light was developing above the eastern horizon of the ocean. Darkness still prevailed from the west, but lights from the mainland seemed like a string of Christmas tree lights stretched from as far north to as far south as one could see. There was even a family of wild horses, less than a half-dozen, grazing at the northern base of the huge dune, waiting to sun themselves at the beginning of another day.

"Now, *this* is the Outer Banks," Ray softly pointed out.

"Sure is."

"God left this spot for those who truly appreciate life."

"Agreed."

The two men turned to the east and watched the brightest part of the horizon. It was a completely cloudless morning, one that would foster a hot, sunny day on the beach, where tens of thousands of children and their parents would enjoy their vacation. The high dunes that separated the beach from the base of Penny's Hill gradually became a darkened silhouette as dawn continued her approach.

"Ray, I have a big favor to ask you, even though I know I have no right."

"I already know what you're gonna ask, but I just can't. Please understand. I gave Crystal my word and that was the deal."

"Yeah, I figured as much. What an unhappy person and I can see why. But, Ray...I think I'm in love with her. She's completely different from when she was in high school. Just as Leeann is now. They just reversed places and well...I thinks she needs me. And I need her. I really do think I love her."

"That may be, but again, I have to honor my word. She didn't get a big sum of money out of me for helping you. Just enough for a new start. That's all she wanted. When my team found out about her from tracking Lawrence, I approached her. The first thing she wanted after we talked was a new identity. I gave her enough money to go anywhere in the world. And the identity to be able to do so. Even I don't know where she is. Also, part of the deal I made with her was to never track her down. She just wanted to start completely over. She wants to be a new person with a new life."

"As you and I have done."

"Right, so's only fair. 'Course in my case I've started over several times but I'm much older than you two."

"Crazy, isn't it? Here I am — thanks to you — with all the financial resources to do whatever I want, but I feel empty. I feel like I won't be happy without her."

"What about that movie star girl? Wasn't that enough to make you forget about anyone else? Did you see that cover shot of her on that magazine? Winking at the camera. She could very well be the most beautiful woman on earth. And she still wants to see you, am I right?"

"She might. But she's probably forgotten all about me by now. She's back on her feet and has all the roles she ever wanted at her fingertips. But even she will tell you how fake that world is. How foolish people are to get excited about them. She would give anything to be able to be like us. Completely unknown, hidden, and camouflaged. We all have these misguided notions of beauty. And most of the time, we all can't even see the beauty that's right under our noses."

"Like this sunrise, for instance."

"Exactly."

"The same way that movie star girl didn't see the beauty of her existence before she became famous, she now probably doesn't see the beauty of her existence now. We all must want what we can't have. What a recurring theme in life. Is that what you're doing now about Crystal?"

Brent remained silent and they both turned their attention back to the eastern horizon just as the first pinpoint of the sun appeared. They watched in silence and awe as the light grew and the sky around it radiated with fresh colors. Soon the sun was completely above the horizon, its base folding out in an optical illusion just as it left the sea.

"You know, Annie tells me that people all the time miss sunsets at the hotel," Brent said. "She says they'll be seated in the lobby pondering over the menu book while a sunset as beautiful as this sunrise is taking place right out back."

"Yep. Good ole Americans. Always in a hurry."

"Anyway, that's what I did these months that I've been back. There was a beautiful sunrise named Crystal and I just let it take place and vanish before I even knew her importance."

"Well, now you're forgetting your — what do you keep calling her? Your stepdaughter Suzanne. Don't forget about her. You have that going forward. Family you thought you had lost."

"Oh, don't worry. She'll always be family to me. She's the daughter I never had and she will always be part of my life. I just think it would be great if Crystal and I could get together. It's not too late for her. Another child would perhaps rekindle her life."

"She told me she just couldn't bear to have another child. She says the world is too bad a place to bring one into. She's still that hurt."

"Life is just so strange sometimes, isn't it? We all handle things in different ways and timing is always so crucial to everything. Especially with relationships. Oh, and the stock market, of course.

"So, Ray, what should I do now? You've given me all the money in the world and all I want is a woman who truly loves me, none of these fake convenience relationships you see everywhere. For money and society. I want something *real*. I want a family. I ask myself if I could find happiness in life without finding that real love and my answer is no. Why did fate pair me up with so much money and power? To enjoy hundreds of millions of dollars at my disposal? To wallow in the phoniness of so much of modern life? Was I given all of this to make up for having lost who I really wanted and that I know I will now never have?"

"I think about the same things. My wife is long gone. I'm past the age of starting over like that. Was this all just a big stroke of luck for both of us? I think not. I've had my spiritual doubts before, but the discovery of DNA cured me once and for all. That can't be random evolution, no way. Yep, there's some kinda superlife out here watching us, judging us, and sometimes even giving us a hand here and there. As to why you and I in particular ended up like this is...maybe it's not for us to wonder...but for us to explore and enjoy. Maybe we need to be like Rhett Butler and forget love, use our money for some remarkable substitutes. Maybe God is giving us a consolation prize."

"You know, I truly appreciate all the money, but I'd much rather have the love I had back before my life became such a crisis. When I was innocent. When I felt at home. Those simple times. That's all. Thanks again, but I didn't ask for this."

Ray shook his head in ultimate agreement, then looked at Brent. He starting laughing, that huge boisterous laughter that carried him through so many dangerous times before. "Well, the heck *I* didn't! I asked for it all right! In fact, I'm all for it. Man, I've been poor. I've been down. Look at you in prison all those years. We should be happy with what we have. We shouldn't even think about complaining."

"You're right, I know that. But I just miss Crystal. She deserves what we have, too. Look at the mental prison she's still in."

"And one that she's going to have to escape from herself. Just like we did."

Brent grew silent. Transfixed at the ocean, he suddenly shook his head and turned his head to the north. The horses were now catching their first light of the sun. They were chestnut with blonde manes, absolutely beautiful. Peaceful, as they stopped their grazing and stared at the sun as it climbed over the dune.

"Brent, look at what we have now. Unlimited opportunity. We have great people around us. We have time. You have much more of that than me. You washed up here and I washed up thirty miles south. But we made it. Beyond incredible odds. We are back in this world and while our next destinations will be different, our goals are good.

"Take your money, your power, your organization and go have some fun. Forget trying to save Crystal now. Either let her save herself or you just go find her. You've got the resources. Yes, it's a huge world out there. But if you *really* and *truly* love her, then you two *will* meet again. It's not up to me. It's up to you. To her. It's up to fate or whatever it is out there that comes in once in a while and steadies our hand, protects us from others, protects us from ourselves."

Brent watched a little foal tiptoe in between a stallion and a mare. Another older foal started romping and kicking a bit, then ran up the dune swiftly though somewhat awkwardly towards his parents.

"Look at it this way, Brent. With all that we've been blessed with, what are we going to say when we appear before whoever or whatever supreme power gave it to us? Are we going to say, 'Hey, sorry I didn't enjoy it, but I was so emotionally hurt that I couldn't have any fun.' I say, 'Hell, no!' I say we go out there and have fun while we can. Help whomever we can while we're doing it! Find someone who needs to be rewarded and someone who needs to be punished. Heck yeah, we weren't given this amount of money just for the heck of it! Don't waste it. I know I won't!"

Brent turned and smiled at Ray and they both starting snickering, then giggling, then bursting into laughter that even drew the attention of the wild horses. The two friends turned their attention to the west, looking out over the Currituck Sound, past Monkey Island and on to the mainland. The rest of the country.

"Thanks, Ray," Brent said. "Thanks for everything."

"You're welcome, son," he said.

Brent looked slowly southward, past the Currituck Lighthouse into the distance and as far down the Currituck Sound as he could. He looked out to sea and then a warm sense of relief and strength swept over him. Ray was right. He was free. It was time to enjoy life. It was time to go find Crystal. It was time to find family. Home isn't geography. Home is freedom. The Count of Cape Hatteras — and Brent Williams — let out a long sigh of relief.

He was finally home.

The saga of The Count of Cape Hatteras will continue in the next book due out in 2011. Be sure to watch for The Count of Cape Hatteras, Inland Run. *For updates and other information about this series, log onto www.countofcapehatteras.com.*